PRETTY PICTURES

NANCY SAVAGE

Print ISBN: 978-1917705400

To my six Rs.

"Here are your keys, I wish the three of you the happiest of days in your new home!" Benton Shepherd's impossibly white smile beams as he passes me a keychain, then turns to high five both of my kids at once.

He's a self-assured kind of guy, just this side of arrogant. Everything you'd expect from a small-town realtor, plus he has the extra selling power of boyish good looks. My daughter seems to have noticed this too, judging by the dopey smile on her face as he talks. Unlucky for her, he's about twice her age. Lucky for me, the legal age of consent in Wyoming is seventeen, one year older than she currently is.

Why must Mory always be attracted to older guys?

Don't kid yourself, Ruby, you were too at sixteen.

"Mory, how about you go take your brother upstairs. You can pick your own bedrooms," I suggest, trying to snap her out of it.

She does the patented teenage groan but picks up on the hint that I want her and Cameron gone, and turns to grab him by the collar before dragging him up the stairs behind her.

"Hey, be gentle with your brother!" I shout after her as he protests and wriggles under her hold.

Benton laughs and puffs out a deep breath. "Kids, right?"

"You got any?" I ask, always eager for tales of worse behaved children than my own.

"God no!" he declares, then seems to catch himself. "I mean, not yet anyway. They're great though, those two of yours. I'm sure they'll love living here in Lonerock. When do they start school?"

"In two weeks. Mory's going to Burwell and Cameron's starting third grade at Whitehill Elementary."

"Hey, I went to Whitehill as a kid. I'll bet you anything crabby old Mrs. Cranston is still teaching there." He grimaces.

"Is it that bad?" I ask, noting he had nothing negative to say about the town of Lonerock when he was still in the process of trying to sell me this place.

"Oh, no no." He flashes that salesman smile. "It's a wonderful school. But you know small towns like this, we don't have a very fast turnover of teachers. And I'm pretty sure Mrs. Cranston started teaching there back in the eighteen hundreds." He laughs.

I'm sure this is a joke he and his buddies would tell on the playground back at school but it sounds juvenile coming from a man in his thirties. Nevertheless, I laugh as I'm expected to.

"Well, Benton, I think the kids and I are just about ready to settle in," I hint, hoping he'll leave before Mory comes back down to swoon over him again.

We finalized the contract at his office yesterday, so he's already made his sale. Now I have the keys, I'm not really sure why he'd want to hang around here any longer. It's an exciting day for me and I'm looking forward to some time alone with my kids to catch up with them and gauge their feelings about the move.

My leap into single motherhood has reached a huge milestone today because after three years of bouncing around short-term rentals, I'm now the proud owner of number 168 Forest Grove: a sage-green, three-bedroomed home with white shutters, a large backyard and a single car garage. At least, that's how it was listed online. In reality, the only reason I was able to afford it was because it's in dire need of modernization. It seems to be living firmly in the eighties with its patterned carpets and sun-bleached wallpaper, while the other houses on Forest Grove that surround it have long since been renovated and updated. This matters not a jot to me, though. I finally have a house I can call my own as well as stability for my children. I'm willing to put the hard work needed into this place to make it our home no matter how long it takes me.

Benton is yammering on about some biannual neighborhood watch meeting as he walks to the door and I stop him when I realize I haven't asked him about a security system. "Is there a house alarm here that I need a code for?"

Benton shakes his head. "No, but you now live on one of the safest streets in the country. I actually live close by, on Abbey Street, and we have a text alert system that covers the whole area. I think there's probably four hundred or so of us on it. I'll add your number, but I'm telling you, the worst you'll get around here is a kid playing knock and run." He laughs.

This makes me feel a little better. The first place I moved into after my divorce was a shabby third-floor apartment that overlooked a park frequented by vandals and junkies, so a quiet neighborhood with people who look out for one another is exactly what I want.

Outside, I feel the late summer sun beat down on my face as I walk Benton to his red Ford Mustang parked at the curb. I shake his hand goodbye.

"Ruby Blake, it's been a pleasure dealing with you. Feel free to call me if you need anything at all, okay?"

I squint a little as the sunlight catches his gleaming teeth. "Thanks so much, Benton."

I wait for him to drive off then turn around and see a woman staring at me from next door. She's sitting on her porch, safely out of the sunshine. I can't place her age, but her face has deep set wrinkles and her gray hair hangs loose around her shoulders.

"Hi." I wave. "We're just moving in today."

I'm sure I said this loud enough for her to hear, but the woman doesn't reply. She scowls then looks down at the magazine in front of her, ignoring me.

Nice lady.

Back inside I find the kids upstairs, Mory talking on her phone while Cameron looks out the window to the backyard.

'Dad,' Mory mouths to me, pointing to the phone against her ear.

I'm surprised it took Aaron this long to call them. He dropped them off at the airport over five hours ago and he usually calls right after they land to make sure they've found me okay. He has Mory keep a tracker app on her phone so he can see exactly when they've arrived. He's a good father to them. I'm lucky.

"Yeah, it's okay," Mory is saying. "It's better than the last place anyway. You want to speak to her? She's right here."

I wave both my arms mouthing 'no', but she shoves the phone in my face and I'm forced to take it.

"Hi, Aaron. How are you?" I say to my ex-husband, giving my daughter evil eyes as she laughs at my discomfort.

"Hey, Ruby. Mory tells me you just got the keys to your new place?"

"Yes. I wanted to wait until the kids got back so we could all move in at the same time. They said they had a great summer with you and Caitlyn by the way, thanks so much for having them there."

"You don't need to thank me for having them, Ruby, they're my kids," he says, a thinly veiled annoyance in his tone. "And there's nothing we love more than having them here with us. We can't wait for Christmas."

That's our custody agreement. Summers and Christmases with Aaron in Arizona, the rest of the year with me. It's not ideal—missing out on two of the most important times of year with my children—but it works for both of us and it gave me time to pack up our rental and start house hunting over the summer.

Mory and Cameron begged me to find a place close to our last one so they wouldn't have to change schools again and that's exactly what I tried to do. But unfortunately I was priced out of the market and had to set my sights further afield. That's when I found the listing for this house. When I drove out to view it, Benton quickly had me sold. He explained the owners had moved away a few years back and it had taken a while for them to put it on the market. And even though I knew it would mean not only uprooting the kids again but also a huge amount of work renovating the place, I didn't have much choice. It's in a great neighborhood and, most importantly, I could afford it. With only a few weeks left until the kids were coming home from Aaron's, I jumped on it.

"You know, I think it's really great that you've found somewhere to settle. Somewhere the kids can call home. I think all that moving about and changing schools was rough on them," Aaron says now.

I don't take this as a dig; he's only voicing what I've been worried about for the past three years. We may be separated, but we both still want what's best for the kids.

I soon pass the phone back to Mory, who promises to call

and text her father often before she passes the phone over to Cameron, who excitedly runs out of the room to talk with his dad again after only being separated from him for a few hours. I know the kid loves me, but I called every day to check on them over the summer and all I got was a rushed hello from Cameron, too busy running off to the pool or some other activity in the sunshine. I can't say it doesn't hurt a little when he shows so much more enthusiasm about talking to his father.

Alone now, I grab Mory by the shoulders. "So, what do you think of the house?"

"It's... okay."

"Just okay? Come on! There's a huge backyard and you've even got your own room, no more sharing with Cam. And you can decorate it any way you like. Paint it black, paint it pink, draw all over the walls with a Sharpie, cover every inch of them in posters, whatever you want!"

Mory's face twists. "I'm good, Mom. The white is fine."

Just when I've started to embrace the chaos and unpredictability of parenting a teenager, my daughter is suddenly the sensible one. At what point exactly did the roles reverse?

2

MORY

Mom's trying way too hard. When she picked us up from the airport today, she was waiting with a huge welcome sign that she'd made herself with glitter pens and glue-on streamers. It was so lame it was almost adorable.

I think she's overcompensating because we've been away all summer with Dad and Caitlyn, and now she's worried we like it better there with them. I mean we do, obviously, but I'm not going to break her heart by telling her that.

At Dad's house we help him and Caitlyn cook dinner around their large marble island every night while listening to music and joking about as a family. My dad says there's a kind of alchemy that happens around the kitchen island that you can't replicate anywhere else, and I think he's right. It's definitely not being replicated here as we eat our dinner now anyway, because what was sold to me and Cameron by our mom as a 'pizza party' tonight is actually just takeout on the dusty living-room carpet.

"Sorry about this, guys. The furniture and our boxes of things should be here tomorrow. The moving guy got the wrong day," Mom explains.

"What are we going to sleep on?" Cam asks.

"I picked up three air mattresses at the store earlier, so it'll be a bit like camping," she says with an enthusiasm I don't think she really feels.

Cameron groans at this revelation and I nudge him hard with my elbow. I can see Mom's trying to make us feel better about moving here but at eight years old, Cameron is thinking only of himself as per usual.

"Ow! Mom, Mory just hit me with her elbow!"

"Mory, leave him alone! He's half your age, for Christ's sake!" Mom yells, then squeezes her eyes closed and lets out a long breath. "Sorry. Sorry, guys, I didn't mean to shout."

Cameron and I say nothing and the three of us continue eating our pizza quietly.

"So, how are you guys feeling about starting a new school?" Mom asks when it feels as though an eternity has passed.

Cameron shrugs, unfazed. "Fine."

"How about you, Mory?" Mom turns to me.

Awful. Horrible. Like I'd rather die than be the new girl at yet another school.

"Yeah, fine," I say.

"Good, good," Mom says before we delve back into silence.

This will be my fourth school in as many years. I used to complain when we'd move house, I'd shout at Mom all the time and tell her I wanted to go live with Dad. I'd tell her I hated her, that I wasn't going to go to school and she couldn't make me. But inevitably I'd end up calming down and getting used to our new situation before we'd up and move again the following year and the cycle would repeat. I think back then, I didn't really see what Mom was going through. All I saw was everything happening to *me*. Then one day I found her sitting in her car, crying, and when I asked her what was wrong, she told me she thought she was a shitty mom and that me and Cam deserved better than what she could give us. I think those words sparked something inside of me because since then, I'm always more careful about what I say to her. There's something about seeing your mom cry, it's really unsettling. I guess everyone realizes at some point that their mom's human, just like everyone else.

So, while I'm glad she's found us a permanent home and we won't have to move again, I'm sure as hell not going to tell her the truth, which is that this house is an old, stuffy museum in a lame ass town and that I miss being at Dad's house already.

When we've finished the pizza, Mom walks us around the house showing us everything she's going to change. "The carpets are going to be coming up. The vinyl flooring in the kitchen and bathrooms too," she explains as we walk into the kitchen. "And I think I'll probably paint all the doors and put in new hardware."

I nod along as though I care about any of this and listen as she goes into way too much detail about kitchen cabinets and shelving the pantry.

"How long's it all going to take?" I ask when she's done. "You know, until this house looks... normal?"

She considers this for a moment. "I think if I throw myself into it, I could have it done in about a year or so. I mean, it would be quicker if I could afford to hire people to do it for me but I think it's better this way. More rewarding. And you guys can pitch in a little, too, if you like?"

"No thanks. I'd just get in your way," I say.

"Can I pull up the carpets?" Cameron asks, ready to start now.

Mom laughs. "Sure! Not just yet though, I think we'll probably do it one room at a time."

"Is Benton going to help, too?" Cameron asks.

The amused expression on Mom's face drops. "Benton Shepherd? The realtor?"

"Yeah, the guy who was here earlier," Cameron says.

"Oh, no, sweetie. He was just the person in charge of selling the house. He won't be coming back here now it's all finalized," Mom explains.

The hopeful look in Cameron's eyes fades to one of disappointment. "Oh. Okay."

I try to keep my expression neutral, but I feel the same way. That guy was *super* hot. He kind of looked like a movie star, all tanned and every hair on his head perfectly styled into place. I keep this to myself though, since my mom would just lecture me about finding a guy my own age instead of always crushing on someone in their twenties or thirties. I think she must be forgetting what sixteen-year-old boys are like. Why would I ever be interested in them? They're as immature as Cameron, sometimes even worse. All the guys in my last school revolved their lives either around sports or video games. Like that was their *whole* personality.

"Sorry to disappoint you, buddy, but Benton isn't going to be helping us out with the renovation. He only does sales," Mom says.

"I liked him. Did you see his car? The red one? It looked like a race car, it was the coolest thing ever," Cameron thrills.

I saw Cam staring at Benton's car earlier, and I've got to admit I may have drooled over it a little, too. That thing must have cost him a ton of money.

Mom rolls her eyes. "Well, I'm sure Benton would be happy to hear that, but I doubt it was eight-year-old boys he was thinking of impressing when he bought it. I mean... I hope not, anyway."

I laugh at this, but it seems to go over Cameron's head.

As night falls, we bring the inflatable mattresses inside from the car and set them up in our empty bedrooms. Mom looks a little sad as she's setting up Cameron's bed and I get the feeling she's having those thoughts again. The ones telling her she's not doing good enough for us. That she's a shitty mother.

I come up beside her and wrap my arms around her waist, resting my head on her shoulder. "I missed you, Mom."

I feel her take a deep breath in, smelling my hair in that weird way she always does.

Her voice comes out a little cracked. "I missed you too, baby."

3

RUBY

The one luxury kitchen item I own is an Italian coffee bean grinder and stovetop espresso maker set.

I treat myself to one glorious coffee every single morning to start my day. The set was a divorce gift to myself and cost me a hundred dollars. I'm not sure if it would count as luxurious to others but for someone like me, who uses pans with broken handles and spatulas that are half melted for years on end without replacing them, my beautiful coffee set stands out in my kitchen. And having gone a full three days at the new house before our boxes and furniture were finally delivered last Friday by the worst moving company ever, I'm very much appreciating my 7am espresso right now.

Week number one at the new house has gone much smoother than I'd been expecting.

Cameron has made fast friends with a kid down the street named Leo, so I barely see him during the day anymore. And Mory seems happier now her things have arrived and she has her own personal space upstairs in her bedroom. I'm hoping she makes new friends easily when she starts school next week.

She's always been a little quiet around new people, and I feel bad for pulling her out of her last school to move fifty miles away just when she'd gotten comfortable there.

I finish my coffee and look at the shopping list I've been jotting down on the back of an envelope. It's not the usual eggs, milk and bread on my list today. Instead, it's brushes and paint, hand tools and sanding equipment. All the things the online videos told me I'd need for a DIY renovation.

This is brand-new territory for me and I feel as though I'm probably out of my depth, but I can't afford to hire tradesmen and since there's a lull in my work right now, I have the motivation and time to do this all by myself. I'm going to work room by room, so the whole house won't end up a complete mess all at once. Starting with the living room. I'm eager to get it done first because the one thing my kids will do with me as a family is sit down to watch a movie once a week, and I want a comfortable space for us to do that in.

"Mom, can I go see if Leo can come out to play?" Cameron walks into the kitchen in his pajamas still wiping sleep from his eyes.

"Cam, it's still early. How about you have some breakfast and get dressed before you go banging his door down?"

He groans, then grabs a chair and hauls it over to the counter to reach the cupboard above him before pulling out a box of cereal and a bowl. Once settled at the table with his breakfast, he scoops it quickly into his mouth, letting the milk dribble down his chin, seemingly having forgotten the table manners I've worked hard to teach him.

"Is that how you eat cereal at your father's house?" I ask.

"We don't eat cereal at Dad's. Caitlyn cooks us breakfast every morning," he says while chewing.

Of course she does. Because Caitlyn is Wonder Woman.

She makes her own sourdough bread, does age-based crafts with the kids, decorates gingerbread men with them, takes them on hikes and plays board games with them. Of course, these are all things that I could be doing myself with my kids, but when Aaron and I divorced I went through a period of depression that sucked all the enthusiasm out of... well, everything for me. I couldn't find joy in any of the things I usually could, and my career as a visual artist went into a huge downward spiral that I still haven't recovered from (if it weren't for our divorce going in my favor, I'd be flat out broke by now). At that point, Mory was in the awkward pre-teen stage and Cameron was five. I still loved them with all my heart but I could barely bring myself to get out of bed each morning, let alone take them out to explore nature and build stick forts in the forest with them. When I finally got myself the therapy I needed, and realized I was just as worthy of happiness as a single divorced mother as I was before my marriage fell apart, I slowly started to regain an appreciation for the little things in life. But Caitlyn was already in the picture doing all the wonderful things with my children that I suddenly wanted to be doing again, too.

So, I tried. I tried really hard. But when I did crafts with the kids, I was told it was boring. And when I asked if they wanted to help me cook dinner, I was told they had homework to do. And when I offered to take them out to do something fun on the weekends, they wanted to see their friends instead.

At first this made me resent my ex-husband's new perfect girlfriend, who never failed to keep my children happy and involved in everything she did. But when that just left me bitter and self-loathing, I came to realize this wasn't Caitlyn's fault at all. She wasn't trying to out-mother me or steal my children's affection. The reason they were happy to do these things with her was because they only spent summers and Christmases there: periods of time where there's no school, no homework, and no friends to distract them, away from home, in Arizona. She and Aaron get the kids' full attention during those twelve weeks of the year, and for the other forty, I wake them up early every day for school, make them clean their bedrooms and eat their vegetables and enforce strict screen time limits. No wonder they think I'm the boring one.

All of this is something I've come to accept simply comes with the territory. And I no longer resent Caitlyn. I now choose to embrace the fact that my children have another reliable adult in their lives who loves them and looks out for them. At least, that's what I'm going to keep telling myself if I want to maintain my sanity.

"Done!" Cameron jumps up and hastily puts his bowl and spoon in the sink before rushing off to his bedroom.

He's soon back downstairs, dressed and turning the house upside down trying to find his shoes. This kid loses his footwear on a daily basis. It always strikes me as ironic that he can never seem to find his shoes, yet somehow he can spot a piece of onion in someone else's food, two houses over.

Before long he's out the door, under strict instructions to return home to Mory if he needs anything, while I grab my bag and head out to the hardware store to collect my new arsenal of DIY tools, fixtures and paints.

Driving through Lonerock I'm impressed with what I see. It's a small town but there's at least a few of the chain stores that I usually frequent and the streets here are clean and well kept. I pass by a large arcade and indoor trampoline center that I know Cameron will love. Just past that is a bookstore-slash-cafe that I think Mory might like. Maybe I can take her there this winter and we can sit together sipping hot chocolate and reading books. These are usually the kinds of images that float through my mind and never end up materializing, but I'm determined now that we've found our forever home to finally have the relationship with my kids that I've wanted for so long.

My hardware store haul is successful but puts me back several hundred dollars—which is nothing compared to how much paying a crew to do the work for me would cost—and I arrive home ready to face this project head on. I run upstairs and put on the new pair of overalls I picked up in town (because every DIY enthusiast needs overalls) and get straight to work.

First things first: the dusty old carpet in the living room needs to get the hell out of here. I know I promised Cameron that he could help me pull it up, but he's still out with Leo. I passed by them on my way home, deep in their own little conversation while kicking around a ball, and I'm too impatient to wait until he eventually decides to come home. I'm dying to see if the original hardwood floors underneath the carpet are still in good shape.

I start by hauling out the couch and TV stand—the only furniture currently in the living room—and leave them sitting in the hall. I then pull up the edges of the threadbare carpet at the far side of the room, rolling it tightly as I go so I can easily get it out to the car later. I'll probably have to pay to leave it at the waste center, but it'll be worth it to have this monstrosity gone.

From the looks of it, the original wooden flooring is in pretty great shape. I feel as though I've struck gold as I keep rolling the carpet, uncovering dusty and scuffed but generally well-preserved wood. With a little sanding and buffing and a fresh coat of stain, I think it should come up nicely.

The carpet roll is growing in size as I reach the other end of the room. It's like an enormous roulade and I wipe my forehead with the back of my hand when I finally reach the end. That was exhausting. And I've barely even started. I sit down and slump back against the Swiss-carpet to catch my breath and that's when I notice it. Something poking out from underneath the roll. It's white and dusty and looks like a piece of paper that's stuck where the carpet had just been lying. I reach down and pull at it. It slides out easily from underneath and I realize it's not a piece of paper, but a photograph. An old one, from a Polaroid camera. It looks just like the kind my mom would take when I was a kid.

A wave of nostalgia floods over me when I think of my mom snapping a photo of me and my brother sitting outside on the wall eating ice cream, then shaking out the photo as it developed, ready for us to see it within a matter of seconds. Of course, this was before we had phones with built-in cameras. I thought it was magical to be able to see a photo so soon after it was taken.

I stare now at the photo in my hand. It's of a young woman. She's got those thick eighties glasses on that age her youthful looks and she's wearing a corduroy dress with a lace collar. She's got a huge smile on her face and is sitting against a wood-paneled wall.

There's a name written in permanent marker on the white strip at the bottom of the photo. *Jessie.*

Was this someone who used to live here? Then it hits me. I've heard about this before! People leaving little mementos around when they're renovating or building a house to be uncovered in years to come by new owners. I'll bet young Jessie didn't think for a second that the carpet they put in wouldn't be pulled up for another thirty plus years. Judging by her age in this photo, my guess is she must at least be in her fifties by now, possibly in her sixties.

This is such a cute idea. Maybe I should get an instant camera and do the same with a photo of me and the kids for a future owner to uncover. Although, it would take a very long time for them to find it because I foresee myself living in this house until the day I die.

I stuff the old photo into the front pocket of my overalls to show the kids later, and begin the near impossible task of hauling the old carpet out to the car as I wonder where this Jessie is now.

4

———

JESSIE

The rain beats down as Jessie leaves Granger's Bar and starts the twenty-minute walk back to her apartment. It's a little before midnight and the streets are already empty. Raindrops fall through the narrow beams of light from the streetlamps and look like little shooting stars.

She was hoping Steve would be walking back to her apartment with her but seeing him cozy up to Katie all night had quashed that hope. She guesses he's not into her after all. His loss. Jessie can do better, anyway. She's got her own apartment, she makes her own money, she has a degree in economics and can speak three languages. Thinking about it now, she realizes that sounds more like a résumé than a reason why guys should be falling at her feet, but she really can't comprehend why Steve would choose ditzy Katie—who probably can't tell a hat from Tuesday—over her; the one who has been working alongside him for over six months, flirting wildly every day. Maybe he's scared of powerful women. That's probably it. Jessie's strength intimidates him. That's the reason he chose Katie over her tonight. Or it could have just been because of Katie's giant breasts.

Jessie's heel catches in a grate and she stumbles when it snaps off. Cursing, she reaches down and picks up the broken heel then carries on her way, doing a pathetic lopsided walk as she goes.

She hears a car approach from behind and slow down to a stop before a voice calls out. "Are you all right? Do you need a ride?"

She turns and sees a man staring out the open window. He has kind eyes and a disarming smile.

"I'm okay, thanks." She smiles back.

"Are you sure? Because it looks like you're limping." She holds up her broken shoe and he laughs. "Come on, hop in and I'll take you wherever you're headed."

"It's okay, really, my apartment's just down the street from here."

She's sure he's just a considerate kind of guy, but she's not stupid enough to get into a car with a complete stranger in the dead of night.

"Okay, well, have a nice night." He winks and begins to drive away slowly.

Jessie continues on and by the time she reaches her apartment the rain has drenched through her clothes. She stands at the top step in front of the door, hand fumbling inside her bag trying to find her keys. Water droplets are falling against her glasses and she can't wait to get inside, strip off these wet clothes and get into bed. She finally finds her keys and brings them up to the lock, but it's so dark she can't see to get the key into the keyhole. From behind her she hears a noise and begins to turn around to see what it is. She doesn't even get a chance to scream before the large object comes at her head with great force and she falls to the ground.

Jessie wakes up in darkness.

Where is she? What's happening? Something is moving, humming underneath her.

She's in a vehicle. She's... she's in the trunk of a car.

She knows this is wrong, she knows the pain in her head is wrong and that she should probably be screaming and shouting and begging for help, but for some reason she can't seem to find a way to make herself do this. She feels heavy, like she weighs twice as much as she usually does and her tongue is sitting weirdly in her mouth, like it's not hers.

She can't tell if her eyes are open or closed because everything looks the same either way and the vibrating underneath her has turned to bumping. She's being shaken back and forth like a rag doll. Why can't she find the strength to move, to scream? What is wrong with her?

This seems to continue for a long time before the bumping turns to thuds and the thuds to bangs as it feels like rocks or stones hit the bottom of the car. Where is she being taken? It feels like a rough dirt track. There's nothing even remotely like that nearby to where she lives, on the outskirts of the city. How long has she been stuck in here?

The bumping slows down and she feels the car come to a stop. With the engine off she can hear the rain hit against the metal above her and she suddenly remembers what happened.

Her keys. She was looking for her keys. There was a guy. A guy stopped to ask if she wanted a lift home. She'd just left Granger's Bar, where Steve was all over Katie. She remembers it all now.

A door slams and a moment later the trunk opens and Jessie stares up into the night sky. Raindrops fall on her face as she squints out into the low light and sees a face looking down at her. It's him. It's the guy who offered her a ride earlier.

She opens her mouth but when she tries to speak no words come out, just a noise that doesn't sound at all like her voice.

"Come on, sweetie, let's get you inside. You're not feeling too well, are you?" he says, pulling her up into his arms and walking her through the rain.

She wants to struggle but her limbs hang loose and useless. What's going on with her?

There's a wooden cabin in front of them now, old and uncared for. Is he taking her in there? No. No. Her mind is screaming out at her to stop him. To stop this and get home. But why oh why will her body not respond to her mind's frantic pleas?

The rusty hinges on the door creak as the man opens it up and walks inside, still holding her like a little child across his arms.

"Okay, darling, I'm going to put you in bed. I think your medicine has you feeling a little sleepy," he says, walking her through the dim, bare main room of the cabin and into a small bedroom.

Medicine? What medicine? Has he given her something? Is that why she's feeling like this, unable to find the strength to move or fight?

He lays her down on a bare, dirty mattress and covers her up with a rough woolen blanket before leaving and going back through to the main room. She can hear him in there, moving things about. The sound of water running and a gas stove clicking to turn on the flame.

She tries to keep her eyes open, but they're drooping further and further to closed. The last thing she hears before she falls asleep is his soft, calm humming from the next room.

"It's a beautiful morning, it's a beautiful day!"

Jessie wakes to the sound of singing, sits upright, and straightens her glasses. There's light coming through the window across from her and the realization of where she is comes crashing down on her.

The man walks over with a tray and places it on the bed beside her. "Orange juice and a bran muffin, just for you."

She grabs the blanket and pulls it closer to her, ignoring the food. "Who are you?"

"You can call me Charlie. And your name is Jessica. I read the letter from your mom inside your bag. She calls you Jessie, though. Would you rather I call you Jessie, too?"

She ignores this.

"Can I go home now, Charlie?" she asks nicely. "My head hurts and I'm supposed to be at work this morning, so people will probably be out looking for me."

Charlie smiles. "Later. Let's just have a nice morning first. Eat your breakfast and then we'll get you dressed."

For a horrifying second, she looks down under the blanket thinking he might have taken her clothes off, but she's still in the same clothes she wore to the bar last night.

"I'm not hungry," she says, knowing this man already drugged her once. "And I'm already dressed, so I think I'm ready to go home now."

"Jessie, sweetie, don't be afraid of me. You have no reason to be scared."

She wants to believe him but he's already knocked her out, drugged her and driven her God knows how far from home out to this dirty cabin.

She looks to the window, wondering how far she could get on foot if she escaped, but he seems to read her mind. "No, no. There's no use running. There are no neighbors around here and it'd take you hours to reach the main road. But if you just spend the morning with me, I'll take you back home afterwards, I promise."

This makes her feel a little better. His smile is genuine, not creepy, and his voice is soft but assured. "Okay."

"Okay! Well, how about we get straight to pictures?" He claps his hands in excitement.

"Pictures?" Her voice wobbles.

"Yes! Now I know you probably want some privacy, so I've left your clothes in the bathroom over there so you can change alone."

She looks to where he points and sees a wooden door.

"Well, go on!" he chimes.

His expectant eyes follow her as she gets up from the bed slowly, a little shaky on her feet, and walks toward the door. There's light coming from inside and she steps in hoping to see a window, but a bulb hangs from the ceiling with a chain string and bare wooden walls surround the doorway. No window.

She closes the door behind her and uses the toilet before washing her hands and assessing herself in the mirror. The top of her head hurts from where he hit her last night but other than that she doesn't seem to have any marks or bruises.

This guy is crazy. She needs to just follow his orders and hope he makes good on his promise to bring her back home afterwards. She sees material folded on the shelf and picks it up. It's a dress.

Just do what he says and get this over with, Jessie.

She takes off her clothes and puts on the dress. The fabric is thick and she's already sweating by the time she gets the zip on the back done up. She looks in the mirror and tries to straighten her hair.

She steps out of the bathroom and finds Charlie waiting for her, leaning against the doorway to the main room. He lets out a gushing sigh and thumps his fist against his chest. "Beautiful! It's perfect. Give me a twirl!"

Jessie spins uncomfortably in a slow circle.

"Okay, we're ready to do this!" He claps his hands and leaves the room for a moment before coming back in with a camera. It's one of those ones that spits out the pictures itself.

He directs her to sit down and shows her exactly how he wants her positioned, casually leaning back against the wall.

"We're just taking a picture and then you're bringing me home, right?" she asks.

"Yes. But, Jessie, this is really important. I need you to smile for me, okay? Because if you don't give me a big, big, *big* smile, then I'm not going to be able to let you leave just yet. Do you understand?"

She nods.

"Okay, are you ready?"

"Yes."

He brings the camera up to his face, and she plasters on the biggest smile she can muster, mouth wide and eyes gleaming. The camera flashes brightly then makes a noise and a square of film slides out the front.

"Oh, my heart! You're so beautiful when you smile. I'm going to keep this forever."

"Thanks, Charlie. So, can I go home now?"

He pulls the picture from the camera and holds it up in the air, squinting at it as it develops.

"Beautiful, beautiful, beautiful," he mumbles, reaching into his back pocket.

He pulls out a black permanent marker and holds the photo up against the wall. He pulls the cap off with his teeth and writes her name on the white section under the photo.

"I'll keep it forever," he repeats again.

"Charlie, can I go home now, please?"

Charlie puts the cap back on the marker and puts it back in his pocket. He looks at the photo again and then tucks that in his pocket, too.

"Charlie, will you please take me home?"

He looks down at her and takes a step closer. But the kindness in his eyes has gone. They're cold. Emotionless.

And it's in this moment that Jessie knows she's not going home.

RUBY

The view from my perch at the top of the ladder is breathtaking. The early morning sunshine beaming over the housetops makes the unappealing task more enjoyable. And with the sun on my skin and my headphones in my ears, cleaning out the gutters is not as awful as I'd been expecting. Though it doesn't do much to keep my mind from the worry of how Mory and Cameron are getting on at their new schools.

Cam strutted out of the house this morning as though he had no worries in the world, but Mory had seemed on edge. I gave her the standard motherly pep-talk about trying to keep positive and to just be herself, and she nodded along as though this was in some way helpful. But I know that nothing I say can soothe the anxiety she's feeling about starting at Burwell High today.

Maybe I'll take the kids out for ice cream after dinner to celebrate their first day at school. I want them to know I understand how big a change this is for them, and that I really do care. I'll use it as a way to get an open conversation going about our feelings, maybe we'll make it into a weekly thing. A family tradition. Or maybe this is all just wishful thinking and when I ask how they're doing they'll just tell me 'fine' with no further details, like usual.

At least we still have movie night.

We just watched our first movie together—*Who Framed Roger Rabbit?*, one of our favorites—in our newly decorated living room last night.

After two weeks here, it's nice to have at least one room that's finished. I was right about the floor, it came up beautifully, and after a lick of paint on the walls and putting in some new curtains the space feels like a whole new room.

One down, many more to go.

My focus today is on getting these gutters cleared out before fall kicks in and they get even more clogged. I doubt they've been cleaned in years because with each scoop of my trowel I'm collecting huge amounts of decayed leaves and debris. The smell is unpleasant to say the least.

I take a break for a moment and twist around to take in the view when I realize there's a police officer staring up at me from the driveway. I wave a gloved hand and make my way down the ladder before placing my trowel and nearly full bucket on the ground.

I take off my gloves, pull my earbuds out, and give him an apologetic smile. "Sorry, I was in my own little world! I didn't see you standing here."

The officer smiles. "That's no problem, I've only been here a minute."

I see his police car parked nearby and feel a spark of concern.

"Is everything okay?" I ask, fearing something bad might have happened at one of the kids' schools.

"I'm just here about a noise complaint we got from a neighbor."

I put a hand on my hip. "A noise complaint? Are you sure you've got the right house?"

"Yes, ma'am. The complaint concerns construction work being carried out on your home late last night."

I laugh and point at the door to the house. "Well, I did use a sanding machine on my front door yesterday, but it wasn't late at night. I stopped around 7pm to watch a movie with my children."

"You weren't using any loud power tools after that time?"

"No. And the sander isn't even that loud."

The officer nods in understanding. "Okay, well that all sounds reasonable to me. We have to follow up on complaints, you see, but a lot of them really amount to nothing."

"Sure, I get it, no problem," I say. "Are you able to tell me who the complaint was from?"

The officer shakes his head. "No, sorry."

He walks back to his car and as he drives off, I look around at the houses nearby. I haven't had the chance to meet any of the neighbors yet but my guess is the complaint must have been from one of the houses either side of ours. There's only a gap of ten feet or so between each property, so I guess they could hear me doing work outside but rather than come and tell me it was bothering them, they called the cops on me. Some people, I swear.

I'm about to put my gloves on and head back up the ladder when I see three women approaching from down the street, hips and arms pumping dramatically. When they see me, they all wave in unison.

I wave back and stay put while they power walk over to me.

"Hi! You must be our new neighbor!" says the woman in the middle. "I'm Felicity Parker. And this is Kendra and Harriet."

Ah, so this is Leo Parker's mom. Cameron has spent so

much time playing with him, I'm surprised I haven't seen her around until now.

Felicity is tall, blonde and beautiful in the kind of way that only wealth can bring. No makeup, no surgical tweaks or fillers, just the delicate skin of a woman who has had the money to take good care of herself her whole life. Her two friends look a little like knock-off Barbie dolls standing next to her.

I wipe the gutter grime from my hands onto my jeans. "I'm Ruby, I just moved in here with my two children a couple of weeks ago."

"Yes, my son Leo talks about Cameron all the time. It seems as though they're the best of friends already!" Felicity's eyes sparkle happily.

"I know, it's so sweet. I was worried it would take Cameron a while to find any friends around here, but he and Leo seem to be glued at the hip already," I say.

I'm aware that as I talk with Felicity about our sons, Kendra and Harriet are looking me up and down, seemingly weighing me up. The three women are so similar in appearance that I fear I'd have a hard time figuring out who was who if they were to quickly change places. They all look a couple of years older than me, maybe forty or so, are wearing athletic wear and have on baseball caps with their blonde ponytails hanging out the back. But where Kendra and Harriet are a little fuller in their figures, Felicity is lean and looks as though she could run laps on them. It's clear she's the pack leader.

"Well, I'm just in the middle of cleaning out the gutters, and I don't want to keep you girls from your morning walk." I smile.

"Oh, we don't usually do this!" Kendra pipes up. Or maybe it's Harriet, I'm really not sure. "Today is day one. We made a pact over the summer that we'd start doing a daily circuit when the kids go back to school."

"Oh, well that's lovely. Best of luck with it," I say, genuinely.

"You should join us! I mean from tomorrow, that is," Harriet says. Or possibly Kendra.

"Oh, I really wish I could but I'm using the time the kids are at school to do up the house. I don't think this place has been touched since the eighties." I sigh.

The three women laugh politely and say goodbye before continuing on with their walk, ponytails bouncing behind them. Every neighborhood has its own mom-clique, I guess I just met ours.

As I turn back to grab the trowel and bucket, I spot a face staring out at me from the house next door. It's that woman, the one who didn't return my greeting on the day we arrived. I'll bet she's the one who called the cops on me. Has she been watching me the whole time I've been out here?

If this woman has some kind of a problem with me, I wish she'd just come over and tell me, because if she's going to be calling the cops on me every time I'm doing work on the house it's going to get old pretty quickly.

I plaster on a huge smile and wave enthusiastically at her, to show her I'm completely unfazed. Her lips turn downward in a scowl before she closes her curtains and disappears from view.

6

———

MORY

I have never felt more invisible in my life than I have today.

Starting a new high school is like going to a foreign country. The language is different, the culture is different, and while everyone walks around the place with purpose, you have no idea where the hell you're going or what you're supposed to be doing.

It took me months to feel comfortable at my last school and it seemed like the second I began finding my place, we had to up and move again. My mom thinks it's as easy as just 'staying positive' and 'being myself' and everything will be totally okay, but what does that even mean? Be myself. Well, I *was* myself today and that tactic got me exactly nowhere. I sat through my classes, I ate my lunch, and talked to no one. Nobody seemed to see me or notice that I was there. Not even my teachers. And it's not as though it's like that for every student: they already know each other. They're already joking around with each other and whispering in class and hanging out in the halls together. If anyone else was feeling as alone and desperately out of place as I was, they were doing a great job of hiding it.

I get off the school bus and make the short walk back to the house, dragging my feet as I walk. I want to go back to Arizona. I want to go back to staying up late and waking up whenever I feel like it. I want to joke around with Caitlyn, tease Dad with her, have barbeques by the pool and compete with Cameron to see who can make the biggest splashes jumping in the water. I want to eat dinner out on the deck in the evenings and talk with Dad and Caitlyn about the future, them taking an interest in the things I want out of life. It was like a dream, being there this summer.

And now I'm in a nightmare. I'm stuck in a town that I don't want to be in, in a school I don't want to be in, I don't know anybody around here, and I'm living in a house that's so ugly inside that I wouldn't invite a friend around even if I had one.

Dad's house is huge and he and Caitlyn made bedrooms just for us when they first moved in. Cameron's has a bunk bed that looks like a castle and there's a dragon painted on the wall. Mine is coral pink and has mermaid bedding and a beautiful white desk. They decorated the rooms back when Cameron was five and I was thirteen, so it's not exactly what I'd choose now but it's still much better than what I've got here. A bare white room with just a bed. I know it's not fair to compare them because Mom is just an artist and doesn't make much money, whereas Dad's got a job at a big-shot company where he gets sent around the world to do business deals and sell products. So, I get that I can't expect the same at Mom's house as at Dad's, but a lot of the time I find myself wishing they'd never divorced so that we could all just live at Dad's house together and be happy again.

At least Mom has finished doing up the living room, which actually looks kind of okay now. I mean, it's not sleek and modern like my dad's house but at least that gross carpet has gone. Mom showed me an old photograph she found underneath it of a girl with frizzy hair and huge glasses and the ugliest eighties dress you could imagine. She thought it was really sweet that someone had left it under the carpet all those years ago for future owners to find and she pointed out how beautiful the photo was. But when I looked into that girl's eyes I didn't see that. I saw pain. I've had to smile through a lot of stuff in the past few years, even when I didn't feel like it. And the smile on that girl's face didn't look genuine to me, it looked forced. Like she was trying to make someone else happy.

As I turn the corner onto our street, I see a guy approaching me. He's got dark blond hair that hangs down over his eyes and as he passes by, he pushes it back from his forehead and smiles at me. I smile back and keep walking. I risk a look behind me and I see that he, too, is looking back to see me again. I snap my head around, embarrassed that he caught me checking him out. He's majorly hot, and I really hope he lives on our street. That might make living here a little easier.

I walk through the door and barely get the bag off my back before Mom is on me, telling me she missed me and asking how my first day at school went.

"Yeah, fine," I say, walking through to the kitchen and pulling a glass from the cupboard.

"Fine? So, it all went well?"

"Yeah, it was okay," I say before gulping down an entire glass of water.

"Did you talk to anyone? Make any friends?" she asks.

"Yeah, I guess. There were a few girls there I was talking to. I ate with them at lunch."

My mom seems to melt with relief at this.

"Oh, Mory, that's great!" She hugs me from behind as I put the glass in the sink and I wait it out until she lets me go. "I knew it would go well for you today! You've got such a strong spirit. I'm not surprised those other girls were drawn to you. You're fun, and approachable."

I almost laugh at this. If I could choose three words that least describe me, they'd probably be strong, fun, and approachable. Apparently, my mother sees somebody completely different when she looks at me. But I don't want to hurt her and I can't bear the thought of her crying over me again, so everyone will be happier if she just thinks things are going super for me. A thought now occurs to me. Is she doing the exact same thing as me? Just keeping her head down, not complaining or making a big deal out of things to make everyone else feel more comfortable? I stand there looking into her eyes for a moment, trying to see it. Is she as miserable as I am?

She smiles and hugs me again. "Mory, my baby, I'm so glad your first day went well. All that matters to me is that you guys are happy."

And I believe her. She once told me that a mother is only ever as happy as her unhappiest child. And since Cameron runs around the place like a squirrel in a nut factory, I'm left with the responsibility of not ruining everything for her by being the unhappy one.

So, I guess school went great, I've already made friends, I have no problem with moving to Lonerock or this gross old house, and I don't want to just shrivel up and die.

7

RUBY

"Mom, my web shooter fell off again!" Cameron cries.

I'm trying to adjust my Cleopatra wig in front of the new hallway mirror when he runs up to me and thrusts a piece of red plastic in my face.

"Can it wait a second? If you want me to come trick or treating then I've got to get my winged liner on first."

Spiderman stares blankly at me. "What's a winged liner? Like an airplane?"

I laugh. "No, it's just makeup."

He groans impatiently and stomps back to the kitchen, probably to sneak another piece of candy from the bowl I have ready for tonight's visitors.

A month ago, I would have been embarrassed opening our front door to strangers and letting them peek in at the mess of the front hall, but I spent most of September working on this space: sanding and repainting the front door, taking up another disgusting carpet, removing wallpaper, painting the walls and skirting, and laying sleek gray floor tiles. The whole thing was so much more work than I'd expected and took nearly four weeks in total, but the transformation is pretty incredible.

So after nearly two full months in this house, we have an entryway and a living room that we can be proud of, and not much else. But hey, it's a start.

I'm hoping that taking Cameron out trick or treating tonight will give me a chance to meet a few more of our neighbors. I've been so busy decorating that I've barely had a chance to get outside. Every so often, I'll see Felicity Parker and her two lookalike buddies power walking by the house in the morning and we'll wave hello and smile but that's about it.

The house to the right of ours is owned by a young couple with no children who drive off in separate cars each morning, both wearing suits. They seem too preoccupied to stop and introduce themselves properly. And the woman living to the left of us, well, I've established that she's not too friendly. Since calling the cops on me that day over the noise of my sanding machine, there have been a handful of other issues come up.

There was the day Cameron left his ball on her driveway, just an inch from our own, and we came home from the store to find it deflated and nailed to our door. Then there was the time the ceramic dinnerware set I'd ordered never showed up. It was meant to replace our old mismatched and chipped plates and bowls, but despite the tracking saying it had been delivered there was no sign of it. Then the next garbage collection day, I saw the box sitting out by that old witch's trash and when I went to inspect it, every one of the plates and bowls inside were broken into tiny pieces. My guess is they were delivered to her house by mistake and instead of bringing them over to us like a normal human being, she decided to destroy them and put them out for collection where I could easily see them. The woman is insane, I'm pretty sure. She'll stand outside her house and stare at me as I unload groceries, no shame whatsoever.

I'm not going to let Cameron knock on her door for candy

tonight, that's for sure, or he could end up being cooked alive inside her cauldron.

My hands shake with anger at the thought of the woman as I apply my eyeliner and my 'wing' turns into a droop.

"Oh, Mom. Seriously?" Mory scolds me as she walks by and she stops to grab the stick from my hand. "Let me do it."

She wipes away the mess I've made then proceeds to draw perfectly neat tips at the side of each eye. She smiles at me in triumph when she's done. "Beautiful!"

"Thanks, Mory. Are you sure you won't come with us tonight?" I ask.

She shakes her head. "Somebody needs to be here for the trick or treaters, anyway."

It's an excuse I can't argue with and I guess I can't expect her to want to join in on Halloween with us forever, but it's the first year she's opted out and it only serves to further remind me of how fast she's growing up.

I leave Mory stocked with a ridiculous amount of candy to hand out and make my way down the street with Cameron, stopping at each house and wishing our neighbors a happy Halloween.

There are graveyards set up in people's front yards, skeletons hanging from trees, and hyperactive kids running around everywhere, screaming. It's such a fun atmosphere and I'm so thankful I still have one child young enough to get wrapped up in the excitement.

Cameron is looking around for his friend Leo and I have to rein him in several times when he nearly runs off without me. By the tenth or so house, his small bag is nearly full to the brim and when I tell him it's time to go home, he pleads with me for just two more houses. I pretend to hum and haw before letting him carry on.

I learned that little trick long ago; tell your child they have to go home before they actually need to, then let them think they've convinced you to let them stay a little longer. They'll feel like they've won and, ultimately, you'll get out of there faster. It works at the playground and the toy store, too.

When Cameron joins several other kids running up to a house with a completely over the top mechanical vampire who laughs and moves about menacingly at the door, a woman dressed up as Alice from *Alice in Wonderland* walks over to me and I recognize her as being one of Felicity's friends.

"Ruby! You make a great Cleopatra!" she squeals.

"Thank you, Harriet. I love your costume, too!"

An awkward smile touches her lips. "I'm Kendra."

"Oh, of course! Sorry, I'm awful with names," I lie, slapping my forehead.

I'm just fine with names. It's the carbon copy soccer moms that I have a hard time telling apart.

Kendra's arm is now being yanked by an impatient little ballerina and she smiles apologetically. "Grace won't let me stop and talk to anyone for more than two seconds tonight!"

We say goodbye and I watch her being dragged off by her daughter to visit more doors when all of a sudden, a pair of hands come down over my eyes from behind and I nearly jump out of my skin in fright. I turn around to see Mory laughing at me, in the same everyday clothing she'd been in when I left her earlier, except she's now wearing a pair of cat ears and has whiskers drawn on her cheeks.

"You came!" I cry.

"Yeah, we ran out of candy at home and it was either this or turn off all the lights and hide until the kids stop knocking at the door. Where's Cam?" She looks around.

I point to the house next to us but when I look, he's not there. I turn around in a circle searching for him but I can't see him anywhere and my heart starts drumming in my chest.

"I... I don't know where he is. He was right there a second ago."

"Calm down, Mom, I'm sure he's fine. He probably just ran off down the street to hit up a few more houses before you could stop him."

She's probably right, but it doesn't stop the panic that's steadily rising in my chest.

I know I usually let Cameron go off on his own during the day but it's dark now and I've heard of way too many abductions starting with a kid getting lost in the hubbub of a large crowd.

I walk quickly down the road, Mory running to keep up with me, and I look at every doorway, every front yard, every group of children, trying to spot my son. It's when I'm approaching the end of the street that I spot him. He's struggling as a man holds on to his arm, pulling him along.

"Hey!" I shout. "Hey! Get off of him! Leave my son alone!"

But before I can do anything about it, the man opens the door to one of the end houses and drags Cameron inside, shutting the door behind him.

8

MORY

I'm panting by the time I catch up with Mom, who for some reason is standing outside a stranger's door, slamming her fists loudly against it.

"Hey! Get out here!" She turns to me, gesturing franticly with her arms. "Mory, call the cops right now!"

"What? Why?" I say, no idea what's going on.

Before she can answer, the door opens and an annoyed-looking man and a guy about my age, who is clearly his teenage son, stand in front of us, confusion painting their faces.

I recognize him immediately; he's the hot blond guy who I passed by that day on my way home from school. The guy who turned back to check me out just as I had been doing the same.

"Can you please stop banging down our door?" the man says. "What's going on?"

My mom steps up close to him, her hands on her hips. "Where is my son?"

The man looks around his driveway, and then back at her. "Uh... I have no idea. Who are you?"

"CAMERON!" my mother shrieks, trying to get a look

inside the house then giving up and pointing a finger at the man. "I saw you take my son. I'm calling the cops right now."

The man looks lost for words and just as my mother pulls out her phone and begins dialing, a little boy approaches the door from inside the house. He's wearing a Spiderman costume with the mask hanging down and I recognize him as Leo Parker, Cameron's friend.

"Um... I think I saw Cam dunking for apples outside the Jensens' house," Leo says, timidly.

Mom's face turns ghost white as she figures out what's just happened. The man says nothing as Leo and his older brother look on awkwardly.

This is the most brutally embarrassing thing I've ever witnessed my mother do. And right in front of the only hot guy in this town. Well, he is if you don't count that realtor, Benton, anyway.

"Oh my God." My mother buries her face in both her hands. "Oh my God. I'm so sorry. I... I thought Leo was my son, Cameron. He's in the same costume, and I..."

The man looks amused. "Don't worry about it. Easy mistake to make. I'm Quinten Parker, Leo's father. And this is Hutch, our older son."

I can't look up; this is too painful to watch.

"What's going on?" a voice comes from inside the house.

A woman who I assume is Leo and Hutch's mother appears at the door, a concerned look staining her beautiful face. Well, it's clear to see where Hutch gets his looks, with parents like these.

"Oh, Felicity, I'm so sorry!" Mom says, nearly crying at this point.

She explains the mistake she made—thinking Mr. Parker had taken Cameron—and the woman is as sympathetic as her husband, but I'm sure this whole family thinks my mom is completely crazy. And, by association, me too.

Felicity turns to her son. "Hutch, can you take Cameron's sister over to the Jensens' to help find him, please?"

"Sure," he says and we both start down the street as Felicity guides my mom inside their house, presumably to help her calm down a little.

The trick or treating has mostly come to an end but there are still kids in costumes playing out on the street and stuffing their faces with candy.

"I'm Mory, by the way," I tell Hutch. "And I'm really sorry about my mom. I can't believe she thought your dad was kidnapping Cameron."

He looks at me, then scoops back a lock of blond hair that hangs down in front of his face. I'm not sure what passes between us in this moment but he begins to laugh and, I can't help myself, I start laughing too. And then we're both walking along, cackling stupidly together and I'm wiping tears from my eyes because I can't believe what just happened.

When we finally get a hold of ourselves, Hutch asks, "Haven't I seen you around?"

"Probably. We've been living here for a couple of months now."

"How do you like Lonerock?" He raises an eyebrow.

"Uh... it's—"

"Boring? I know," he cuts in.

We both laugh again and I feel instantly at ease with him. In the short time it takes to get to the Jensens' house, Hutch tells me he's turning eighteen in a few days, he's a senior at Hyde Academy (a private school where I'll bet each term costs more money than my mom makes in a year) and his passion is robotics.

At the last part, I perk up. "Really? Me too! I took a robotics program they ran at my last school. It was kind of basic but it was the only class I ever looked forward to. I'm the only person I know who actually likes that kind of stuff."

"Well, I guess there's two of us." His eyes sparkle in the moonlight as he talks. "My dad and I do builds together every weekend. You should come over and join us sometime."

I don't want to seem too eager at this, an offer that sounds like the best thing I've ever heard. Getting to spend time with one of the hottest guys I've ever met while building robots? Is life pranking me right now? This kind of stuff doesn't ever happen to me.

"Sure, I'll give you my number. Just tell me when to come over and I'll be there." I work hard to keep a big goofy grin that's trying to break through off my face.

We arrive outside the Jensens' where several unattended kids are playing a game of pin the tail on the witch's cat, which I literally have to drag Cameron away from, digging my fingers into his arm to keep the brat from squirming out of my grip.

When the three of us return to Hutch's house, we find Mom, Felicity and Quinten inside the kitchen drinking tea and talking.

The Parkers' house is easily twice the size of ours, maybe bigger. It's got huge glass windows, beautiful stone floors and there's not a speck of dust or dirt anywhere. It reminds me a little of my dad's house, not the style exactly, but it has that kind of put together look, a bit like a showroom you'd see in a catalogue. As though a lot of thought has gone into placing every item where it is. One thing's for sure though, if this is where Hutch lives he'd be horrified by the inside of my house, which looks as though the eighties walked up and barfed all over it.

As soon as we're inside, Leo immediately grabs hold of Cameron and drags him off to go compare their candy haul.

Hutch stands next to me a little awkwardly, before he turns

to his father. "Hey, Dad, can Mory join in on our build this weekend?"

Quinten turns to me. "You like robotics?"

"I do." I grin. "Hutch told me about the builds you two do, they sound really cool."

"Well, we'll be making an ant with head sensors this weekend, if you want to help out?"

"I'd love to, thanks!" I turn to Hutch and we both catch each other beaming, then quickly rein it in.

I don't want Hutch to know how excited I am about this. I never thought blonds were my type, but this guy is hot as hell, and I've now got a date with him this weekend.

9

———

RUBY

This morning, when I got home from dropping Cameron off at school, I found the woman who lives next door standing on my doorstep. Her name is Bernice Fisher. I learned a lot about her from Felicity and Quinten Parker when I talked with them on Halloween night.

Bernice has been living on this street for over thirty years and in that time has not made one friend. Quite the opposite, apparently. The Parkers told me that everyone on this block has their own stories of run-ins with Bernice. I'm not even close to the first person she's called the cops on and I doubt it was the first time the officer who'd spoken to me that day had been sent out because of a call Bernice Fisher had made.

Quinten told me she'd once reported him for dealing drugs to children after she'd seen him passing his son a packed lunch outside their house. Another time, she'd accused him of breaking and entering when he'd been out helping families tidy up the neighborhood after a bad storm. The feeling around these parts, I take it, is that Bernice Fisher is stark raving mad. And I have the special honor of living next door to her for the rest of my days.

Seeing her on my doorstep from inside my car this morning —arms crossed against her thin frame, eyes narrowed and waiting—I strongly contemplated reversing my car back down the driveway and ignoring her completely.

When I'd finally found the courage to get out and face her, she ordered me to remove the bird feeder that's been sitting in my backyard for the past two weeks. The bird feeder that Cameron made at school and is so proud of.

According to Bernice, the bird feeder is attracting more birds into *her* yard and she plans to hire somebody to come over and power wash her back deck due to the mess they've made. She then demanded that I give her two hundred dollars to cover the cost of this. And since I don't have two hundred dollars to spare (and wouldn't give it to her even if I did), I politely declined. But I did agree to take down the bird feeder.

Cameron will be disappointed. He's been enjoying watching the sparrows and goldfinches fly in and out of the yard from his bedroom, but I've got so much to do already that it's easier to just avoid any more confrontation with Bernice.

At the top of my list of things to do is starting work on the kitchen. Seeing Felicity and Quinten's house the other night left me feeling even more deflated about the state of my own home.

A knot forms in my stomach when I think about Halloween night. I can't believe I accused Quinten of trying to kidnap Cameron and was about to call the cops on him. Am I any better than Bernice Fisher? Is this where she started before it all went downhill for her, accusing her neighbors of everything under the sun, terrorizing the street for the past thirty years?

It really was just a simple mistake—I mean the kid was wearing the exact same costume as Cameron and they're pretty much identical in size—but my reaction was completely over the top and I can't count the number times I apologized to both Quinten and Felicity that night. They were more understanding than I would have been in their place, that's for sure.

It doesn't help me feel any better that they're this perfect couple with two beautiful children (who both attend private schools, of course) and a huge house and money to throw around. Felicity even coaches Leo's little league team while Quinten works on science projects with their older son, Hutch, on weekends. They're the family Aaron and I wanted to be. We never did manage it, though. I don't for one moment regret our divorce—which went quite amicably—but that doesn't stop the little stab of pain I get when I see families who not only make it all work but have so much to show for it, too.

I can't offer my kids a home with two parents, or a huge house, lots of money, or to coach them in their extracurricular activities. But I can try my damnedest to make this home one that they don't hate returning to each day or feel ashamed at the idea of bringing friends over to. I'm tackling it one room at a time and today I'm going to show this kitchen who's boss.

I've had my morning coffee, the kids are back at school, and I'm armed and ready with a tool that looks a whole lot like a crowbar. It might actually be a crowbar, I'm not sure, but I'm ready to pry the old yellowing laminate countertops from the otherwise decent cupboards and drawers sitting underneath. All the cupboards need are a lick of paint and then I can affix to them the secondhand (but good as new) countertops I scored for next to nothing online. Then I just need to replace the old grapevine patterned tiles with the plain white ceramic ones I picked up from Home Depot and voilà! A whole new kitchen for less than four hundred dollars.

I'd planned to wait until the weekend to start this particular task because I thought maybe we could all do this one room together as a family, but after learning that both my children will be spending this entire Saturday over at the Perfect Parkers' house—Mory doing robotics with Hutch, and Cameron on a Lego playdate with Leo—I figured I may as well just get started all by myself.

I'm not sure how much longer I can wait for this magical future I've been envisioning to arrive. The one where my children and I spend one full day together, bonding or playing or just hanging out. At some point I might have to accept that my kids just don't want to spend the precious little spare time they have with their mother.

I suppose I'm happy about Mory finding a friend so close by, though. Hutch seems like a good kid. Mory told me she has a group of friends at school she hangs out with, but I've noticed that she never goes out with them at weekends or over to any of their houses. I'm starting to wonder if they really exist.

I know that despite Mory's genuine interest in robotics, the real reason she wants to go over to the Parkers' this weekend is to get closer to Hutch. He's got a Disney Channel kind of face and the floppy blond hair to match. I saw the look in her eyes at their house, the girl is crushing hard and it's adorable. And since there'll be some parental supervision involved, I have no issue with her spending time with Hutch over there.

Then again, if it all ends in tears—as it so often does with teenagers—she'll be stuck living on the same street as Hutch until they move away for college. But love and heartbreak are all par for the course at her age and I won't be the one to get in the way of her path. Not that she'd let me if I tried.

I start on the far side of the countertop, wedging the bar underneath and levering it upwards. I hear a little crunching noise and the side of it lifts up a little. That was easy. This might not take as long as I'd expected it to. I move along to the middle section and do the same, but this time when I move the counter upwards a tile on the wall at the back of it shifts and falls over, as though it was already loose.

When I go to pick it up, I see something stuck to the rear side of it with a piece of tape. It's another photo.

I smile and lift it up. I'd almost forgotten about the one I found under the living-room carpet. I'd shown it to Mory when she got home from school one day and suggested we should get an instant camera and do the same ourselves as we renovate the place, but she hadn't seemed interested.

I take the tape from the photo and turn it around. It's just like the last photo, but this one is of a different young woman. She's wearing a red and white flowery dress with big puffed-up sleeves, the kind my aunt would always wear to church when I was a child, along with a wide-brimmed summer hat that would block the view of the people in the row behind.

It's weird, though. This girl bears no resemblance to the one in the last photo. Her hair is much lighter in color and straighter. She's sitting in seemingly the same place and in the same pose— against a wood-paneled wall and smiling wide for the camera— but I can't imagine she's related to the girl from the last photo. Jessie, I remember it had read.

This one has another name written below, in the same writing as the last. *Sandra.*

I stare at the photo and the same questions run through my mind as with the last. Did it occur to these people that these photos might take another thirty or so years to be uncovered? And what I'd really love to know is; what exactly was it that Jessie and Sandra were so happy about?

10

SANDRA

Sandra wakes to the sound of footsteps in the next room. Her limbs are heavy and her head is spinning. For a moment she thinks she's at home in her own bed, before she smells the musty odor of damp wood and the terrifying reality sets in.

He brought her here last night. He told her his name was Charlie and that he worked for Manning Models as a talent scout. He showed her his business card and a black binder full of models signed to their agency. Sandra even recognized some of them. That was when he asked her to come to his studio. His enthusiasm was so infectious that when he promised this was the start of an amazing future for her, she believed him. Like an idiot.

She knew by twenty minutes into the drive that he wasn't really a model scout. His avoidance and vague answers to all her questions tripped the alarm in her mind and she knew she needed to get away from this man, and fast. It's not like she hadn't seen the warning signs when he first approached her but stupidly she ignored them, so badly wanting to believe.

The thing is, when a guy like Charlie picks you out from the crowd and tells you you're one of the most beautiful girls he's ever seen and that he's going to make you a household name... well, you should walk away right then and there. And maybe fifty other girls did. But Sandra didn't. She wanted to believe that this was the *something* she'd always felt was around the corner for her. That this smooth, handsome man was telling her the truth and that in just a few months' time she'd be in London or Paris, walking the catwalks in the latest big-name designers' clothing and being paid thousands for it.

She can hear how phony it all sounds now, but when Charlie looked into her eyes it felt as though he was unlocking something deep within her, a part of her which nobody else had ever accessed before. But by the time she found the courage to speak up and tell him she'd figured him out it was too late, because whatever was in that Diet Coke he gave her had left her limbs slack within minutes. He'd drugged her. It's obvious now, but for some reason that wasn't as clear to her as she sat in that car feeling each part of her body gradually failing to respond. She'd wanted to pull her bag from the footwell below her, open the car door and jump right out. But all she could do was blink at the headlights on the road ahead that were blinding her. Those headlights became fewer and fewer until there were no other cars around. Or houses. Just a dirt track that felt as though it wound on forever.

By the time they arrived at the cabin she could barely keep her eyes open and when she tried to speak, her mouth just couldn't form the right shapes. The last thing she remembers before she'd fallen into a deep dreamless sleep was a shadow kneeling down beside her and cold eyes fixed on hers.

Now, in the early morning light, she tries to lift her head from the mattress and listen closely to the sounds coming from the next room. The fog that's been clouding her mind begins to clear but with that, the gravity of the mistake she's made hits fully. She doesn't know where she is, she doesn't know who the man really is and they're so far from civilization that there's nobody around to save her.

She sees a bathroom across the room and forces herself to sit up. Her head is pounding and her mouth is bone-dry. She's never needed a drink of water so badly. She slides her feet over the edge of the bed and onto the floor. There are no shoes on her feet, he must have taken them off her. Thankfully she's otherwise still fully dressed, a welcome consolation amidst the nightmare she's found herself in.

The wood floor shifts noisily under her feet as she moves and she only makes it halfway across the room before a figure appears in the doorway. The smile that was used to so easily convince her yesterday now drives a dagger of fear deep into her chest.

"Good morning, Sleeping Beauty." He crosses his arms and leans back against the door frame casually.

Sandra freezes where she stands, not knowing what to do or say.

"Go on." He extends an arm. "Go to the bathroom. I'll wait here."

She keeps her eyes on his as she moves forward and reaches for the handle. The light is already on inside and there's no lock when she closes the door but at least there's an illusion of safety inside here that she can cling on to. She turns the rusted faucet and pulls her hair back, ducking down to drink greedily from the flowing water. She then splashes some on her face before taking a few breaths, trying to figure out what she's going to do next. She wishes she'd told somebody where she was going or who she was with, but after Charlie introduced himself to her, everything happened so fast that she didn't get a chance.

There's a knock at the bathroom door and her whole body goes rigid.

"Sandra, put on the dress." His muffled voice from outside the door is quiet but firm.

She looks around and finds something folded up on the shelf. It unfolds as she pulls it down. It's a red dress with white flowers and large puffed-out shoulders. It's made of a cheap, crinkly kind of fabric and it's hideous. She doesn't want to put it on, but there's a voice shouting inside her head not to make this man angry. If she wants to get out of here, she needs to stay quiet and do as she's told. Then maybe he'll let her go.

Each little movement takes her full concentration as she gets out of her clothes and into the dress. Her whole body is threatening to collapse but she tries to stay strong. She just needs to play along with this and everything will be okay. She looks at herself in the small mirror above the sink. Her skin almost matches the dress: her face is pasty white and her eyes rimmed with red.

She can hear his footsteps out there, pacing. The last thing she wants to do is leave the bathroom and face the man waiting for her in the other room, but she has no other choice. She takes a deep breath and slowly opens the door. She jumps in fright when she sees he's right outside, his face so close she can smell his stale breath.

"You look beautiful." His eyes come to life, and he runs a finger down the material at her shoulder.

He's holding a camera in one hand and uses it to gesture to the wall across from the bed. "Sit down over there."

"I... do I have to? Can't we go outside?" she croaks.

"Sandra, a little advice. If you want a good picture taken, never argue with the photographer." There's an impatience in his voice that scares her.

Sandra knows he didn't bring her here just to take photos, and she can only pray that she finds a way to escape before his real plans are revealed. She walks to the side of the room and sits down slowly against the wall, looking up at the lens pointed her way.

"No, no, no." Charlie lowers the camera from his eye. "Come on, sweetheart, you've got to smile."

She tries to morph her features into a smile but it's as though she's forgotten how.

"Did you not just hear me, Sandra? Smile!" he shouts and she flinches.

"I just want to go home," she whimpers, her words sticking together as she speaks.

"Sandra, this was supposed to be nice. You're my model, remember? And I just want to take one photo. That's all."

She swallows down a lump in her throat. "Okay."

She uses everything she has to force herself to smile.

"Bigger. Bigger. Come on now!"

Sandra stretches her mouth until it's painfully wide. A sudden flash of light goes off before a photo slides from the front of the camera and he holds it up like a prized possession. "Don't you feel better now, for co-operating?"

She nods as a tear runs down her cheek.

There's a darkness to his eyes as he studies the photo and mutters to himself. "I'm going to keep this forever."

It only takes a split second for Sandra to make the decision. She prays that her legs will hold her as she rises up and begins to dash for the door, but she's too slow and in seconds he has her in a tight grip. She tries to kick and scream but he just pulls her in tighter toward him and she looks up to see the same smile she saw on his face yesterday. Except now the kindness in it is gone, replaced by something darker. Something terrifying.

"You're not going anywhere, Sandra."

I pull up outside Cameron's school just after lunchtime. In my rush to get over here I forgot to grab a jacket, which I'm now regretting as I get out of the car and make the short walk to the front entrance, the chilly breeze biting through the thin fabric of my sweater.

When Cameron told me yesterday about a small scuffle he and another boy had gotten into at school over a wolf sticker, I hadn't thought it anything serious. He'd said he'd planned to put the wolf sticker on the picture collage he'd been working on and had left it on his desk while he went to go sharpen his pencil at the trash can. When he returned, he found the boy had taken it and stuck it firmly to his own collage. Cameron had gotten angry and tried to pull it off the boy's paper and the boy had shoved him, resulting in Cameron telling the teacher on him. Your typical eight-year-old squabble.

But the call I got from the principal thirty minutes ago, requesting that I come in right away to meet with him about another incident Cameron was involved in with the same boy has me worried. Cameron is not the kind of kid who goes around starting fights. He's gentle, considerate and tends to make friends with every kid he meets, so this leads me to believe the problem isn't him, it's this other child. Cameron seems to love going to this school, so I don't want anything to ruin that for him.

Inside it strikes me, as it has done in the past, how strange it is that every single elementary school smells the same. Like markers and floor cleaner mixed with teachers' despair.

I quickly find the main office and explain why I'm here to the school secretary, and she directs me to the principal's office down the end of the hall.

When I knock on the door and poke my head into the room, Principal Sailsbury is sitting behind his desk talking on the phone. He looks up and smiles at me apologetically, flashing five fingers my way. I close the door and sit on one of the two chairs outside his office. After a moment, a woman walks by and glances my way. She smiles and when I smile back, I realize it's with an almost shameful expression. It doesn't matter how old you get, sitting outside the principal's office will transport you right back to your childhood.

"Mind if I sit?" I'm shaken from my thoughts when I see a man with dark hair and work combats approach me and point at the seat next to mine questioningly.

"Go ahead." I smile.

"Thanks." He sits down and leans forward, clasping his hands together. "In trouble with the principal?"

I laugh. "That's how it feels."

I get a hint of this man's scent and discreetly breathe in deeper. He smells great. Like freshly cut pine mixed with soap.

"I'm Justin Thomas, by the way. Xavier's dad." He holds out his hand.

I'm not sure who he's referring to for a moment before it

clicks that he's here for the same reason as me, and I reach out to shake his hand with a hesitant smile. "I'm Ruby Blake, Cameron's mom."

I see Justin's eyes flicker almost imperceptibly down at our hands, likely noticing—as I do—that neither of us wears a wedding ring.

"So, uh..." Justin grimaces. "Do you know what happened?"

"No, I just got the call a little while ago to come in. I hope it was nothing too bad."

"I'm sure it's just another disagreement. Xavier told me about yesterday's incident with the wolf sticker," he says.

"I heard about that, too. And don't worry, Cameron didn't seem too upset about Xavier pushing him."

Justin laughs. "Uh... I wasn't worried. Because Cameron was the one who pushed Xavier."

I cross my arms. "That's not what I heard."

"Well, I guess you heard wrong then." There's a playful smile on his lips. "And we should have no problem getting to the bottom of this because Principal Sailsbury used to be a criminal defense lawyer."

I raise a brow. "Used to be?"

Justin nods and lowers his voice before leaning in conspiratorially. "The rumor is that he was disbarred for misuse of client funds. I heard he was ordered to repay over fifty thousand dollars that he'd already blown on gambling."

My mouth drops. "Noooo."

"Yep."

"And they just let him be principal here?" I whisper.

"Uh-huh. I mean, he's not a danger to the kids or anything but... you know. It's hard to respect a guy who would do something like that."

I want to ask more but the door to the office opens up and Principal Sailsbury calls us in. We both stand up and walk inside, and he gestures for us to sit across from him at his desk.

His office is small but bright, with a window overlooking the playground. And judging by how clean and impossibly neat the room is, I take it Daniel Sailsbury is an organized man.

He takes his seat across from us and clasps his hands together on the desk. "Mr. Thomas, Miss Blake. Thanks for coming in. As I told you both on the phone, there was another incident this morning with Xavier and Cameron, the second in two days. Their teacher, Mrs. Jacobs, recommended I bring the parents in to try to resolve this issue at a base level."

"What happened exactly?" Justin asks.

"Well, I'm told that during reading time this morning, Mrs. Jacobs found the two boys fighting over a book and some name calling ensued," he says gravely.

Justin tuts. "Surely there's a rule saying teachers can't do that?"

This doesn't elicit so much as a smirk from the principal. "It was Xavier and Cameron who were doing the name calling, Mr. Thomas."

I don't really want to say it out loud, but I mean... that's it? That's what I left my kitchen remodel to come in and talk about? I know it's been a long time since I was at school but my memory is that boys of that age would routinely throw names back and forth at one another, get each other in headlocks, then be back to friends by lunchtime. This doesn't feel like a call-the-parents-in kind of situation, and I can't help but suppress a chuckle over the idea of Daniel Sailsbury going from questioning witnesses on the stand to mediating a discussion where the subject is two boys calling each other poopy heads.

It appears that Justin is on the same train of thought as me. "Did either of the accused physically assault the other?"

Principal Sailsbury clears his throat. "This is not a versus issue, Mr. Thomas. And no, there was no physical fight. But I believe there was an incident yesterday where one of the boys shoved the other."

"Yes, that was Miss Blake's son, Cameron. He shoved Xavier over a *wolf sticker*." Justin shoots me a raised brow, daring me to contest him.

"Not true. It was the other way round," I say.

"It's not important who—" Principal Sailsbury doesn't get to finish his sentence as Justin turns to me, ignoring him.

"Not only that, but I put it to you that your son is a repeat offender. Xavier told me he once saw Cameron skip line for a pudding cup in the lunch hall," he says, clearly enjoying this.

I scoff and cross my arms. "Oh, please. Unreliable witness."

Justin nods, as though he's onto something. "*And* I heard that he routinely toots and blames innocent bystanders."

"Oh, objection!" I can't stop myself.

"On what grounds?" Justin tips his head, daring me.

"Relevance." I turn back to the principal. "And I'd like that remark stricken from the record."

"I'm not keeping any records of this conversation, Miss Blake." Principal Sailsbury sighs.

"Actually, I'd say it's quite relevant to establishing your son's character," Justin posits.

It seems as though we might be grating on Principal Sailsbury's nerves because he leans back in his chair and tries to rein the conversation in. "I think you're both missing the point here. I'd just like to reiterate that this is not a versus issue. We try to foster a cohesive structure in our classrooms and what we're looking for is a way to encourage that in both of your boys."

Justin nods in agreement at this and scoots his chair forward. "If I may approach the desk?"

"You're a mere two feet from it, Mr. Thomas. But sure." He squeezes the bridge of his nose, completely unamused.

Justin nods. "Thanks. I think that a *cohesive structure* is what we all want, but I'm sensing a lack of co-operation from the defense." He shoots a thumb back at me.

"If you two have just about finished this..." Principal Sailsbury seems at a loss for words. "*This.* Then I would suggest you try working through your children's issues by giving them the opportunity to get to know each other outside the school setting."

It's not long before the principal dismisses us both with a very reluctant handshake and the moment we close his office door behind us, Justin and I both crack up.

I have to muffle my laughter in my sleeve as I wave goodbye to the secretary when we pass by the office.

"I think that went really well," Justin says chipperly as we walk out the door into the cold outside.

I raise an eyebrow. "Well, I don't think he'll be calling either of us into his office anytime soon again, anyway. He looked like he wanted to punch you."

"You mean *cohesively structure* his fist with my face?"

I laugh at this. "Schools have changed since our day, huh?"

"You can say that again. I once got pushed into a huge mud puddle by the biggest kid in my school. My principal saw it with his own eyes and you know what he did?"

"What?"

"Nothing. He just held out a hand to pull me back up and told me to go clean myself off."

This about tracks with what I remember from childhood and I'm so glad things have changed since then. I'm happy that bullying is no longer tolerated, but on the other hand I think calling in parents for every squabble or disagreement only stops children from learning how to resolve conflict themselves.

When I reach my car, Justin stops next to me. He leans against the hood and crosses his arms. "I think Principal Sailsbury might be onto something though, maybe we should get the boys together."

I pause. "Oh. Well, sure, I guess. If you give me your number, we can arrange something soon. Maybe take them out for ice cream, if you want?"

Justin smiles. "Great. It's a date."

12

—————

MORY

"Okay, Mory, you want to pass the body shell over?"

I pick up the shell and pass it to him. "Here you go, Mr. Parker."

"I told you, call me Quinten," Hutch's dad says, placing the shell around the body of the ant, hiding the magic we've been working on all afternoon underneath it.

"Sorry," I say, then look at Hutch next to me and make an oops face.

Hutch laughs, and his dimples show.

There's no denying it, he's cute. Freshly eighteen this week, he's two years older than me but he's already taller than his father and has a maturity beyond which I've ever seen in a guy his age.

Spending today at the Parkers' house, working on this robotic ant project with Hutch and his dad has been the best experience I've had since moving to this crappy town. And judging from the sounds coming from downstairs, I'd say Cameron enjoys being at the Parkers' house better than ours, too. He and Leo are supposed to be doing Lego down there but

63

I'm pretty sure they've just been having a Nerf fight for about an hour now.

In our house there would be no room for both a delicate robotics project and an all-out Nerf war to coexist, but the Parkers have a dedicated project room upstairs that holds everything from Felicity's sewing machine and reels of fabric to a completed seven-thousand-piece Lego Millennium Falcon, which Hutch and his dad built. There's a huge wooden table in the middle of the room with benches either side of it and a wall with shelves the whole way up that has every kind of craft supply imaginable. This is a family who do things together. Create things together. It shows, too, in Hutch's relationship with his father. And I've been trying to put my full attention into this build but when you're working right alongside a guy this hot your mind begins to wander.

"Okay, kids. I think you can take over from here. I've got to go check on the boys, they probably have the whole house covered in Lego by now. Hutch, you show Mory how to work the remote," Quinten says, then leaves the room.

I notice he leaves the door open a little, probably to make sure that robotics are all Hutch and I are doing in here.

Alone with him now, I scoot a little further up the bench closer to Hutch as he explains the controls. "Okay, you just move this up and..." He smiles as the ant moves forwards.

"This is so cool," I say. "Way more advanced than what we did back in my old school."

"My dad and I started with the basics as well, about a year ago, and we've just kind of been working our way up from there," Hutch explains.

I take the remote and move the little ant back and forth, and Hutch is so close now that I can hear his breath near my ear. At the press of a button the ant turns and walks in the other direction. I try to focus but my thoughts are elsewhere.

I wonder if I'm on his mind as much as he's on mine. I know he's attracted to me, too, it's obvious with the little looks he's given me today. Even so, I can't come on too strong because I'm afraid of what his reaction might be. But since that day we walked past each other and both looked back at the same time, he's been on my mind. His blond hair, his deep blue eyes, and the wanting look on his face when he glances my way.

Hutch's fingers graze mine as he picks up the ant, which threatens to fall off the table and we both pull our hands back as though a bolt of electricity passed through us. We laugh nervously and get back to playing with the ant as my mind begins to drift again.

If things do ever go further than flirting, I know that nothing can happen here at his house. Not with his whole family here.

"I'm really glad you came over today," Hutch says.

"Me too." I grin as our eyes meet.

"Have you been to Lonerock Falls yet?"

"What's that, a waterfall?"

Hutch nods. "Yeah. And it's pretty great. It's only about five minutes from here; I go there all the time. I can take you there sometime if you want?"

"That sounds great," I say.

We hear footsteps approaching and without saying a word we both instinctively move a little further from one another just as Quinten comes back into the room.

"How are you kids getting on? Is the ant working okay?" he asks.

Hutch clears his throat. "Yeah, I think so."

Quinten leans between us and picks it up. "You two did a great job. Should we bring it down and show the boys?"

"Sure." Hutch gets up and I follow him.

We walk side by side as we follow his dad downstairs. We find Cameron and Leo in the kitchen eating ice cream straight out of the container and when we show them the ant, they immediately want to give it a try outside. Hutch passes over the ant and the controls to his little brother with strict instructions not to break them, then he turns to Quinten who's collecting up dozens of Nerf darts from all over the floor. "Hey, Dad, is it okay if I take the car out? Mory hasn't seen Lonerock Falls yet and I thought I could drive her over there real quick to show her."

"Sure, I don't see why not. Just drive carefully, okay?" He pulls his car keys from his back pocket and flings them to Hutch who catches them.

Outside, we walk shoulder to shoulder down the driveway. "I didn't know you had your license," I say.

"I got it last year." Hutch grins. "Passed first time. I'm saving up for my own car, but for now my dad lets me borrow his every once in a while."

I sit in the passenger side and Hutch starts up the engine. I feel a little nervous about being in a car with a newbie driver behind the wheel but Hutch seems really mature for his age and I doubt he's the type to try to impress me by driving too fast. Either way, I make sure I'm buckled up tight before he carefully backs down the driveway.

We're only driving for a few minutes before Hutch parks the car on the side of the road. We get out and descend a slope on foot—Hutch catching my arm when I nearly fall—and we soon come to a clearing in front of a rushing waterfall. With the embankment hiding the road behind and the water sparkling in the sunlight, it's like suddenly stepping into a painting, too perfect to be true.

"It's beautiful," I breathe.

Hutch steps in front of me and takes hold of my hands. "Not as beautiful as you."

This is by far the sweetest thing a guy has ever said to me. With second place going to the time Jimmy Farnsley at my old school told me I was a solid seven out of ten, with makeup on. Which was rich coming from a guy who looked like he'd stop you on a bridge and make you solve a riddle in order to pass.

Hutch closes in the distance between us and just as his lips are hovering above mine, his phone starts to ring in his pocket and we both let out a nervous laugh before he pulls it out and answers.

I walk over to the waterfall and let the tiny droplets of cast-off wash over my face as he takes the call. After a moment, he walks over and tells me his dad needs the car soon to go collect dinner. With the moment between us passed, we walk back to the car and make the short drive back to his parents' house.

Inside, I find Cameron in the living room with Leo playing a video game and I tell him we have to leave. As usual, he refuses to listen and I have to drag him along by the arm.

Hutch is in the kitchen with his dad, returning the car keys, and I thank them both for letting me help out with the project. Hutch insists I come over again next weekend to help him and his dad with another one.

On the way out the door, pushing Cameron in front of me, I look back and see he's watching me leave. I smile and he winks at me, sending my heart soaring, and I don't think next weekend can come soon enough.

Luckily, it won't have to, because the second Cameron and I arrive back at our house I hear my phone buzz and I pull it out, surprised to see a text signed with his name, reading:

Meet me back at Lonerock Falls at midnight.

13

RUBY

"Okay, you can stop laughing now," I plead.

Justin tries to rein it in, but his pursed lips only stay sealed for about three seconds before laugher bursts out of them again and he doubles over.

"I'm sorry! I'm sorry!" He wipes away a tear. "I just... Oh God, I wish I could've been there to see it. I mean, the image of the guy opening the door to find Cleopatra, Queen of Egypt, standing outside his house accusing him of kidnap!"

I'm starting to regret telling him about what happened on Halloween night.

I cross my arms. "Trust me, it wasn't at all funny in the moment." I struggle to maintain a straight face but a smile slowly creeps across my reddened cheeks. I suppose it is *kind of* funny.

Taking Principal Sailsbury's advice, Justin and I arranged to get Cameron and Xavier together outside of school, giving them a chance to get to know one another better. I'd wanted to take them out for ice cream, but when Justin found out I'd just moved into a fixer-upper he'd insisted that he and Xavier come over, eager to take a look around. I'd been a little apprehensive at first, since my kitchen currently resembles a building site—what with the countertops still missing and the floors all ripped up—but saying this to Justin over the phone had only served to further his excitement about seeing the place.

He'd shown up with two tubs of Ben and Jerry's for the boys and a fully stocked toolkit for me, tied up with a red ribbon. I'd gratefully accepted it, being woefully under equipped for many of the tasks ahead of me, even after my hardware store haul. It seems Justin's a real DIY enthusiast because he's only been here thirty minutes but in that time he's shown me a whole new vision for the place. He's got unusually strong opinions about things like light fixtures and storage solutions.

We're now sitting on the back step, drinking coffee, watching the two boys as they work together to climb the large tree that sits at the end of the yard. Xavier is holding Cameron's foot to give him a boost up. You'd never know they'd been the cause of such problems in their classroom. I suppose Principal Sailsbury was right, they just needed to get to know each other in a different setting.

Justin pushes back his dark hair. "So, you've just moved here. Two kids. Doing this all by yourself. What's your story?"

It's becoming increasingly obvious to me that Justin is a walls-down kind of guy. It's a little intimidating, but also kind of refreshing.

"Divorced. My husband left me for another woman." I shrug. "That old story."

"Ouch." He scrunches his face up.

"It's fine." I sigh. "He really levelled up. She's the domestic goddess I never was. And honestly, both our lives are better for it."

Justin looks as though he's sizing me up, trying to figure me out. I doubt he'll have any luck; I've been living in my skin for over thirty-eight years and I still haven't figured out exactly who I am.

I haven't had to ask Justin about himself because he freely handed out all information up front. He's a man who doesn't beat around the bush. At forty years old he's a carpenter, a widowed father to eight-year-old Xavier and a lifelong resident of Lonerock. He lives close by, in a house he and his wife, Elle, built themselves before she passed away when Xavier was just a baby. All this he shared unreservedly with me, a woman he's only met once before.

My own observations are that he's strangely upbeat for a guy who has faced great loss. He's funny, he's almost too handsome, and seems like a great father. So, naturally, I'm wondering what his deep dark secret is. There has to be something wrong with him.

"So, your daughter, Mory. How is she liking Lonerock?" he asks.

"Hmm," I sigh, "I don't think she's liking it that much at all. Although she met a boy recently so that seems to be helping. He lives down the street. He just turned eighteen and apparently just got his driver's license."

Justin raises an eyebrow at this and I laugh, knowing what he's thinking. Because in truth, it terrifies me.

I was a teenager once. I remember boys with cars. I remember what happens with boys in cars. Although, according to Mory, Hutch is as squeaky clean as they come. He's the model son, the model student, and she says he even drives carefully. Not the kind of guy Mory is usually interested in, but I think his influence might be having an effect on her. I've noticed she's ditched her usual grungy teenager vibe in favor of a cleaner, more preppy style. Gone are her ripped jeans and messy hair, now replaced by a more pulled together, clean appearance. And as much as I think she looks great, I'm worried she's so enamored by Hutch that she's trying to mold herself into what she thinks he wants. I just don't want my daughter to compromise anything about herself in order to try to please a boy. Hutch may be clean-cut and well-spoken but underneath it all he's still an eighteen-year-old male, just like any other, so there's a strong potential for Mory to get hurt.

I watch the boys now as they scramble their way off the tree and run around the side of the house with Cameron's skateboard.

"This guy she's met is from the same family who kidnapped your son?" Justin asks.

I roll my eyes his way but answer anyway. "Yeah. The Parkers. They're so perfect it's enough to make you want to vomit."

"Is this Quinten and Felicity Parker?"

"Yes. You know them?" I ask, surprised.

Justin nods. "There aren't many people in this town I don't know. And yeah, you know when people are that perfect, they've got something to hide."

I laugh. "Funny. I was just thinking something similar about you."

"Me?" Justin points to his chest in disbelief.

"Yeah. I mean, you're doing this all by yourself, you're juggling work and a house and raising a kid, I mean—"

Justin holds out his palm to stop me. "Hold up. You're doing all that, too. Is it somehow more commendable just because I'm a man?" His voice is defiant but there's an amused look on his face.

"Oh stop. That's not what I meant at all." I narrow my eyes at him. "It's just... what with losing your wife, it must be even more difficult. I mean, I get some time off when my ex-husband takes the kids. You don't get that. And you seem as though you just take everything in your stride. Don't you ever just... break?"

Justin shakes his head. "Nope."

"No? Never?"

"Ruby, the thing you're going to learn about me is that I live an unexamined life. I'm not one for introspection. Call that unhealthy if you like. I kind of just get on with things and ignore the naysayers."

"How many naysayers are there exactly?" I ask.

"More than you'd think," he says quietly.

I want to ask more but the boys have reappeared and are running full force toward us.

"Mom!"

"Dad!"

They shout in unison.

"What's up?" I ask Cameron, concerned by the look on his face.

"She took my skateboard! I was showing Xavier a trick and she just came and stole it from me!" he shouts, his voice wobbling as though he's trying not to cry. "She took it inside her house and won't give it back!"

"What? Who are you talking about?" I ask.

"The mean lady from next door!" Cameron shouts.

Generally, I might presume that Cameron was telling me the abridged version of how and why his skateboard was confiscated, but since he's referring to Bernice Fisher, I totally believe it. I give an apologetic look to Justin before I get up to follow Cameron.

I'm starting to wish I'd been told about this woman before I bought the place. Bernice has been nothing but a pain in my ass since we got here and the thought of living next door to her for the next twenty or more years until she croaks sounds exhausting.

I get to her front drive, Cameron right behind me, and march up to her door. "Mrs. Fisher!" I shout and knock loudly.

I ring the doorbell a couple of times for good measure, then wait. The old witch is hiding in there, and apparently she's not coming out. I open up her mail slot and shout through. "Bernice! I know you're in there. My son wants his skateboard back!"

Cameron and I wait another minute before we see Justin walking toward his car with Xavier behind him. Giving up on Bernice, I walk back around to our driveway.

"Sorry about this. The woman next door to us has been giving us a hard time since we moved in. I don't know what her problem is."

"It's okay, we'd better be getting home anyway," Justin says. "I hope you manage to get that skateboard back."

"Yeah," I say. "But then it'll just be something else with her tomorrow."

Cameron runs around the side of the car to say goodbye to his new friend and Justin takes a step closer to me. "So, next time Xavier and I come over, I'm going to install that new countertop for you."

"Is that right? *Next time?*" I say, a little shocked by how forward this guy is.

"Yep," he says, popping the 'p' at the end. "We'll see you sometime next week."

He winks at me as he gets into his car and I watch, mouth agape, as he drives off. I'm not sure I've ever met a guy like Justin before. So cocksure and uninhibited.

Cameron pulls at the side of my top. "Mom, I really want my skateboard back."

I look back at our neighbor's house, then nod to him. "You go inside. I'll get your skateboard back for you."

Cameron runs into the house and I metaphorically pull up my sleeves as I—a mother scorned—march right up to Bernice Fisher's house ready to stand up for my son.

But the strangest thing happens when I get to her door. My hand is out, poised to knock, when the door swings open and Bernice stands there, a dark look clouding her haggard face. She shoves the skateboard into my hands and looks right into my eyes as she speaks quietly. "Do not trust Justin Thomas. *He* was the one that did it," she says before slamming the door in my face.

14
———

MORY

If you'd told me when Mom first moved us out here three months ago that I'd soon be dreading leaving Lonerock to go to my father's house in Arizona, I'd have said you were out of your mind. Certifiably insane.

But it's been two weeks since I first visited Lonerock Falls, and since then I've been back four times. Each time after nightfall, when Mom and Cameron are asleep. I stay up some nights, my phone in my hand, waiting for the text to come. And on the nights it does, I make the fifteen-minute walk in the dark to the waterfall, where I find him waiting for me.

The first night I snuck out to meet him there, he'd leaned down to kiss me and it felt as though my legs might drop out from underneath me. But each time we get together, I feel more and more comfortable wrapped up in his arms. And the fact we're keeping this a secret from everyone makes it all the more exciting. And on the weekends, when I go to the Parkers' to join in on the robotics builds, the best part of the day is when we find a stolen moment together to share a kiss.

So, the thought of Christmas break being just around the

corner and having to leave him behind and not see him for over two weeks feels like torture. I may as well be stabbed in the heart right now.

My mom knows that I find Hutch cute, I've told her, of course, and she teases me about it when I go to his. But if she knew the truth about the make out sessions, I know she'd put a stop to me going over there.

My mom still thinks of me as a child. She even calls me 'baby' for God's sake.

I love my mom and I know she's trying really hard to make our home better, but it's a complete mess. And I'm so much happier when I'm at the Parkers' house. I think Cameron is, too.

Last Saturday, after our latest robotics build with his dad, Hutch had waited until we were alone and pulled me by the hand behind the door. His face was just inches from mine. "Will you stay for dinner tonight?"

I felt his fingers lace with mine and I smiled. "I'd love to."

So, with Hutch's mom's blessing (and a text reply from my own mom saying it was okay) both Cameron and I had joined the Parkers for dinner that evening. Cameron and Leo sat next to each other, pretending their slices of garlic bread were airplanes crashing into the broccoli rainforest while Felicity and Quinten had conversed with me and Hutch as though we were their equals.

We discussed history and what places in time we'd love to have seen, and Quinten had even proposed a question to everyone at the table: if you could meet anyone in the world, dead or alive, who would you choose? Felicity had said Marilyn Monroe, which I thought was funny because she kind of looks a little bit like her but with long hair, and Quinten chose some physicist that I'd never heard of. Then Hutch chose Abraham Lincoln, and I chose Ada Lovelace—which Quinten and Hutch both said was a great answer—although if I had been honest, I probably would have said Taylor Swift but I thought they'd be less impressed by that.

After, we'd all had dessert (home-made apple pie with whipped cream) and the whole evening was just so great that when it was time for me and Cameron to leave, going back to my mom's small, messy house and dealing with her annoying questions (*what did the Parkers make for dinner? Did Cameron remember his table manners? Did you both say thank you to Felicity and Quinten before you left?*) was the last thing I wanted to do.

The only consolation was that before I left their house that evening, we'd quietly made a plan to meet again later, since it's the last chance we'll have before I leave for Arizona in few days. We're going to meet at Lonerock Falls again, our usual spot, at midnight. Mom always falls asleep at about ten, and Cameron— who spends his whole day bouncing around the place like a kangaroo on a pogo stick—is dead to the world from eight o'clock onwards every night. So, I have no worries of either of them catching me sneaking out.

When I step out of the house, I pull my coat firmly around myself and watch my breath steam out into the cold December air. Walking by each house, I take in the twinkling Christmas lights and lawn decorations, which make the whole street feel festive and alive.

My mom hasn't put up any decorations this year. She says there's no point because it'll just be her alone there until we get back from Dad's house after New Year. I don't know if she realizes how much of a guilt trip she's laying on me and Cameron when she says things like that. It's not like we choose to go to Dad's house for summers and Christmases. That's what *they* agreed, without ever asking me or Cameron what we wanted. Although, if they had, we would both have just chosen to stay with our dad all the time. And I can't even imagine the guilt trip my mom would lay on us then.

Spending so much time at the Parkers' recently has given me a glimpse into the type of life that I never had the chance to get. The big house, the attentive parents, the dinners around the table together. I mean, we get some of that at my dad's, and Caitlyn is great and all, but I've forgotten what it feels like to have both of your parents together. It felt safe, I remember that. But then, Mom and Dad fought so much that as time went on, that feeling of safety grew less and less stable, until one day everything just crumbled and fell apart. Now me and Cameron go where we're told to, when we're told to. And if that means Mom spends Christmas alone, that's not our fault.

Hutch doesn't have to deal with flights back and forth between his parents' homes, or his parents asking thinly veiled questions about the other one, wanting to know what they're doing and who they're seeing without actually having to come out and ask it.

As I climb down the embankment and hear the falls rushing close by, I look around in the dim light that comes more from the streetlights on the road above than the nearly full moon in the sky, and I see that he's not here yet.

I walk over to the bench to wait for him. I pull out my phone to see if I missed a text, but there's nothing. It's quiet on the road above, there's barely any cars out at this time of night, and it's so cold that after a few minutes I begin losing the feeling in my fingers. I'm wondering where the hell he is when I hear a twig snap behind me and then a pair of arms creep around my shoulders. I jump in fright but laugh when I turn around to see him smiling at me.

"Hey," he says and kisses me softly on the lips.

After a moment I pull away. "You kept me waiting."

"Sorry, I had to make sure everyone was definitely asleep."

"I guess I forgive you," I tease and then laugh as he grabs me and pulls me up into the air, spinning me around before lowering me back down and kissing me again.

This is where I'm happiest now. Right here, in the moonlight, with the water roaring nearby. It's like we're the only two people in the world.

"I don't want to go to my dad's house. I don't want to leave you. You're so lucky you don't have to deal with any of this. Your family is perfect," I say.

I get a side eye for this. "Trust me, our family isn't as perfect as we might seem."

Maybe he's telling the truth. But whenever I look at Hutch, I see a guy who has two perfect parents, the perfect home and seemingly no roadblocks in his way of living an incredible, balanced life. My life is a mess in comparison.

"I'm going to miss you." He rests his forehead on mine before pulling me closer, holding me tightly.

We stand there for a while, embracing the short amount of time we get to spend alone together, and soon it's time to leave again.

By the time I reach my house, it's after one in the morning. I slot the key in quietly and close the door behind me before taking my shoes and coat off and putting them back in their places. I'm two steps up the stairs when I hear her voice.

"Mory, in here please."

I curse under my breath and slowly walk into the living room where I find my mom sitting in the low light of a lamp, a book open on her lap. She puts it down next to her and sighs. "Where were you?"

There's no point in me making up some kind of over the top

ridiculous lie, like I was sleepwalking or that I thought I'd heard a burglar outside, she'd just see right through it.

"With Hutch." I sigh.

She rolls her eyes. "Well, I figured out that much myself. Where?"

"We just met up nearby," I say, not wanting to out our special spot.

"Mory, I know he's only a couple of years older than you, but technically he's an adult and if you two are—"

"We're not having sex, Mom," I say. "Hutch is sweet and respectful and you have nothing to worry about."

"So why the sneaking around?" she asks.

I try to find the right answer to this. "It's... I don't know. There's always other people around when we're at his house. We just want a little time where it's just the two of us, you know?"

Mom nods in understanding. "Okay. I get it. You know it's not *that* long ago that I was a teenager."

I have to look down at my feet to stop myself from rolling my eyes. The amount of times Mom has reminded me that she and Dad were high school sweethearts and that she was only twenty-two when they had me, and that she's a 'young mom' is embarrassing. It's as though she thinks it makes her cooler or more relatable in my eyes, but if there's a difference between her and the older moms around the place, I don't see it.

"I'm sorry for sneaking out. It's just this was my last chance to see him and I'm going to really miss him when I go to Dad's next week," I say honestly.

Mom gets up from the couch and hugs me tight, then kisses my hair.

"That's really sweet. I know Hutch is a nice guy, and I trust that you have good judgment. But with the age gap, it's important that you wait at least a few months, until you're seventeen, before you and he consider taking your relationship any further, okay?" Her voice is kind but there's no hiding the underlying sternness to it.

"Just like you and Dad did, right?" I can't resist.

Mom looks down at her bare wrist, eyes wide. "Gosh, it's late. We should really be getting to bed."

15

———

RUBY

And just like that, Mory and Cameron are gone again.

I dropped them off at the airport this morning and clung on to them until they pried themselves away from my grip. Their father will get to enjoy the holiday season with them and I'll be wishing them a happy Christmas over the phone again. The same for New Year.

When I arrived back from the airport alone and listened to the deafening silence that filled the house and looked around at the clutter of unfinished odd jobs and works in progress around me, I knew I had two choices: spend the holiday period wallowing in my own self-pity, or roll my sleeves up and throw myself into getting this house renovated.

I half-heartedly chose the latter and now, as I'm hauling a box of broken old tiles outside to the trash, I glimpse Bernice Fisher at her window, watching me. She sees me look at her and turns away, closing the curtains. That woman must have absolutely no life of her own, because she seems to spend her time waiting at her window for something—anything—that she can log a complaint with someone about. I don't know what capacity Bernice knows Justin Thomas in, but her warning to me a couple weeks back that '*he did it*' could have been referencing anything from cutting in line at the grocery store to single-handedly pulling off the Kennedy assassination. Luckily, her dislike of Justin seems to be as unfounded as her dislike of, well, everyone else.

Justin has been a saving grace for me, coming over and helping me install the new countertops in the kitchen and then again to help with tiling the backsplash. Xavier comes along with him to play with Cameron, and Justin always brings ice cream for the two boys and some kind of DIY related gift for me. After the toolkit, it was a stud finder and then a set of wrenches, each time wrapped up with a red ribbon. I'd have to be blind not to notice his flirting, the man doesn't have a subtle bone in his body. I was wondering how long it would take him to actually make a move when I finally got a text from him yesterday:

> You, me, that kitchen sink waiting to be
> installed and a bottle of wine tomorrow night.
> I'll be over at seven.

I didn't have much choice but to agree. I've been putting off installing the new sink I bought for the kitchen and the offer was very much appreciated... and the fact that I've since meticulously shaved, exfoliated, blow dried my hair and bought myself a brand-new set of lace underwear is purely coincidental.

Since my split with Aaron, I've only been on one date. It was a blind date—set up by a mutual friend—and it was going great until midway through our meal when he got a text from his ex-wife asking him to come over to help fix her laptop. He literally got up mid plate of spaghetti, threw three twenties on the table, apologized, and left. That kind of put me off the whole dating thing for a while. And since I haven't really been putting myself out there at all, it's been a long time since I've had any prospective suitors. So, the fact that there's now an attractive man who not only knows how to take the lead but has taken it upon himself to help fix up my house is a new development in my life you won't find me pushing back against. And I guess there's no ex-wife to compete with here, because she's dead.

Oh God, did I really just think that?

As I mentally beat myself up for this, I haul sections of the old kitchen countertops into the back of my car ready to dispose of just in time to see Felicity and her two gal pals approaching, out on their morning walk. It's hard not to notice they're all wearing Santa hats, and I suddenly feel a little self-conscious about my decoration-free house.

The three women slow down as they reach me and, as usual, Kendra and Harriet hang right by Felicity's side as she speaks. "Ruby! How are you?"

"I'm good, thanks." I wipe my hands on the back of my jeans and cast my eyes back and forth between the Stepford Trio. "You all look very festive today."

"Just spreading a little joy." Felicity laughs and then her face darkens. "Ruby, is it true what I heard? That you're dating Justin Thomas?"

Wow. Word spreads fast around these parts.

I notice there's a hungry look on both Kendra and Harriet's faces, like a couple of piranhas waiting to be fed by the latest piece of gossip on the street. I decide not to feed them today. "I think you must have heard wrong, because he's just helping me fix up the house. Cameron is friends with his son, Xavier."

Felicity delicately places a hand to her chest, seeming relieved. "Oh, good."

I don't know why she'd have an opinion about who I choose

to date, but she doesn't give me a chance to ask before she quickly changes the subject.

"You know my boys are really going to miss Mory and Cameron over the holidays. Especially Hutch. You know I think there's a little love story brewing there." She cups her hand to the side of her mouth as though she's divulging a secret.

"Yes, Mory's very fond of Hutch, too. The robotics sessions with him and Quinten are all she ever talks about. It's so nice of them to include her," I say. "And thank you for letting Cameron come over to play with Leo so often."

Felicity waves this away. "No need to thank me, we just love having them both at our house. It's starting to feel like they're family, we see them so often."

This comment, although I'm sure meant warmly, sends an icy dagger through my heart. I'm used to Mory and Cameron preferring their father's house over mine, but now I have a whole new set of competition closer to home. The simple fact is that my kids seem to want to spend time with anyone, anywhere, rather than be with me in our new place.

The three women—having successfully spread their joy—carry on down the street and I spend the next hour pulling furniture and toys out of Cameron's room in order to access the floor. Like the rest of the original wooden floors in this house, they're in rough shape and will need sanding down and staining. I won't get all of that done today, but I'm determined to get a start on both the kids' rooms in the hope I can have them looking great for when they get back. The downside to this is that the upstairs hall is small enough already without more clutter added to it, and now I'm going to have to climb over a bed as well as a mountain of action figures and building sets in order to access the stairs each day until I have the rooms finished. But I know it'll all be worth it in the end.

Once I have Cameron's room completely cleared out every

movement I make inside there echoes sadly around the bare walls. I try to pump myself up a little by setting up a portable speaker and putting on an upbeat eighties playlist. I figure everything else in this house is stuck in that decade, why not just go with it?

As the synth-pop sounds of A-ha's 'Take on Me' start blasting out, I dance around the room with my dustpan and brush sweeping up the random bits of debris I find.

There are pieces of yellow card that Cameron seems to have cut up into hundreds of tiny squares and left lying around. There's a withered apple core, which he must have thought was a good idea to fling into a corner rather than bring down to the trash and—most annoyingly—there are various foam stickers stuck to the floor, chunks of which stick stubbornly to the wood when I try to pull them up.

I'm kneeling down, working on scraping at the remnants of a monster truck sticker, when I rest a hand on the floor beside me and one of the boards creaks as though it's not properly attached. I stand up and move to the speaker to turn off the music, then walk back over to the same floorboard and rest a foot on it. With the music off, the creaking sound is louder and I'm surprised I haven't noticed it before until I realize it's sitting right where Cameron's bed usually is. I'll just have to nail it back in.

I'm about to go fetch the toolbox Justin gave me when a thought creeps into my mind. And when I reach down to pull at the top of the board, lifting it up, I somehow already know what's waiting for me underneath. But this time, when I look down and see the photo lying in the dust, right where I'd somehow known it would be, it's not intrigue that I feel—as I had with the last two—because I can no longer make sense of what it is that I'm finding. It's starting to feel like these aren't just little keepsakes that were hidden away all those years ago to surprise the next owners, but some kind of dark pattern that I can't decode. Because this photo isn't of Jessie, like the first one I found. Or of Sandra, like the second one I found.

This one is of another girl, in another dress, smiling brightly up at the camera from the same unknown spot as the last ones, along with the same black writing below.

And this girl's name is Erica.

16
———
ERICA

Erica walks into the movie theatre alone. She collects her ticket alone. She goes up to the concession stand alone and picks up a large popcorn, a large Pepsi and a huge Hershey's chocolate bar all for herself because she really doesn't give a damn anymore.

Maybe Bobby is right. Maybe she *has* gained some weight recently. Maybe she'll gain some more, see how he likes that. Maybe if he was a better boyfriend and didn't stand her up so often or break their plans just to go and hang out with the guys instead, then she might be inclined to watch what she eats a little more to please him. But since he can't even be bothered to come watch one freaking movie with her, she's just going to eat the whole lot and forget all about Bobby Granger.

Erica's mom once told her that if a man really loves you, he'll move mountains to be with you. Bobby won't even move his behind off Eddie's couch to come meet her two blocks down the street, so that says a whole lot about how he feels about her.

She's going to break up with him. She doesn't need him. She's said this before, but this time she really means it. She's done with Bobby for good.

She takes a sip from her drink as she shuffles along an empty row of seats to the sweet spot right in the middle, then places it in the holder as she settles down into the plush red velvet seat. The lights go down and the trailers begin to play, but rather than pay attention to the new movies coming out, she can't stop thinking about Bobby.

This is how it always goes. Erica tells him she's done, he says 'fine' and then after a few days one of them calls the other and they get back together until the cycle inevitably repeats. It's been nearly a year of this since she first met him, and between that and him always having something to say about how she looks or what she's wearing or what she eats, she's just sick of it all. This will be the very last time that Bobby Granger stands her up.

She's so lost in her own thoughts that when she sees a guy sitting a few seats across from her in this otherwise empty row, she wonders how she didn't notice him come in.

There's barely anyone else in the theatre, just a group of noisy teenagers who don't even look old enough for a slasher movie like this and a couple down the front occasionally getting pelted with popcorn by the rowdy teens. If Erica were those two, she would get up and go thump those brats but the couple just seem to be trying to ignore it.

As the opening credits start, the man on her row moves up into the seat right next to her. "Hi," he whispers in the darkness. "I think I might have joined the wrong room, is this not the new Schwarzenegger movie?"

"No. This is screen four, *Clover Hill Massacre.* The Schwarzenegger movie is playing on screen two."

"Dammit. And I'll bet I've already missed the start of that, too."

"You're not missing anything, trust me, I saw it last week and it's one long cheese fest from start to finish."

The screen suddenly lights up brightly, illuminating the

man's face. He's clean-cut, smoothly shaved and has a strong jaw that offsets his boyish features. He's drop-dead gorgeous.

"You know, I hear this movie is pretty good though, if you like slashers," Erica says. "You may as well stay in here now that it's already started."

He seems torn for a moment before he looks at her and smiles. "Sure. Why not?"

"I'm Erica, by the way."

"Charlie." He holds out a hand and she shakes it.

Charlie stays where he is and settles back into the seat as he puts his drink into the cup holder beside him.

The movie gets into the real gory stuff right away—exactly the kind of thing Erica loves—with a group of college kids running through an abandoned warehouse, a crazed maniac in a dark mask chasing after them. One of the guys (a tough-looking jock) gets cornered and a knife flashes on screen before a river of blood begins to run.

Erica laughs without meaning to. She doesn't know why, but horror flicks always have the opposite effect on her. The characters are always dimwits, the girls are just vapid shells with loser boyfriends who treat them like crap, until the killer cuts him up and we watch as the girl runs around cluelessly in the wrong direction, right smack bang into the killer. This movie is no different than the others she's seen and she's loving every second of it.

"Oh my God." Charlie puts a hand to his mouth. He looks as though he's going to get sick.

"Are you all right?" she asks, worried he'll barf all over the floor next to her.

"Yeah, I'm okay." He tries to take a sip of his drink but it gargles, the cup empty. "Crap."

"Here, have some of mine." She passes her cup to him and he takes a sip, holding on to it like a lifeline.

"Thanks, I'm just not used to watching these kinds of movies. It's so graphic." He grimaces.

That's cute. But Erica doesn't want to make him feel stupid for having a reaction to the sight of fake blood and violence, he's obviously just a sensitive guy. "You just have to think of it like a comedy."

"A comedy? I don't know. All the stalking and killing kind of freaks me out, if I'm honest, Erica. Sorry to sound like such a wimp," he says.

"You don't sound like a wimp." She smiles. "I think that's sweet."

He smiles back, still clutching her drink. They return their focus to the movie and watch as a girl runs up a set of stairs screaming as a dark figure approaches slowly from behind.

"See, it's funny because she's basically falling right into the killer's trap," she says to Charlie. "She's doing exactly what he wanted her to do. Now he has her trapped."

"Is that right?" he asks.

"Yep. And she'll die off screen as we hear her screams ring out from behind a closed door. I know these movies well enough to know what's coming up," she explains.

Sure enough, not one minute later the girl is dead and they see blood trickle out from the room on the screen.

"See?" Erica says.

"You're good," he says and passes back her drink.

"Thanks." She takes a long gulp, her mouth parched from the entire bucket of popcorn she's finished off.

As the movie goes on, Erica explains to Charlie—who confesses he's never really watched the genre before—about the common clichés used in horror movies. He's impressed by her knowledge on the subject and as they continue on, engrossed in conversation, she finds herself forgetting all about Bobby and his stupid friends.

This is the kind of guy Erica needs. Charlie is sensitive and interested in what she has to say. Although, for some reason, as she's explaining about jump-scare killer resurrection scenes she finds it hard to get her words out properly. She guesses this is what happens when she talks uninterrupted for any length of time. She wouldn't know, given that Bobby always tells her to shut up when she goes on about anything she's interested in.

Charlie is leaning close to her now, and she can smell his aftershave. A soft smoky smell, with woody undertones. It's sexy. Their eyes are no longer on the movie but locked on each other's and when the final credits begin to play and the lights come up, his hand is resting gently on hers. They get up and walk up the steps of the movie theatre, but it takes a lot of effort for her to stay co-ordinated. It's like she has to think about every single movement as she goes.

Charlie seems to notice this as they make their way through the lobby and looks concerned. "Are you okay?"

"Um... I don't know. I think so," she answers, confused by what she's feeling. "I think I just need to get back to my car."

"No problem. I'll walk with you." He smiles and his eyes glisten happily.

As they walk out the main entrance of the movie theatre, her legs become a little numb and she stumbles as she steps out onto the sidewalk. She holds on to Charlie's arm to catch herself, embarrassed.

"Sorry, I... I don't know what's wrong with me. I feel a little dizzy."

Charlie puts an arm around her waist and speaks softly into her ear. "That's okay, Erica. You can just lean on me."

17

RUBY

Justin arrives at seven on the dot, bottle of wine in one hand, a laser-level wrapped in a red bow in the other.

I take both from him when he holds them out. "You know, you can't always bring me something every time you come over. Soon I'll have more tools than a hardware store. But thank you."

"Don't ever let it be said that I don't know the way to a woman's heart," he says, walking through to my kitchen as though he owns the place.

This is the first time Justin has come over without his son in tow. Having left Xavier with a sitter for the evening, Justin seems to have a different air about him now that he's not on daddy duty. It could easily be mistaken for arrogance, but the impression I get is that Justin is a guy who doesn't have the time or patience for ambiguity. If he wants something, he'll tell you. He has the confidence of ten men, and I'm surprised by my attraction to this particular quality.

I follow him into the kitchen to find him rummaging in the drawers. "What are you looking for?"

"Corkscrew," he says.

"In here." I budge him over with my hip and pull a drawer open.

He pulls it out and I take two glasses down from the shelf while he opens up the wine.

"Okay, here's the plan," he says, passing me a full to the brim glass. "First thing we've gotta do is disconnect the old sink and remove it." He points to the old, corroded fixture. "I can handle that part. Your job is clearing out the cabinet below. Make sure there's enough space to fit in the new one."

I take a large gulp of wine and salute him, before kneeling down to clear out the cabinet, removing pots and pans and setting them aside.

I've never been on a date like this, so casual and productive, and I've got to say, it's a lot more relaxing than any dinner at a fancy restaurant. For one thing, I'm wearing jeans and a T-shirt, and Justin is even more causal in work combats and a hooded sweatshirt.

As we work alongside each other, I have a flashback to my earlier conversation with Felicity. And when Justin heaves the old sink out, and I've got space cleared for the new one, I take my chance to broach the subject with him as we take a break.

"Something strange happened today," I say, sitting at the table.

"Oh?" Justin joins me, wiping his hands on a cloth as he sits.

"Felicity Parker asked me if you and I were seeing each other... romantically."

Justin's lip twitches up into a smile. "That *is* strange. Because I was going to ask you the exact same thing."

I laugh. "That wasn't the strange part. You see, I told her that we're just friends. She and her friends are busybodies and I didn't want to fuel that gossip train."

"Oh. I can't say I'm not disappointed." Justin lowers his head.

"Well, that's just the thing," I say. "Felicity wasn't. She kind of seemed relieved when I told her that you and I weren't an item."

"Huh," he says, apparently unsurprised.

"And strangely enough, I had another neighbor—Bernice Fisher from next door—warn me off of you, too. Why do you think that is?"

Justin's face darkens. "Well, I think I can take a wild guess."

I tip my head, confused.

Justin doesn't say anything for a few moments and I'm beginning to worry when he finally looks up at me. "There was a rumor, after my wife Elle passed, that I killed her."

My mouth drops open, but no words come to me.

"Yeah. Crazy, right?" Justin says. "They all thought it was impossible that such a beautiful woman, with a nice house, a loyal husband and a brand-new baby could ever take her own life."

I place my wine glass down and put my head in my hands. "I'm so sorry, Justin. I didn't know. When you said your wife had passed, I'd assumed she was sick."

"She was sick," he says gravely. "She had postpartum depression. She was battling the hardest thing she'd gone through in her life and I was the only one who could see it. To everyone else she was Elle Thomas, the proud new mother who always wore a smile as she showed off her baby boy."

I've never seen Justin's mood resemble anything close to serious before and I feel awful for bringing this up. I can't believe anyone could think that he would hurt his own wife. I've only known him for a short time, but he's been so selfless and giving and he's obviously a wonderful father to Xavier.

"I'm so sorry that people thought that about you, Justin. To compound the pain of it all for you like that..." I trail off, not knowing what to say.

Justin looks down at his hands for a moment before he taps the table and gets up. "That's all in the past, we don't need to talk about it."

I nod silently, then watch him snap back into work mode as though nothing just happened. "All right. We have the old sink out, now we need to make sure the plumbing is in okay shape." He picks up a wrench from the toolbox. "You hold the pipes steady while I work on them."

I'm a little thrown by what I've just found out, but I try my hardest to regain my composure and join him at the sink. When Justin finishes tightening the last bolt, he wipes his hands on his jeans before turning to me with a proud smile.

"All done," he proclaims, beaming at the sleek stainless-steel fixture that now adorns my countertop.

"I'm impressed. You really know what you're doing."

"I aim to please." He shoots me a sly wink.

We clean up the mess we've made, then move through to the living room. Once we're settled beside each other on the couch, I reach into my pocket.

"I want to show you something."

I pull out the three photos I found and pass them to him. He takes them and flips through them, studying each one, a puzzled look on his face. "Well, these three girls sure do look happy. Who are they?"

"Jessie, Sandra and Erica."

He nods. "I see that."

"Do you recognize any of them?" I ask. "Did any of them used to live around here?"

He looks closer at each girl before passing the photos back to me. "No. Why?"

I sigh. "I'm sure it's nothing, but I found them hidden around the house. At first I thought it was just a cute little hello from the past, left for future owners to find. But now I'm not so sure. I mean, they look to have been taken in the eighties, so I kind of thought you might remember these girls from living around here when you were small."

"Nope, sorry," he says. "You could ask the previous owners of the house?"

This hadn't occurred to me, but now that I think about it, it might be a good idea. "I guess I could get their number from my realtor, Benton."

"Benton Shepherd?" Justin asks.

I laugh. "Wow, you really do know everyone in town."

A frown creases his forehead. "Well, a lot of people know Benton. He's not the kind of guy to slip under the radar. You've seen his car, right?"

I roll my eyes, remembering how impressed Cameron had been by Benton's flashy red Mustang. "You think he's compensating for something?"

"Yeah. A heart." Justin scoffs. "That guy has some questionable business practices. He might be all clean-cut and smooth, but he's as shady as they come. A wolf in sheep's clothing, my father would have called him."

"What do you mean?" My interest is piqued now.

"Benton makes his living pressuring people into selling their homes for far less than they're worth, convincing them it's the best offer they'll get. He has no problem with lying about the condition of properties, covering up major issues. He's only interested in his commission, fast sales, and will do whatever it takes to get there." Justin shakes his head.

"You think he's a crook?" I ask.

"I mean, if it looks like a duck, waddles like a duck, quacks like a duck..." He shrugs.

"Well there was no fast sale on this house, anyway," I say. "He told me it was empty for a few years before he eventually sold it to me."

Justin looks around. "Well... that one's hardly a shocker."

I grab a cushion and throw it at him. "Hey! I happen to love my little time capsule. Although, I'll be happy when it finally starts looking a little less outdated."

"That's what I'm here for. Free labor." Justin throws the cushion right back at me.

"You know," I say, "I meant to clarify earlier on that I only told Felicity that we aren't seeing each other because I wanted to avoid gossip. *Not* because I'm not interested in you."

Justin's eyes dart around as he pretends to calculate the double negative. "So... that means—"

I don't let him finish before I lean in and kiss him. He's taken the lead in every other way so far. Now it's my turn.

18

RUBY

I pour my morning coffee, still half asleep, and stumble my way over to the kitchen table. Sitting down, I take a much-needed sip of the dark, life-giving liquid and proceed to neatly line up the three photos on the tabletop.

I run my fingers over their smiles. Identical. The wide eyes. The huge grins. The hideous but on-trend dresses for that time.

Who are you? Why are your photos hidden around my house?

I was disappointed last night when Justin told me he had never seen these girls before. He knows everyone around here. He's lived in Lonerock his whole life. At forty years old, he may have even been an infant when these photos were taken, but if any of these girls were still around Lonerock by the time he was a young child, surely he'd recognize a photo of them? And the fact that he doesn't leads me to two possible conclusions. One of which must be true.

The first: these women were not from Lonerock.

The second: they *were* from Lonerock, but they were no longer here by the time Justin grew older.

Neither of these explanations brings me any further to understanding why their photos have been hidden around this house for decades. Three young women who look to be of no relation to each other. Three identical poses, in the same exact spot, which doesn't even seem to have been inside this house.

It's not making any sense to me.

And then there's that nagging question in the back of my mind. The one that won't go away: *are there more?*

I'm not sure what exactly comes over me as I look down at these photos. Maybe it's the double espresso that I've just chugged down on an empty stomach; maybe it's the fact that I'm missing my kids so badly that it feels like half my heart has been ripped out and is over there in Arizona with them; maybe it's these goddamn huge grins on these three girls' faces that seem more and more tortured by the second as I stare down at them— but before I even know what I'm doing, I'm tearing the house apart, bit by bit, trying to find another photo.

I pull off skirting boards, I test every floorboard and tile, trying to find something loose that might hide another maniacally grinning girl behind it. I'm pushing out dressers and beds, leaving a trail of destruction in my wake. It's like I'm possessed. I don't even know what I'm trying to prove or how another photo might help me figure this out, but for some reason, the mere idea of another one of these photos living secretly inside my house as I go about my day, unaware of its existence, makes me feel as though my spine has grown a thousand little centipede legs that wriggle around under my skin.

I can't stand it. I don't know who these girls are. I don't know why their photos were left here, but it's no longer cute. It's no longer fun. Their smiles are burned into my mind, their mouths wide in a macabre grin, taunting me.

I don't know how much time has passed when I hear my phone buzzing on the kitchen table and I run downstairs, nearly tripping over the mountain of things piled up on Cameron's bed, which still sits in the upstairs hall. Any progress I've made on the house pales in comparison to the absolute chaos the rest of the place is in right now.

By the time I get to the phone, I'm sure I'm going to miss whoever is on the other end but when I look at the screen, I see Mory's name and I quickly swipe to answer. "Mory!"

"Woah, Mom. Dial it back a little. Are you okay?"

I try to calm my breathing, realizing that I must have sounded like a madwoman to my daughter. "Sorry. Sorry, Mory. It's just so nice to have you call. I figured you'd be busy with your father and Caitlyn. Are you guys having fun?"

"Yeah, um. I guess."

That doesn't sound reassuring. "You guess?"

"Yeah. I mean..." Mory pauses, something clearly on her mind. "Well... I miss him, Mom."

"Miss wh—" I cut myself off as I realize exactly who. "Oh. Hutch."

There's quiet on the line. Then the sound of sniffing. Mory is crying.

"Oh, honey. You really miss him, huh?" I say, wanting to reach into the phone and hold my baby girl close to me.

"Yeah," she sobs. "I miss him so much. I just want to come back home, Mom."

I try not to take this personally. Neither Mory nor Cameron have ever called me up from their father's house to tell me they miss *me*, or that they want to come home to me. But it is one of life's fundamental facts that there are no stronger emotions in the world than those of a teenage girl in love.

"Mory, baby, I'm sorry. I know you miss Hutch, but you'll be home in just a couple of weeks and you two can catch up then. And you'll have so much to talk about after the break."

The sobbing at the other end of the phone continues and it's torture for me, not being able to hold my daughter and kiss her hair and tell her it's all going to be okay.

It's completely irrelevant that in a year from now she will probably have forgotten this boy and have moved on to another. The fact is, at her age, love is all consuming. Every hour of every day is spent thinking about that person who makes your world go round.

It's been a long time since I've had feelings like that, but I remember those days. I even remember having those feeling about her father, Aaron. Hard as it is to imagine now.

And when Justin lingered at the door last night, his lips still hungry on mine as we said goodbye, I sure can't say my feelings for him felt at all tepid. In fact, the whole night was pretty damn steamy, let me tell you. But I'm not *in love* with Justin. And that's the difference between sixteen and thirty-eight. I'm able to separate my hormones from my emotions.

I spend the next fifteen minutes pouring supportive words into the phone until Mory's ragged breaths become more stable and she eventually calms down enough to tell me that she really is having a great time over there, despite being utterly lovesick, and that Cameron is so immersed in a Christmas movie that he can't even make it to the phone right now to say hello.

When we eventually hang up the call, I have a realization that sends a warm glow all the way through my core: Mory and Cameron might enjoy being at their father's house more than being here with me, they might have more fun there, they might love to cook and eat meals with Caitlyn and their father, play games and do endless wonderful activities... but when my daughter had real feelings—overwhelming ones that were eating away at her heart—she called *me*. She needed my voice to soothe her. She needed her mom.

This alone is enough to pick me up and carry me through the rest of what already promises to be a very long day.

19

RUBY

"Hmm." Felicity shakes her head, her blonde hair swishing around her narrow shoulders. "No, I don't know them."

My heart sinks. I'd come over to the Parkers' house after speaking with Mory to ask them about the photos, but Felicity had insisted that I come in and try a slice of her home-made cinnamon cake. I'd been hoping Felicity or Quinten might be able to tell me who these girls are. My manic searching this morning didn't turn up any additional photos, but I just can't shake the feeling of unease that's settled over me.

I don't know who these women were, or how their pictures ended up in my home, hidden in the most obscure places, but their haunting smiles seem to follow me in my mind wherever I go, seared now into my consciousness.

"Honey, how about you?" Felicity calls her husband over from where he pours us coffee.

Quinten hands both me and Felicity a cup then sits down, pulls on a pair of glasses and picks the photos up to study them. He holds one of them out to Felicity. "This kind of looks like the woman who works at the auto shop, don't you think?"

Felicity shakes her head. "No. The ages don't line up.

Judging by when these photos look to have been taken, these women would be in their sixties by now, and she's late forties at most."

He makes a throaty noise. "I guess you're right."

"The dark-haired one looks a lot like Miss Tammy, Leo's old kindergarten teacher, it's possible this could be her mother," Felicity suggests.

Quinten shakes his head. "No, Miss Tammy's mother is the secretary there, remember? She was the one who showed us around that first day."

"Oh, yes, that's right," she muses. "It's been so long, I forgot. Wasn't she the one that sang us the class rules in the tune of 'Twinkle Twinkle Little Star'?"

The couple both laugh at this and I can see this is getting me absolutely nowhere.

Felicity passes back the photos to me. "Sorry we can't be of more help. You could always try contacting the previous owners, Stan and Anita Desmond."

"You know them?" I ask, sliding the photos back inside my handbag.

"Used to," Felicity says. "But they moved away a long time ago."

"You don't happen to have a contact number for them, do you?" I ask in hope.

"No, sorry. I used to be in touch with Anita, but she's since changed her number and I don't have the new one. But Benton Shepherd sold you the house, right? He should have it."

This brings me right back to my conversation with Justin last night. Although after hearing about Benton's somewhat shady practices, I can't say I'm all that enthusiastic about the idea of getting back in contact with the man.

When our coffee cups are empty and Felicity and Quinten walk me to the door, I can't help but share with them my conversation with Mory this morning, and her emotional reaction to missing Hutch.

"Oh, that's adorable." Felicity clutches her chest. "Those two make such a cute couple, don't they, honey?"

Quinten smiles. "Well, I know Mory certainly has our Hutch's heart, anyway. They're texting all the time. He never stops talking about her."

Felicity puts a hand on my shoulder and lowers her voice. "I want you to know, I did have a talk with Hutch about the age difference. And he told me he's waiting until she turns seventeen next month to officially ask her out on a date. Something a little more romantic than a robotics session with his father!"

"That's sweet," I say.

I don't have the heart to break it to them that Mory and Hutch have been secretly meeting up for weeks behind their backs.

When I get home, I don't waste any time trying to find Benton's number. With one week until Christmas, he'll likely soon be out of the office until the new year, and I want to get to the bottom of this before the kids get back from Arizona. After emptying my handbag out onto the coffee table, I find Benton's business card amongst the rubble and type the number into my phone.

The photos stare up at me from the coffee table as I pace the living room, my call ringing out unanswered. The eyes of the girls in the pictures seem to follow me as I go, watching me.

After everything Justin told me about Benton Shepherd last night, he's not someone I particularly want to be calling for a favor right now, but I don't have much choice. He must have a number for the previous owners of this house and I don't know where else to find it. I tap my fingernails impatiently against each other as I wait for him to pick up.

"Shepherd's Real Estate, how can I be of help today?" Benton's voice finally comes through the line, smooth and slick.

"Benton, hi, it's Ruby Blake," I say, my voice steady.

"Ruby! It's great to hear from you. How's everything with the new house?"

"It's wonderful." I stretch the truth tight enough to snap. "But there's something I hoped you could help me with."

"Fire away," Benton prompts.

"I need to contact the previous owners, if that's possible. I have some questions for them."

"Questions?" Benton sounds curious.

"Yeah. You know, just about the history of the house and such," I say.

"Oh, well, I can tell you all of that. The last owners moved in when it was built in the early eighties, they moved out to live closer to their grandchildren a few years back and were the only owners of the property until they sold it to you last August," he explains.

"Yes, thanks. You mentioned all this when we met before. But I have some more in-depth questions I'd like to ask the last owners myself, if you could give me their number?"

I hear Benton exhaling between his teeth. "No can do, sorry. Giving out clients' personal information goes against our policy here, I'm sure you understand."

I had a feeling this would be the answer, but I was hoping Benton would be the kind of guy who wouldn't care too much about bending the rules.

"The thing is, Benton, I'm concerned about some... items that I've found around here," I say.

There's a moment of silence on the other end of the line. "What kind of items, Ruby?"

I don't feel like sharing anything more with this guy. "Just some personal things that I'm sure the last owners would like to have back."

Benton now speaks softly. "Well, that's no problem at all. If you drop them into my office, I'd gladly pass them on."

Something about this offer sets my senses on alert and I have a strong feeling that giving these photos to Benton would not be a good idea.

"You know what? It's really not that important. I'm sure they took everything they wanted from the house," I backtrack.

"Are you sure, Ruby? Because I don't mind—"

"Yes, it's fine," I rush. "I've got to go. Happy Holidays."

I end the awkward exchange feeling a little rattled.

Why did it seem like Benton knew exactly what the 'items' I was referring to were? I mean he couldn't, could he? He was easily born a full decade after those photos were taken.

A part of me just wants to throw the damn photos in the trash and forget all about them, but I know that wouldn't shake the questions from my mind.

Who are these girls? Why does nobody around here remember them? And why were their photos left hidden here?

Despite their beaming faces, I can't escape the suspicion that something bad happened to these women. And what's more, after our phone call just now, I can't shake the feeling that Benton Shepherd somehow knows more about this house than he's telling me.

20

RUBY

"Can I ask you something?" Justin turns in his seat to face me.

"Shoot," I reply, glancing from the road to him and then back.

"What did the brake pedal ever do to you?"

I roll my eyes and ignore him, tunnel vision on the red light ahead of me, waiting for green.

"No, seriously," he continues. "You seem to hate that thing, kicking at it every time you need to come to a stop. My whole life, I've never felt a seat belt have to work this hard."

I sigh. "And let me guess, you're a perfect driver?"

Justin shrugs. "I'm all right. I mean, enough to know that a brake pedal doesn't work like a light switch..."

If this guy wasn't both achingly handsome and endlessly helpful, I'd likely kick him out of the car right about now, but since I was the one to ask Justin to keep me company while I make the drive out to Arlington Mills, I have no choice but to take his driving critique in the half-serious manner in which it's meant.

"I'll try not to be so heavy footed with the brakes," I say sarcastically, then sigh. "I'm just a little nervous."

After my call with Benton yesterday, I was afraid I'd hit a dead end in my search to find out the identities of the smiling girls, until I realized that thanks to Felicity and Quinten, I already had the previous owners' names. And an online search for Stan and Anita Desmond had brought up an address in Arlington Mills, about a three-hour drive from Lonerock. Without thinking it through long enough to hold myself back, I'd called Justin and asked if he could find Xavier a sitter so he could join me on a road trip. In typical Justin fashion, he'd said yes without even asking me where we'd be going or what we'd be doing.

In truth, there are two reasons I asked Justin to accompany me today. The first, because I enjoy his company and this is a chance for us to spend some time alone together, and the second because a little voice in the back of my head is telling me that if I'm right, and that something may have happened to these girls all those years ago, then I should probably have some backup when I drop in on these people unexpectedly.

The best-case scenario is that this couple are happy to be reunited with the photos and can tell me who the girls are.

"So you think this couple will have the answers?" Justin asks.

"Well, if they don't then I think I need to consider bringing it to the police," I say. "I mean, the Desmonds were the only ones who owned the house before me, which means if they have no explanation for the photos or how they got there, then somebody else put them there."

Justin seems to think on this. "Why would somebody do that?"

I have no good answer to that, and as the road stretches out endlessly before me, my hands grip the steering wheel tightly. With every mile that passes, my anxiety grows. What if they refuse to speak to me? What if they've never seen these photos before? There's no good evidence to suggest that anything bad happened to these girls, but my gut is telling me that something is very wrong about this whole thing.

"Ruby." I hear Justin's concerned voice beside me as I signal to exit the freeway, an hour now from our destination. "I think you've worked yourself up about this. It's probably nothing. I mean, if you ask me, those girls look as happy as can be."

I sigh, trying to calm my nerves. "Yeah. I'm sure you're right."

"You know what else I think?" Justin's voice is uncharacteristically serious. "I think it's a week before Christmas, your kids are out of town with their dad, and your mind is just finding a way to distract you from the hurt that causes you."

"Don't analyze me," I say. "Or I might have to do the same to you."

I can't imagine it's all that easy for Justin at this time of year either, as a single father of an eight-year-old who doesn't even remember his own mother. It puts it in perspective for me, at least, the fact that my children still have their father and get to spend this time with him. Even if that leaves me alone for the holidays.

Justin laughs. "I'm not going to deny that it's a difficult time of year for me, but I'm not the one turning into Inspector Clouseau over here just to escape my feelings."

He may have a point, but I'll be damned if I'll admit it.

Before long my phone tells us we're just minutes from the Desmonds' home and as I drive through the tree-lined streets of this quiet Arlington Mills neighborhood, all I see are exquisite houses with manicured lawns and perfectly trimmed hedges. Each home is unique in its architecture and design. It's the kind of place you don't get to live in without a very healthy bank account and it's quite a step up from my little outdated home on Forest Grove, where Stan and Anita moved from.

"I get the feeling that Christmas here is more of a competition than a celebration," Justin remarks, looking out at the excessive number of lights and decorations around the place.

When we arrive at the address I step out of my car and take a moment to stretch out my legs as I look up at the beautiful house in front of me. The white exterior is offset by dark shutters and a perfectly manicured lawn showcases three wooden reindeer statues. There's a small deck out front and a wicker couch with patchwork cushions on it. The whole place is the perfect mixture of modern and rustic and it's hard to believe that a couple who used to live in the time trap that I call home now own a place like this.

Justin puts a confident arm around my shoulder. "What are we waiting for?"

We walk up the stone path toward the front door and before I get a chance to linger, Justin rings the doorbell twice and winks at me. We wait patiently, my stomach churning a mixture of anticipation and nerves. Moments later the door swings open, revealing the friendly face and warm smile of a woman who I'd guess is in her sixties.

"Hello, can I help you?" she asks.

I'm suddenly wishing I'd practiced what I might say when I got to the door, but it's too late for that now. "Hi, are you Anita?"

"Yes."

I smile. "My name is Ruby Blake, and this is my friend Justin." I indicate to him. "I'm sorry to drop by unannounced like this but I'm the person who bought your last house, in Lonerock. And I wondered if you have a moment to talk with me?"

She seems a little surprised, but her smile widens. "Well sure, come on in."

21

———

RUBY

I know that our intentions here are good but I'm a little concerned that Anita is trusting enough that she'd welcome two strangers into her house so easily.

As she ushers us in, she calls up the stairs. "Stan! We have guests."

She walks us through to the kitchen and on every inch of wall we pass are family photos hanging proudly, glass frames buffed to within an inch of their lives and not a speck of dust on them. Anita offers us a seat and refreshments, and I feel relief at her warm greeting. Despite my initial nerves, I know I made the right decision to come here. I look to the doorway and see a man with a thick gray mustache and reading glasses hanging from his neck.

"Stan, this is Ruby, the new owner of the house in Lonerock, and this is her friend, Justin," Anita says as she lays out a plate of cookies on the table.

"Hi." I get up and shake his hand before Justin does the same.

"How interesting." Stan moves slowly to sit down across from us, a hint of a hunch in his gait. "What brings you here?"

I see no point in wasting any time so I pull the three photos out of my bag and lay them down on the table. "I found some old photos that I think you might have left at the house."

Stan pulls his glasses up to his eyes and Anita comes to look over his shoulder as he picks up the photos. They both look through them and I can see immediately that there's not a hint of recognition in their eyes.

"No, not ours," Stan says. "Unless you know who these people are, Anita?"

Anita shakes her head. "No. I've never seen these girls or these pictures before."

My heart drops and my disappointment must be obvious because Anita looks at me with sympathy in her eyes. "Did you drive all the way out here just to find the owner of these photos?"

I nod and sigh. "I have no idea how they ended up in my house. They were there when I moved in. I've been finding them hidden behind tiles and under flooring as I've been renovating the place."

"That's quite an undertaking." Stan puffs out his cheeks and blows. "The place hasn't been touched since we first did it up in eighty-five."

"No matter how many times I told Stan here that we needed to redecorate, we never did, so it was outdated even by the time we moved out." Anita laughs.

I smile. "It had definitely gathered some dust in the few years you'd been gone, that's for sure."

Stan and Anita share a glance before turning back to me, the same expression of confusion on both their faces.

"It's been more than just a few years since we moved from Lonerock," Anita says. "We've been living in Arlington Mills for the past sixteen years."

Something pulls tight in my chest.

"I... that's not what Benton said when he sold me the house. He said you just moved a few years back."

Stan shakes his head and tsks. "Benton Shepherd. We're not his biggest fans. When we moved from Lonerock, we kept hold of that house for a few years. Our first grandchild had just been born and we wanted to be closer to family out here but weren't yet settled on the idea of selling. Then, when we made up our minds about ten years ago and first approached Benton about selling the house in Lonerock, there were some issues that had to be taken care of before it could be put on the market. At first he told us it would take six months or so, but he kept stringing us along, with various other issues arising which always meant it had to be put off."

"For nearly ten years?" I ask in disbelief.

"I can't really say I understand how these things work, but yes," Anita confirms. "First it was that there were issues with the property's deeds, then he convinced us to wait for market conditions to improve, to get the best price. Then it was various other things that he said needed sorting before selling the house. Anyway, January this year, he finally called and told us the house was on the market and then by August we had the news of its sale. So all's well that ends well, I suppose."

None of this sounds right to me. There are no issues that take ten years to prepare a house for sale. Benton not only strung this nice couple along for years on end for reasons that likely only benefited him, but he also lied to me about how long the house was empty for.

Stan is still turning the photos around in his hands and looking carefully at them, his glasses exaggerating his curious eyes behind them. "You know, what I find most interesting about these photos are the dresses."

Anita rolls her eyes at this. "Maybe you're forgetting the

eighties, Stan, but these were the exact kind of thing I used to wear back then, too."

Stan places the photos back down on the table. "Yes. That was the style *then*, but these photos weren't taken in the eighties."

"What... what do you mean?" I ask.

"I mean," Stan points at the photos, "look at the back of them."

I quickly snatch them up, sure that if somebody had written a date on them I would have seen it because I must have looked at these photos a hundred times by now. And, looking at the backs of them again now, I see that I'm not wrong. There's nothing there.

I look up at Stan, confused. "There's nothing written there."

"Look closer," he says, and points to a serial number printed on the back of the film.

It's a jumble of numbers and letters, but there's no date there.

"I don't understand," I say.

Stan's eyes are lit up, clearly excited to explain to us something only he knows here. "See, some Polaroid photos have a unique serial number on the back which contains information. It might not look like much, but it actually represents the camera model, production batch, and the date that the photo was taken. And if you look right here," he taps the back of one of the photos, "at the last two digits, the year is right there."

I stare down at the last two digits on the photos, and my heart begins to drum in my chest. I have to squint to be sure I'm not reading these wrong, because the numbers that stare back at me paint a very different picture in my head than everything I thought I already knew about these photos.

Stan is right. They weren't taken in the eighties. Not even close. These photos were all taken within the last seven years.

22

RUBY

Shepherd's Real Estate office is situated in a brand-new commercial business park on the east side of Lonerock. It's a step up from what I gather was Benton's last place of business, judging by the worn sign on the small office building that sits empty next to the drug store in town. I guess he's moving up in life.

I pull into the parking lot and take a deep breath to calm my nerves. Having used up his babysitter miles, Justin is home with Xavier today, unable to join me on this particular mission.

Since leaving Arlington Mills yesterday, I've had some time to think and I've come to a few conclusions. Namely, Benton Shepherd is not only a crook but he's also the only person who has had access to the house since Stan and Anita moved out years ago and therefore must know something about these photos.

I find a spot near the entrance and turn off the engine before stepping out of my car. Cold rain beats down on the asphalt and bounces off the roofs of the vehicles. I have to hold my hood up against the rain as I make the short dash toward the entrance. The exterior of the office is modern with large windows that I'm sure on a nicer day lets in plenty of natural light. I can see a couple inside, chatting to a woman behind a desk. A sign above the door proudly displays Shepherd's name, and I push open the glass door to enter.

Dripping on the carpeted floor, I wait my turn to approach the reception desk. The walls are full of photos of properties for sale, and the soft scent of fresh coffee floats through the air. When the couple in front of me leave, the young woman behind the desk greets me with a polite smile. I introduce myself, only to be told that Benton is out but shouldn't be too long. I'm offered a seat and a coffee while I wait, and gladly accept both.

I sit down next to the window and try to think through how to best approach Benton with what I know. There's one fact that he can't escape; he told me the last occupants of my house had moved out only a few years ago. I now know from Stan and Anita that it was actually closer to sixteen years ago. This doesn't necessarily change how I feel about the house but not being truthful about the length of time it had stood there abandoned was clearly a misleading tactic to make the house seem less undesirable.

As for the photos, maybe he has a good explanation for them. Maybe they're friends of his, or girls he dated in the past.

But like Stan Desmond said yesterday, the old-style dresses in the relatively new photos is the thing that stands out as weird. And it's this, along with the fact the photos were hidden around the house, that gives me the creeps.

"Here's the man himself," the woman behind the desk singsongs before I spot the red Mustang parked outside and the door opens.

Benton walks in, shaking the rain off his shoulders. He doesn't see me at first and approaches the desk with a lowered brow. "*Atkins the Asshole* pulled out of the Clayton sale at the last minute today. Didn't I tell you he was a—"

The woman coughs loudly, interrupting him and gesturing my way. "Mr. Shepherd, Ruby Blake is here to see you."

Benton's head whips my way and I watch the frown on his face morph seamlessly into that salesman smile I remember. "Ruby, what a pleasant surprise. What can I do for you?"

I don't return the warmth. "I was hoping we could talk. Alone."

"Sure thing. Jane, can you hold my calls for five minutes?" He doesn't wait for her reply before ushering me toward his office at the back of the room.

Inside, he closes the door behind us and gestures to the chair in front of his desk. "Please, have a seat."

He sits down across from me and beams, white teeth glistening. Men like Benton have spent years practicing this winning smile, effortlessly sealing the deal with clients who can't resist his charisma and good looks. But I won't be letting his charm distract me today. This man is a liar.

"So." He leans back in his chair, casually. "What's up?"

"Benton, I'm not going to waste either of our time." I get straight to it, pulling out the three photos. "Who are these girls and why were their photos hidden around my house?"

Benton's curious eyes go straight to the photos on the desk. He picks them up and I study his face like a hawk, looking for any spark of recognition.

"Isn't it obvious?" he finally says. "It's Sandra, Jessie and Erica."

"You know them?" Relief washes through me.

He cracks a crooked smile. "Never seen them before in my life. Just going by what's written on the photos. You say you found these at the house?"

My heart sinks and I nod, not taking my eyes from his.

"Well, they probably belong to the last owners. But like I

told you on the phone the other day, I can't give you their information. Sorry."

"Stan and Anita Desmond, Arlington Mills." I sit back, crossing my arms. "Nice couple."

Benton's mouth falls open. "You—"

"Found them? Yeah. Beautiful house. Lovely neighborhood. And they've never seen these photos before, because as noted in the serial codes on the backs, they were all taken within the last seven years. And, as you know, the Desmonds moved away from Lonerock sixteen years ago."

Benton brings his hands together, wordlessly. I can see his mind working. He knows I've caught him out on at least one lie, and it may well cause the others to crumble.

"Yes, well, the Desmonds and I have been working closely for some time to—"

"Benton, you told me the house was only empty for a few years!"

Benton nods. "Well, it was."

I scoff in disbelief before tapping my imaginary broken watch, trying to fix it.

"Okay, so we disagree on how many a *few* is," Benton concedes with a smirk. "But it was on the market for less than a year when you bought it."

"Because after Stan and Anita told you they wanted to sell, you strung them along, lying to them for another ten years!"

Benton's smile falters for a split second before his mask slips back into place. "I'm not sure what you're talking about, Miss Blake. I assure you, I have never lied to any of my clients."

I think my last nerve must be located in my forehead, because it's now ticking.

"Don't bother lying. I know you manipulated that sweet couple to keep their house from selling. And since you have a reputation in this town for a fast turnover, I can only imagine it had something to do with you wanting that house empty. And why exactly *was* that, Benton?" I seethe, looking pointedly at the photos.

Benton sighs and leans forward, resting his arms on the desk. "Ruby, I'll level with you. That house had a lot of issues that needed seeing to, a lot of red tape, a lot of road blocks, most of which were out of my hands. Could I have pushed to speed the process up? Probably. But I always try to get the best price possible for my clients. And in the end, it was an outdated house and the Desmonds benefited from waiting until the rest of the street caught up with the modern world before selling."

He seems to have an answer for everything.

"The photos. They were put there while you had the keys. How do you explain that?" I tap them again now.

Benton sighs and picks them up again. "Well, I guess it's possible that one of the contractors or cleaners who came in over that time left them there. They're just photos though. Are they important in some way?"

"I don't know," I admit. "I think it's very strange that the house was left empty for years, and yet these photos ended up hidden there."

"That *is* weird. But you know, I've found stranger things in old houses, believe you me." He grins suggestively. "If walls could talk, huh?"

I don't buy this act for a second. Because the walls in my house *are* talking. And they're screaming Benton Shepherd's name.

23

RUBY

It's three days into the new year and for me, Christmas came and went in a blur of sanding, staining and painting Cameron's bedroom, all the while firmly pressing down the empty feelings that come from spending the holidays alone.

Justin turned up at my door on Christmas Eve with a bottle of wine and a new light fixture for Cameron's room, telling me that his rule is to never leave my house before fixing something up or helping out in some way first. He'd stayed for a few hours before we eventually untangled ourselves and he left to return to Xavier and his parents, who he had staying with him over the holidays.

Every phone call I've had with Mory or Cameron recently has been so short that I'm starting to feel as though I'm forgetting their voices. There's always something more exciting to see and do than talk with their mom on the phone. At least Mory seems to be feeling a little better about being away from Hutch. I'm sure when she returns, it'll be him that she's most excited to see, not me. But I'm long used to playing second fiddle in my kids' life, and as long as my babies are home with me, I'll be happy.

With so much spare time on my hands recently and a keen determination not to spend it on self-reflection out of fear of getting to better know myself (Justin and I really do make a great couple), I've been spending an uncharacteristic amount of time online. Namely, looking for answers about who those girls are. I started by cross referencing the names 'Jessie,' 'Sandra' and 'Erica' with 'Lonerock' and when that came up with nothing promising, I expanded my search to a wider area. Then, finding myself no closer to identifying them—and following an instinct which has been slowly gnawing away at me—I eventually started searching for missing persons who share their first names. But without last names or any other details about these women, I've yet to find any matches online.

I realize I've become obsessive about this, and when Justin suggested that I should drop it for my own wellbeing I half-heartedly promised that I'd try. But within twelve hours I was back online again, searching.

I've considered bringing it to the cops, but what would I say? *Hi, here are some photos of three really happy girls. How soon can you set up an investigation room?*

But I don't even see their smiles anymore. In fact, when I place my finger over the lower half of their faces, all I see is terror in their eyes.

I'm starting to realize I may never know who these girls are or how their photos ended up in my home. All that my conversation with Benton Shepherd did was confirm to me that he's about as trustworthy as a small child with a permanent marker. The man lies like the rest of us breathe. And if I'm right about my suspicions and he is lying about those photos, there's only one reason: to protect himself.

But then the question remains, why would he have left those photos in the house if he was going to sell it to me? If he wanted to keep them hidden, surely he would have taken them out before giving me the keys? Benton may be many things, but stupid isn't one of them.

None of this adds up.

I find myself yet again pondering on this never-ending circle of unanswered questions as I take my trash outside. I step onto the driveway and feel the crisp January air against my skin. A lot of people in the neighborhood have already taken down their Christmas decorations, which I'm grateful for since every twinkling light is another reminder of a holiday I no longer get to celebrate with my kids.

As I haul the black sack into the trash cart I spot Bernice—my sociably challenged neighbor—making her way down her driveway toward me, and I can already sense trouble brewing. She comes to a stop, a scowl on her wrinkled face as she stares my way. I can feel her eyes boring into me and I'm reminded again that this will be my life here, forever, until the old cow finally drops dead one day.

"Good morning, Bernice," I say, trying to keep my tone neutral.

She ignores my greeting, her face twisting into a frown. "I want you to know that I'm going to be bringing a list with me next week, to the meeting. I'll be raising my concerns there."

"What meeting?" I put a hand on one hip.

"The Residents' Biannual Safety Forum," she snaps, then shoves a piece of paper my way. "This is a copy of my list."

I scan the words and feel my anger rise. "For God's sake, Bernice, you can't be serious."

She scoffs. "As a heart attack, lady."

I take a deep breath, trying to keep my frustration in check, and glare at her retreating back as she shuffles away, muttering curses under her breath.

I look down at the piece of paper in my hand. There are fifteen infractions listed, all in relation to my household. From kids playing too loudly in the garden to men showing up in the late hours of night and even dates and times listed. The whole thing is ridiculous.

I shake my head. Living next door to Bernice has been a nightmare. I'm so tired of constantly tiptoeing around her. I guess I don't have much choice but to try to find out when and where this meeting will be, so I can go along to defend myself when she pulls out this stupid list.

I hear a car horn beep twice behind me and look back to see Felicity and Quinten pulling up, their car window rolling down.

"Ruby!" Felicity leans over her husband to call out.

"Hi," I say, making my way to them.

"We just wanted to stop and say Happy New Year!" Felicity coos. "How are you doing, all alone over here?"

"Great, thanks." I swallow down a less kind response.

A woman like Felicity, with her handsome husband and two perfect sons, probably can't comprehend why such phrasing might cause upset, but I can't hold it against her that her life worked out perfectly and mine didn't.

Quinten leans an arm on the side of his window. "So, when are the kids home? Hutch is about to go crazy waiting on Mory to come back."

Felicity echoes this. "Oh, Ruby, you should hear the boy talking about her. It's love, I'm sure!"

I laugh. "That's sweet. They're back on Friday, so I'm sure she'll call over during the weekend. Cameron will be excited to see Leo, too."

"It's so nice to have new neighbors with kids the same age range as ours," Felicity says. "Hutch was just a baby when we moved here, and the kids on the street were all older. And now that he's grown up, it's all babies and toddlers on the street. All Kendra and Harriet talk about are diapers and playgroups, while I'm here worrying about driving licenses and college applications!"

I don't want to ignore Felicity's ramblings, but it suddenly comes to me that the Parkers might know something about this meeting Bernice was talking about. "Hey, do either of you know anything about the upcoming residents' meeting?"

Quinten nods. "Sure, the Biannual Safety Forum. It's kind of a mix between a neighborhood watch meeting and a friendly get-together. It's held at Lonerock Community Hall."

Felicity leans forward in her seat again. "Aren't you on the community text chain? There was a message sent out the other day with all the information."

"I'm on the text chain, but I didn't get any message about a meeting," I say, confused.

"Strange, Benton usually sends them out to everybody," Felicity muses. "Well, anyway, it's at seven o'clock, Monday night. Maybe we'll see you there."

Felicity and Quinten wave goodbye and drive off, leaving me with my mind quickly connecting the dots.

Benton, who lives close by on Abbey Street, is in charge of the text thread for our community. I know I'm on it because I've already gotten several texts about missing pets and weather alerts since I moved here. But for some reason I didn't get the text about the meeting. It's almost as though Benton doesn't want me there after I confronted him about the photos a couple of weeks back. Like he's afraid I might come along and start asking more questions.

Well sorry, Benton, but I'm going to be at that meeting. And you can bet your ass I'll be bringing the photos along with me.

24

MORY

I never thought I'd say it, but it's actually kind of good to be back home in Lonerock.

Dad dropped me and Cameron at the airport this morning. I know for a fact that he had his tracker app for my phone running because he texted me about two minutes after we got into Mom's car, saying he was glad we got home safe and that he missed us already.

The only thing is, I was kind of expecting Mom to have made more progress on the house, but when we got there and I stepped inside I had to bite my tongue to keep from saying anything that might upset her. The place is no better than when we left. There's stuff everywhere. It's like she started a bunch of projects and just gave up halfway through. Most of the walls are still coated in the same gross, peeling wallpaper, and other than a couple of changes in the kitchen, there's not much sign of any new additions or improvements.

To add to that, there's a weariness in my mom's eyes that I can't ignore.

"I thought you were going to make the house look good?" Cameron blurts out.

I shove him hard in the back. "Shut up, Cam! She is. It just takes time."

Mom gives me a stern look for pushing my brother, then her eyes soften. "It's okay, Mory. And yes, Cameron, I know it doesn't look very good yet but go upstairs and look at your bedroom."

Cameron's eyes light up and he practically falls over himself in his haste to get up the stairs. Ten seconds later we hear a shout of "Woah, cool!" coming from his room and Mom laughs.

"Before you ask, I haven't gotten around to your room, yet, sorry," she says.

"That's fine," I say.

There are bags under Mom's eyes and I'm starting to wonder if there's something wrong, other than having spent Christmas alone.

"So, tell me everything!" Her enthusiasm seems forced. "What did you guys get up to over the holidays?"

I tell her about the raffle I entered at the Christmas fair and how I won a huge stuffed reindeer and about Cameron's new obsession with Mario Cart, and the caroling trip that Caitlyn dragged us all along on (which actually turned out to be kind of fun), and a few other funny things that happened while we were there. I intentionally leave out one very important detail of our time there, because Mom really doesn't look like she needs to hear about it right this minute.

"If it's okay, Mom, I'm going to go see Hutch," I say, one foot practically out the door already.

"Wow, you lasted all of ten minutes here, I'm impressed." She laughs before holding out her arm, gesturing for me to leave.

Twenty minutes later, I walk down the path leading away from the road, and the sound of vehicles fades away, replaced by the gentle rushing of the waterfall. The air is crisp and cold, and I pull my coat tighter around me as I emerge from the trees into a clearing. My breath catches at the beautiful sight before me. Water cascades down the rocks, glistening in the sunlight. The surrounding area is covered in a thin layer of frost and a light mist hangs in the air, making the whole place look like it's right out of a fairy tale.

He's already waiting for me and I run up to him full force, a grin on my face. He catches me and spins me around. I bury my face into his blond hair and when I finally let go and he places me down, I can feel the waterfall spray on my face, the cold water droplets tingling on my skin.

"I missed you," he says, kissing both of my hands in turn.

"Not as much as I missed you." I laugh.

We sit down together and catch each other up on everything that's happened in the three weeks we've been apart. The smell of damp earth and fresh water fills the air while we sit, watching each other's eyes light up as we joke and laugh and have fun just being with each other. I could spend all day here with him. But unfortunately, it soon comes to an end when we both have to leave to go home to our families.

Back home, Mom is putting a huge pot of mac and cheese out on the table, which she knows is both mine and Cameron's favorite.

When I sit down and begin piling my plate up, she leans closer to me. "How'd it go with Hutch?"

I suppress a grin. "Fine, Mom. We just talked for a while."

"Good." She smiles. "You know I have it on good authority that you can expect to be asked out on an official date next month."

"Next month?" I ask, confused.

"When you turn seventeen." Mom nods.

"Oh," I say, understanding now.

I guess Hutch must have shared with his folks that he's interested in me as more than just a friend. I doubt that was a shocker, with the amount of time we spend together. But the idea of Hutch and I going out to dinner or a movie alone together seems kind of weird now.

"Mom, guess what?" Cameron says, mouth full of cheesy pasta.

"What?"

I kick Cameron under the table and give him *shut up* eyes.

"Ow! Mom! Mory kicked me!" he wails.

"You were talking with your mouth full." I glare at him. "And I think you should shut up."

Mom stares from me to Cameron and back. "What's going on?"

"She doesn't want me to tell you about Dad and Caitlyn," he says.

"God, Cameron, you are such a brat!" I kick him again.

"Mory! Stop it. What are you guys talking about?" Mom demands.

I put my head down and scoop another forkful of food into my mouth. I guess she's going to find out sooner or later anyway, I just didn't want anything stressing her out even more right now.

"They're having a baby," Cameron says. "We're gonna have a little sister."

In the three seconds following Cameron's words, I see Mom's eyes glaze over and her face form an expression I don't recognize. Then just as fast, she jumps up from her seat, a painfully big smile on her face.

"Congratulations, guys!" She hugs Cameron tightly and then me. "A new sibling. That's just wonderful news. I'm so happy for you both!"

But I don't think she is, really.

I search her eyes as she sits back down. Despite the grin pinned firmly on her face as she listens to Cameron talk on and on about what he's going to do with a baby sister, all I see is pain in her eyes. It's like the photos of the women she showed me before. Her face is split into two parts. On the bottom, her lips turn upwards, happy. But on the top, it looks as though she's being tortured.

25

———

RUBY

I pull into the parking lot of Lonerock Community Hall, my hands gripping the steering wheel tightly as I search for a spot among the throng of cars already here. The sun has set and in the orange glow of the parking lot lights I can see people milling about, their voices carrying through the air. I finally find a spot and turn off the engine, then sit back, rigid in my seat.

"You want to talk about it?" Justin asks.

"What is there to talk about? My kids are getting another sibling, and that's a great thing."

"And?"

"And what?" I turn my head to glare at him.

I'm starting to regret asking Justin to come along with me to the meeting. He doesn't even live in the catchment area. But I thought it was a good idea to have someone in my corner, just in case things go south tonight, and Mory agreed to minding the boys for us this evening so here we are.

Now he's psychoanalyzing me, when I'm already on the brink of a meltdown, and I don't have much patience for it.

"You know, it's okay to have some feelings about your ex-husband having another baby," he says.

"Is it?" I turn to him, eyes wide. "Is it okay for me to want to scream? Is it okay for me to despise the thought of my kids getting a new baby sister? Is it okay for me to hate Aaron and Caitlyn, and seethe with jealousy over them adding a precious new baby to their family, while somehow simultaneously being completely content with not having any more of my own?"

Justin mulls this over for a second. "Yes. I think that's okay. I'd dare say it's even... normal."

I slam my head back against my seat and take a deep breath, letting it out slowly while I collect my thoughts. "Parenting is the most beautiful and cruel experience there is in life," I say, my voice breaking a little. "One day, you give your child their last bath or read them their last bedtime story and the occasion isn't memorable. You don't even notice it. Then at some point, you realize that period of your life just slipped by and now lives in the past, gone forever. And in that moment, right there, you finally realize that all those small things that seemed so mundane and even frustrating at times... well they were actually the most valuable moments of your entire life."

There's silence in the car for too long, until I finally look over to Justin. He's just staring out of the window into the dark. After a moment he turns to me, his eyes glassy. "Christ, Ruby."

"Sorry."

"Don't be. But you can apologize to Xavier in advance when we get back, because I'll probably end up hugging that kid way too hard before bed tonight."

I crack a smile at this and open the door to get out. Right now I need a distraction, and this meeting should be the perfect thing for that.

We walk through the parking lot, the streetlights casting long shadows that seem to follow us as we make our way toward the hall. I see the glow of light spilling out from the windows of the building and my heart begins racing with anticipation.

There's no escaping the fact that what I'm here to do tonight will stir up a hornets' nest in this small community. Somebody here knows something about these pictures, and I'm going to shake the hive until the truth comes out.

Justin reaches for the handle of the heavy wooden door and pushes it open, holding out his arm for me to enter first. Inside, the room is filled with the buzz of conversation. The scent of coffee and old wood fills the air, and it's immediately clear that everyone here already knows each other, their conversations flowing easily as they mingle around the snack table.

Feeling a little out of place, I stay close to Justin as we each grab a cup of coffee and try to blend in. I notice that every once in a while, someone will look from Justin to me and back again, frowning, before quickly turning away.

I grab his arm as he's about to stuff a glazed donut into his mouth. "We should probably try to mingle."

"No talk," he grumbles. "Free food."

I leave the caveman to it and try to seek out any familiar faces. I've been living here for five months now, and I'm wondering how long it will be until I won't feel like such an outsider. Finally, I spot someone I recognize as a blonde woman shuffles through the crowd toward me. "Ruby, hi! This must be your first time coming to one of these meetings."

I smile. "Hi, Kendra! Yes, it is."

She laughs and taps my arm. "Harriet, actually."

"Oh! Of course, I knew that. Sorry." My cheeks redden. Harriet and Kendra are so blandly indistinguishable. They really should wear name tags.

As Harriet and I make chit-chat, I can't help but notice her eyes flicker to Justin every now and then.

It's starting to really bug me now. Either Justin is so good-looking that nobody (including the local pastor) can keep their eyes off of him, or these are the judging eyes that he told me about before. I can't even begin to wrap my head around how anyone could think that he murdered his own wife, he's one of the most kind and gentle men I know.

When everyone is ushered to the seating area, I catch him by the arm and speak quietly. "Have you noticed the looks?"

He laughs as he licks his sticky fingers. "Only every damn time I've left my house for the past eight years."

"Don't you feel like telling them all to go to hell? How do you deal with this?" I ask.

He looks into my eyes. "I know the truth. That's all that matters."

We weave our way through the crowd, past rows of chairs set up facing a stage with a podium at the front and pick seats close to it. After a minute, Felicity and Quinten sit down next to us. A flicker of judgment passes across Felicity's eyes when she sees me with Justin, but she says nothing and proceeds to make small talk with me as usual.

The room is filled with chatter and laughter, the air buzzing with energy, but it quickly dies down when Benton Shepherd walks onto the stage, commanding everyone's attention with his dazzling smile.

"Hello and good evening, everybody." He waves, eyes scanning the room. "It's great to see so many familiar faces here tonight. I appreciate all of you taking the time to join us for this meeting."

As he begins speaking passionately about the community he's known as his home for many years and a new development project for a children's playground that he's excited to get behind, I feel a cold sensation prickle down the back of my neck and I turn around to see a pair of dark eyes right on mine. Bernice Fisher's scowl could peel paint off a wall as she glares at me from the end of the next row back, her eyes brimming with pure, unadulterated hate.

I roll my eyes and turn back to face the front of the room again, listening as Benton reads out some stats given to him by the local police chief about the impressively low crime rate in our area. Benton is all but patting himself on the back for single-handedly making sure his neighborhood stays safe.

This guy thinks he's Batman, I'm sure of it.

When he's done making sure everyone knows this night is mostly about him, it's time for some others to take the floor and, with each person that faces the room, a better picture of the community builds in my mind. There's Tom and Andrew, who are setting up a Men's Shed and encourage the guys in the room to stop by. There's Angela, who needs more volunteers to help tend the flower beds at the entrance to Forest Grove, which I (along with several others) gladly raise my hand to. And there's Elijah, who very kindly reminds everyone how nice it is when they make the effort to pick up after their dogs.

Everyone seems so nice and friendly, and I'm starting to feel proud to have joined such a balanced and connected community.

Unfortunately, that feeling is extinguished when Bernice Fisher gets up to have her say.

26

RUBY

It's impossible not to notice the hushed groans and displeased whispers around the room as Bernice walks slowly up to the podium. Evidently, I'm not the only person around here who is tired of this woman's caustic attitude.

"Here we go," I hear Felicity sigh.

I sink down a little in my chair, trying to stay calm as Bernice takes the podium, list in hand. I knew it was only a matter of time before she'd get up there and start spouting off about me, but now that I see her sour face staring out into the crowd, I want to shrivel up and disappear.

"I've been raising my concerns for months about a new resident on my street," Bernice starts, with no introduction or pleasantries. "And since she refuses to listen to me, I have no choice but to address it here."

There are some groans from the audience as Bernice pulls her glasses up from around her neck and opens her list. "The new resident at number 168 Forest Grove has consistently been—"

Bernice is cut off before she's barely begun by a panicked-looking Benton who rushes the stage. "Bernice, I'm going to have to stop you there. I understand that you have concerns, but there are proper channels for addressing personal disagreements, and this meeting is not one of them."

My cheeks are burning. I'm sure all eyes in the room are fixed on me right now, but I daren't even look.

Bernice crosses her arms and holds her place firmly as Benton closes in on her. "You expect me to stay quiet as Ruby Blake invites a killer into our neighborhood?"

Justin's dry laugh beside me is nearly drowned out by the murmurs that float around the room.

Benton now has Bernice by the arm and is guiding her away from the stage. She struggles with him and manages to pull free from his grip.

"Fine! I'll sit back down," she shouts, before turning to the crowd again. "But I know as well as everyone else here does that Justin Thomas killed his wife!"

I begin to rise in my seat to defend Justin, but he pulls me back down and shakes his head. "She's not worth it, Ruby. Don't bother."

An awkward silence falls over the room as Benton returns to the podium. He brushes down his suit and clears his throat. "Well, I think that's it for our speakers. Thank you to everyone for coming out tonight, as well as for your continued participation in keeping this community safe and connected."

As the crowd claps and Benton blesses everyone with a gleaming smile, I take a deep breath and stand up.

A few people are getting up to leave now and I make a dash for the stage. Benton is just starting to walk down the steps and he gives me a strange look as I rush past him.

"Excuse me! Sorry! Everyone!" I speak loudly.

Those who have already gotten up out of their seats begin to sit back down, brows raised. Benton, standing at the end of the row I just exited, crosses his arms.

"I just have an enquiry to make." I open my bag up and pull out three printed sheets of paper.

I had the forethought to scan the photos and print them out large before coming tonight, in order for everyone to get a better look.

"I moved into number 168 Forest Grove a few months back, and I found these three photos in my home." I hold each photo out in turn to the perplexed crowd in front of me. "Does anyone know who these girls are?"

I wait a few moments. There's a little chatter amongst the audience but no raised hands or voices.

"Doesn't anyone recognize even *one* of them?" I plead.

Benton starts back up the steps and I'm sure he's about to haul me off like he did Bernice. I can read the expression on his face, he doesn't want me showing these around.

"Wait!" I hold my palm out to him, and turn back to the crowd, desperate now. "I think something bad happened to these girls, and somebody is trying to cover it up."

There are confused murmurs from the crowd, but I just speak louder. "Somebody left these photos hidden in my house, and I think these are the smiles of people under duress. If anyone knows something, it could—"

"It was him!" A shout cuts me off. "He did it! He left them there!"

Everyone turns to look at Bernice, where she stands screeching. She's pointing Justin's way again. "I've seen him come and go from the house for years! I've tried to warn you all but nobody ever listens to me!"

Fire shoots through my veins at the sound of her high-pitched voice. What is that woman's problem? Why has she got it in for Justin?

Thankfully, nobody seems to give Bernice's panicked squawking much mind, and an elderly man sitting next to her takes her by the elbow and gently leads her away as she continues shrieking incoherently in Justin's direction.

Benton rushes up to me, teeth gritted. "It's time for you to leave."

Most people are getting up and gathering their things now, eager to get away from the circus that's broken out. This is a mess. I haven't accomplished anything here, and now my neighbors think I'm a match for Bernice in the crazy department. I look down at Justin who remains seated, seemingly unfazed by the repeated accusations against him. I shove the photos back into my bag and push past Benton, ignoring him. I don't believe for a second that nobody here knows a thing about these girls.

Especially Benton Shepherd.

I walk down the steps as Felicity and Quinten are getting up from their seats and I see Felicity look up at me, sympathy in her eyes.

"Sorry you didn't get your answers," she says, then leans in close and whispers in my ear. "But you might want to listen to Bernice, just this one time."

I pull away from Felicity, my eyes narrowed as she walks away. I expect this kind of crap from Bernice, but Felicity? This whole town seems to have found Justin guilty of a crime that wasn't even committed. The poor man lost his wife, the mother of his child, to suicide. And this is how they treat him?

"Let's go." Justin slips a hand in mine.

Stepping back out into the parking lot, the bitter cold nips at my face.

It's quiet outside, a welcome contrast to the heated atmosphere that had filled the meeting room just moments ago. The whole thing has left a weird feeling in the pit of my stomach. Somebody there knew something about those girls, I know it. And there's a reason they won't speak up.

"Well, I don't know about you," Justin says. "But I think that went great."

I let out a strangled laugh. "Yeah, except now everyone thinks that I'm crazy and you're a murderer."

"We make a good pair." He stops me where I am and pulls me in, kissing me on the lips.

"What was that for?" I ask when he finally releases me.

He sighs. "It's for you being the only other sane person in this entire town."

I pull him in by his collar and kiss him again before we walk hand in hand back to the car. But when I start the engine, Felicity's warning begins to play over and over again in my mind, and I can't help but begin to wonder if there's something that I'm missing.

If Justin's wife was depressed and took her own life, and no criminal charges were ever brought against him, then why does everyone seem so damn sure that he killed her?

27

RUBY

I'm cutting carrots for soup when I hear a low, urgent wail in the distance. The unmistakable pitch rises and falls, growing closer, setting the hairs on the back of my neck on high alert.

I put my knife down and wipe my hands on a dishtowel before moving to my front window. A few locals I recognize are standing on the street outside, concern etched on their faces as two police cars pull up in front of Bernice Fisher's house.

I throw the dishtowel over my shoulder and step outside just in time to see an ambulance blare its sirens up the street and park right next to the police cars.

"What's going on?" Mory's voice comes from behind me.

"I don't know," I say, looking around at the chattering mouths and crossed arms of the bystanders outside.

A large crowd has now gathered and it's evident that something is going on inside Bernice's house. I spot Felicity across the street, her usual shadows, Harriet and Kendra, right by her side. Instructing Mory to stay inside with her brother, I open the door and make my way across the street. Felicity turns when she spots me and I can see from the look on her face that it's bad news.

"What's going on? Is Bernice okay?" I ask.

Felicity shakes her head, her eyes glistening. "Oh, Ruby. It's terrible."

"Bernice is dead," Kendra says. "Tom Griffin, the mailman, found her this morning."

My heart hammers inside my chest and I can't find any words to speak.

"He told me he'd noticed her mail was piling up for the past two weeks." Harriet's eyes light up perversely as she speaks. "He tried her door and it was unlocked, so he let himself inside. He found her decaying body in the kitchen."

"Murdered," Kendra adds. "And nobody has seen her since the night of the meeting, so presumably it was just after that."

I feel my legs go weak.

Felicity holds out a hand to steady me. "Are you okay?"

"I... I can't believe it," I stammer. "What happened to her?"

"Tom said it looked like she'd been strangled," Felicity says. "But I guess we'll have to wait for the official word from the coroner."

The three women continue talking amongst themselves, their words muffled in my ears as everything around me seems to go gray.

It's not like I haven't noticed how quiet it's been around here in the two weeks since the community meeting. But thinking of Bernice lying there dead, undiscovered for so long, turns my stomach.

It's no secret that I didn't get along with the woman, but this isn't what I wanted. She didn't deserve this.

The police are now cordoning off Bernice's house and asking the crowd to move back to make space.

"It could be a break-in gone wrong," Felicity suggests.

"Oh, come on, Felicity, you don't believe that any more than I do." Kendra shakes her head.

"What... what do you mean?" I find my voice.

They glance silently from one to the other, before I realize what's going unsaid.

"You all think Justin did this," I mutter in disbelief.

Nobody speaks.

"I can't believe you all!" My voice rises. "Why would Justin do something like this? He barely even knew the woman!"

"Ruby, he—" Felicity starts.

"No! You know what? Justin is the kindest, most selfless man I've ever known. He didn't kill his wife, and he definitely didn't kill Bernice Fisher!"

I storm off in the direction of my house, shaken by the ignorance of women who are old enough to know better than to jump to conclusions. Inside, I shut the front door behind me, my head spinning.

"Mom!" Mory is running down the stairs, panicked. "Mrs. Fisher is dead!"

"I know." I grab her and hug her tightly, then pull away to look at her. "But... who told you?"

"Hutch," she says, holding up her phone. "He said that she was killed!"

"We don't know that for sure yet." I try to calm her down. "Let's just wait for the police to do their job before we start adding to the rumors."

Mory lowers her voice. "Hutch says his mom thinks Justin killed her. And that he killed his wife years ago, too."

I sigh. "Sweetie, there's no truth to that. Trust me, Justin is a great guy. I wouldn't let him into our lives if I thought for a second that any of that was true."

"I know," Mory says without conviction. "Can I go over to Hutch's house?"

I can see she's seeking comfort and since she doesn't seem to be getting it from me, I agree to her request and try to busy myself by returning to preparing vegetables as I had been before this whole afternoon went haywire.

But as I stand at the counter peeling potatoes, I can't get the image out my head of Bernice lying dead in her kitchen for the past two weeks, while we've all just been living our lives as normal.

That woman was spiteful and mean, but that doesn't take away from how horrible it is for her death to have gone undetected for so long. That nobody cared enough for her to notice her absence and check in on her. I wonder who the police will be looking at, as a suspect in her death? I cast my mind back to the meeting two weeks ago, the last night she was seen. She ruffled a lot of feathers that night, mine included. But one face pops into my head now. Benton. Might he have had motive to kill Bernice? There's a lot I don't trust about that man, but could he really be capable of murder? I already suspect that he knows more about the girls in the photos than he let on to me, so if my instincts are right, and he did something to those girls, I suppose it's plausible that he could have killed Bernice, too.

But unfortunately, Benton is not the one who people will point the finger at for Bernice's death. Justin will be.

Bernice was vocal at the meeting about her belief that Justin was guilty of killing his wife, and even pointed him out as being responsible for leaving the photos of the girls hidden in my house—claiming to have seen him coming and going over the years. But... that can't be true. Justin didn't recognize those photos when I showed him them. And he told me that his wife, Elle, had taken her own life after a short but devastating battle with postpartum depression.

I haven't broached the subject with him since he first told me because it's obviously a very painful part of his life that he'd rather not speak about. But I do remember wondering, right after the meeting, why it seemed that everyone—and not just crazy old Bernice—had been wary of Justin. The looks, the whispers. I might have asked him more about it had I not been so distracted over the last two weeks. The news of my children's impending new sibling, the house renovations, and Mory's upcoming seventeenth birthday have all been keeping my mind busy. I've not even had time to dwell on the photos of the girls. It seems like that chapter closed for me the night I left the meeting, my questions unanswered.

But now that the neighborhood gossip train has taken off yet again, this time accusing Justin of murdering Bernice, I'm starting to wonder if it's possible there's some piece of information about the death of Justin's wife that I'm missing. I mean, as sad as it is, hundreds of people take their own lives every single day. And unless there's great evidence to the contrary, their loved ones don't just get accused of having been the one to kill them.

My mind suddenly in overdrive, I slide my phone out of my pocket before I can stop myself. I pull up Google and type *Elle Thomas Lonerock* into the search bar. If there was anything more to her death than what Justin told me, surely there must be something about it online.

I take a deep breath and press the search button, then watch in horror as headline after headline pops up on my screen.

28
———

MORY

Hutch and I sit next to each other at his kitchen island, my head resting against his shoulder.

"I can't believe Bernice is dead," I mutter. "It's so crazy. I mean, who do you think would want to kill her?"

Hutch shrugs. "Everyone?"

I lift my head and narrow my eyes at him. "That's not funny, Hutch!"

"It wasn't meant to be. And I'm not trying to be mean, but everyone hated that woman. I don't think anyone will care that she's gone."

This strikes me as just about the saddest thing I've ever heard. But I met Bernice a couple of times, and Hutch's statement tracks. And even though I know my mom would never admit it, I bet she's just a *little* relieved to never have to deal with Bernice's complaints about her again.

It's the first time Hutch and I have been alone at his house. His dad is at work and his mom has gone out for the afternoon with Leo, so he invited me to come over and keep him company.

"So, do you think it'll be weird for you, getting a new baby sister?" Hutch asks me.

I think about this. It's hard to wrap my head around the fact my dad is starting a whole new family without me and Cameron. I mean, of course we're part of that family but Dad and Caitlyn will be spending all their time with the baby, and only summers and Christmas with us. Up until now, from the second me and Cameron arrive at his house to the second we leave, it's all about us. But I don't think that will be possible anymore once the baby arrives. Caitlyn will be busy looking after the baby, and my dad probably won't have as much energy as usual. I guess there wasn't much chance it was going to stay the same forever.

"I don't know," I say. "It's kind of cool. But I'll be seventeen when the baby is born, and once she's my age I'll be like, really old."

"I guess," Hutch says. "Hey, speaking of you turning seventeen... I was wondering if you wanted to go out on your birthday. I can borrow my dad's car and we could catch dinner somewhere, maybe see a movie?"

"Your mom made you wait to ask me out, didn't she?"

"Yup."

I think it's sweet that Hutch still follows his mom's rules at eighteen. He's a really great guy. We've been hanging out at his house for so long now that it would feel kind of weird to go on an actual date. But I think it's important to him that I say yes.

"I think that would be fun, thanks." I smile.

He's looking at me with that warm gaze that makes me remember how cute he is.

He's always been so respectful of the fact I'm only sixteen and he's eighteen. Most guys wouldn't care. I mean, *I* don't even care—what difference does it make if I'm sixteen years and eleven months old or seventeen? What magically happens between those two times that makes it more appropriate for us to date?

But Hutch is a guy who follows the rules, and I know he'd never push any boundaries or make me feel uncomfortable in any way. That's just the kind of guy he is. It's sweet and endearing, and it only makes me like him even more.

Hutch suggests he make us some food, and I watch as he rummages through his fridge, pulling out various ingredients to make sandwiches. His messy blond hair falls into his eyes as he focuses on the task and I can't help but smile at how adorable he looks, even when he's just making us lunch. As he spreads mayonnaise on the bread, I lean against the counter and stare at a photo stuck to the fridge door.

"Is that you and your grandmother?" I ask, pointing to the picture.

Hutch looks up, his eyes softening as he nods. "Yeah, that's me and Nana at Disneyworld. She passed away when I was a kid."

I can hear the sadness in his voice. "It looks like you two were close."

"We were." He keeps his focus on the sandwiches. "Leo's too small to remember her, but she used to take me everywhere. On vacation, to the theatre, to bingo nights."

I laugh at this. "You liked going to bingo nights?"

"I liked going with Nana," he says, meaningfully.

"Sounds like she was an amazing woman."

He puts a plate down in front of me and I thank him before taking a bite of the sandwich.

Hutch nods, his eyes avoiding mine. "She was. You know, nothing's been the same since she's been gone. She was like the glue that held my family together."

I don't get what he means by this. Hutch's family is perfect. Like a TV family, where everyone always looks amazing and their house is stupidly big.

"It always seems to me like you've got the kind of family everyone wishes they had," I say.

"Yeah." Hutch looks down at his hands. "My mom works really hard to make sure of that. She even sets up these family photoshoots once a year with a photographer. Smiling and happy. But that's not how it really is at home. My parents fight all the time. My dad works so much and my mom blames him for everything that ever goes wrong. She tries to make things seem perfect on the outside, but it's not."

"At least your parents are still together," I point out.

"Is that such a great thing?" he asks.

I have to stop and think about this. "I don't know. I mean, when my mom and dad split, my dad got a new girlfriend straight away. That was kind of weird. Although, I'm used to her now. But now my mom is suddenly dating again. And there's all these rumors the guy killed his last wife…"

"Do you believe it?" Hutch asks, taking a bite of his sandwich.

"No way." I shake my head. "He's a good guy. He's been helping my mom out with the house, and he's got a kid the same age as Cameron."

"You ever heard of Ted Bundy?" A sly smile touches his lips.

"Yeah, but didn't he stalk and kill random women? Not just his wife and an old lady everyone hated."

Hutch shrugs. "My point is that even a guy like Justin, who looks like a nice family kind of guy on the outside, could secretly be a psycho murderer."

I'm suddenly turned off my sandwich. "I don't think Justin is like that. Plus, my mom said his wife wasn't killed, she was depressed and ended her own life."

"Well, nobody really knows, do they?" he says.

His tone catches my attention. "What do you mean?"

Hutch pushes his plate aside and leans in closer to me, his voice low. "What I mean is, how could anybody know what really happened to her, if they never found her body?"

29

RUBY

Lonerock Woman Missing.

Search Launched For Missing Lonerock Woman.

Lonerock Woman Missing For Seven Years Declared Dead.

I scroll down through the search results that span back over eight years. Article after article, each one a fragment of a story that slowly begins to form a clearer picture as I read through them, leaving me with an ice-cold pit of dread deep in my chest.

I pull up three tabs on my screen, each one a local news article from years past, and work my way from oldest to newest.

The first is from eight years ago.

Authorities have launched a search for Elle Thomas, a wife and mother from the Lonerock community who was last heard from on the evening of July 17th, when she was on her way to meet her husband, Justin Thomas, for dinner. Justin became worried when Elle never arrived and reported her missing to the authorities when efforts to reach her by phone went unanswered. Elle's car was later found abandoned on Springdale Road near a river. Friends and family of Mrs. Thomas are urging anyone with information on her whereabouts to come forward and help bring her home safely.

Justin never told me that his wife went missing. In fact, he never told me how his wife even died. He just said she took her own life, and I felt it would be stepping over the line to ask how she did it.

I read on, but the next article is even more concerning.

Six months have passed since Elle Thomas, a beloved member of the Lonerock community, went missing. The young wife and mother was last heard from on the evening of July 17th, on her way to meet her husband, Justin Thomas. However, she never made it to her destination and was reported missing the same day. For weeks, officials led a ground and water search spanning several miles around where her vehicle was found, which turned up no clues to her whereabouts. Authorities had been working under the information that Mrs. Thomas was suffering from depression following the birth of her first child and may have been having thoughts of self-harm. But it seems they are now shifting their focus to her husband's potential involvement in the disappearance, since it was reported that Elle and Justin had been fighting earlier that day.

Justin was investigated in Elle's disappearance. They thought he killed her. Why didn't he tell me this? It explains why everyone in Lonerock seems to hate him. Not only do they think he murdered his wife, they think he disposed of her body, too.

My heart thudding in my chest, I switch to the third article.

It's startlingly recent—from only months before I moved to Lonerock.

> The small town of Lonerock is in mourning after the decision was made to declare missing local woman, Elle Thomas, legally dead seven years after her mysterious disappearance. Elle's husband, Justin Thomas, filed for the declaration after the minimum seven years had passed with no new leads on her whereabouts. Authorities investigating her disappearance over the years initially focused on Justin as a potential suspect. However, after an extensive investigation there was no evidence to link him with any involvement. Elle's car was found abandoned on Springdale Road, near the river, prompting authorities to conclude the new mother may have taken her own life as it had been known she was suffering from postpartum depression since the birth of her first child just months previously.

It's a good thing I'm sitting down already, or else I might just crumple to the floor. Who is this man that I let into my house? Into my bed.

Justin lied to me.

Well... I guess he didn't exactly lie, but when he told me that his wife had taken her own life, I presumed she had died from an overdose or some other tragic self-infliction. I didn't pry any further, because I knew it was a deeply painful subject for him. He never once offered up the information that his wife had gone missing, never to be seen again. And he definitely didn't share that there was a police investigation into his involvement.

It seems suspicious to me that a husband would be so quick to conclude his wife had taken her own life, when there's a possibility she may have been kidnapped or killed by somebody. I guess the police thought that too.

Everything is suddenly beginning to add up.

The whole community is scared of him; he seems to have no friends here. And there I was, new to town, just months after his wife was legally declared dead—a newcomer who didn't know the truth. Fresh pickings. Did he really think I wouldn't find out that he was once a suspect in his wife's disappearance?

Then a dark thought runs through my mind. If Justin had something to do with Elle vanishing, it really is possible he had something to do with the photos I found.

Bernice stood up at that meeting and pointed him out as being the one to have come and gone from this house before I moved in. I thought the old bat just had it in for him, but now I'm starting to wonder. Did Justin kill those girls like he did his wife?

Before I can think my reaction through, I'm grabbing my keys and running out the front door. Bernice's house is still cordoned off with various official vehicles parked outside, but the crowd has since dispersed and I spot Cameron playing ball alone in our front yard.

"Get in the car," I shout, sitting in and buckling my belt.

"What? Am I in trouble?" He sits in the passenger seat, still holding the ball.

"No, sweetie, sorry if it sounded like you were. I just have to go see Justin, and I can't leave you alone here while Mory is at Hutch's house."

Cameron's eyes light up. "Cool! I've never seen Xavier's house before. He said he has a full-size basketball stand."

I've never been to their house, either, now that I think of it. Justin and I have been seeing each other for months, but he always comes to mine. It just makes sense, because of the work he's been doing here. But now I'm wondering if there's a reason he's never invited me over to his place. He kept the truth behind his wife's death from me, so I'm starting to question everything else he's ever told me about himself. Which is shockingly little. But I do know his address, since it was on a package of electrical fuses he once brought over after ordering it for me.

My fingers grip the steering wheel tightly as I navigate the winding roads leading east of Lonerock. I've not been out here before and the area is unfamiliar to me. As we get further from town, passing houses becomes less and less frequent, and the trees seem to close in on the road. I make the turn to his house and find myself driving down a long gravel driveway. A small pond to the left glistens in the hazy afternoon sunlight, and tall trees surround a vast area of land.

"This place is cool," Cameron remarks. "Is this where Xavier and his dad live?"

"I... I'm not sure," I mumble, confused.

It's not possible all this could be Justin's land... is it?

But a glance at the map on my phone tells me I'm on the right path. And fifteen seconds later as I pull to a stop, I have my suspicions confirmed that there's a lot I don't know about the man I've been seeing.

Because that cozy little house that he told me he built with Elle all those years ago—the house that he lay the foundations for and hung the shutters on while Elle painted the bedrooms— is not a *house* at all.

30

RUBY

I stare up at the sprawling two story mansion—this monstrosity —in front of me as I step out of the car. With a wooden balcony overlooking a pond and huge glass windows, which must frame the surrounding grounds beautifully from inside, it's a far cry from the image Justin put in my head when he'd told me about the starter home he and Elle built for themselves all those years ago.

As I step out of the car onto the perfectly kept grounds to the front, the door to the house opens and Xavier runs out. "Cam!"

Cameron jumps out of the car excitedly and the two boys waste no time running off around the side of the house, probably to a tennis court or an outdoor theatre, or a huge pool around the back—it wouldn't surprise me at a place like this.

Why did Justin downplay his home to me? Why hasn't he ever invited me over here? Most guys would be falling over themselves to impress the woman they're seeing by taking her back to his huge countryside home. But not Justin.

Nothing about him says 'money.' Every time I've seen him,

he's been in work combats and a hoodie, and the Ford he drives is practically on its last legs for Christ's sake. Everything about him screams working-class Joe. There's a glaring disparity here and something clearly isn't adding up.

I realize that I've been standing beside my car, trying to process the fact that I apparently know nothing about the man I've been dating, when I see the door open again and Justin walk out slowly. His brow is raised, clearly surprised that I've shown up unannounced. "Ruby? What are you doing here?"

There's about ten feet between where we stand and I stick firmly to my spot by the car, not wanting to get any closer to him. "You lied to me."

He crosses his arms. "How so?"

"Your wife, Elle. You didn't tell me she went missing." I keep my voice low, steady. "And that you were a suspect."

Justin sighs. "That?"

"What do you mean *that*? Yes, that!" I yell.

"I figured you already knew." Justin shrugs, as though everyone in the world has been accused of murder at one point or another. "Lonerock loves to gossip."

He starts walking toward me, but I hold out a hand to stop him. "Don't come near me."

His nonchalant attitude about this is grating on my nerves. Shouldn't he be defending himself? Or trying to convince me that he had nothing to do with his wife's disappearance? I've seen people more passionately defend themselves after being accused of passing wind.

"Nobody told me anything, Justin," I say. "You could have told me the truth. Instead, I had to find out about this on the internet."

He scratches his head. "It's a time of my life I don't like to talk about. My wife went missing. As her husband, the blame was pointed at me. What can I say? It was hardly surprising."

He stops and sits on the bottom step of his porch. It's made of solid oak with intricate carvings along the railing and I expect he probably built it himself, being a carpenter. The whole house is just picture-perfect in every way. Every detail looks like it was thoughtfully planned out. And I'll bet the view from that balcony upstairs is something else.

How much of this was Elle's labor of love?

I'm suddenly brokenhearted for this woman who built a perfect life—the picturesque house in the countryside, the husband, the baby—and never even got the chance to live it.

"Did you do it?" I ask, not taking my eyes from his.

"Kill my wife? No," Justin says, unblinking. "And I'll forgive you for asking."

"And what about the pictures of the girls?" I'm not letting up easily. "At the meeting, Bernice accused you of coming and going from the house in the years that it was empty."

Justin's laugh is dry. "I told you, I don't know who those girls are. And somebody seriously needs to put a stopper in that old bag's mouth."

My jaw drops involuntarily.

"What?" he asks, frowning. "Why are you looking at me like that?"

"You haven't heard?"

"Heard what?"

The inside of Justin's house is just as impressive as the outside. His kitchen is nearly the same size as the whole downstairs of my house. The space is obnoxiously big for just him and Xavier, but something tells me that when he and Elle built the place, they'd had plans to fill it up.

"I can't believe someone killed her," Justin says, passing me a mug of coffee. "I mean, she was truly awful but to strangle her to death? Somebody must have really hated her."

My stomach turns at these words. "It's not official that she was killed, yet. That's just what the mailman who found her told Harriet."

Justin walks to a window overlooking a field-sized backyard, where the boys are chasing each other around a huge wooden jungle gym.

"They'll all think it was me," he says, casually. "I mean, she died just after the community meeting where she came straight out and accused me of being a murderer. Plenty of witnesses."

I don't want to confirm his suspicions that, yes, his name has been thrown in the hat already—at least within Felicity's clique—but I know Justin didn't kill Bernice. And I don't think he killed his wife, either.

Justin takes a seat beside me. For a man who is probably about to have the cops come knocking on his door in a murder investigation, he looks remarkably unconcerned. I'm starting to wonder if he's got a stash of horse tranquilizers somewhere around this ranch of his that he keeps himself topped up with daily—the man just can't be rattled.

"Justin, I thought you were a struggling carpenter," I say, looking around the place. "What is all this?"

"I'm a carpenter. I have struggles." He shrugs.

I narrow my eyes at him. "You told me that you and Elle built your first home together. That you spent every cent you had, that you did most the work yourselves just to be able to afford it."

Justin sips his coffee slowly. "That's all true. It's not my fault if you pictured the house differently to what it is."

"It's a freaking mansion!" I yell, incredulously. "You drive around in a beat-up old car, you always have holes in your shirt and I happen to know you're a cheap date. So, what gives?"

Justin leans forward. "Sure, I'll tell you. If you want to listen."

"I've got all day." I cross my arms.

31

RUBY

And he does.

He tells me about the day he and Elle finally moved into this house. It had taken them years of saving and another four long years of building, a lot of which was a combination of their own hard work mixed with cashing in every favor they had around town.

It was Elle's dream home. She'd always wanted a big family, and Justin was eager to provide.

He tells me about the positive pregnancy test that she wrapped up in gift paper and surprised him with on his birthday. And of how they brought Xavier home from the hospital to this house, where family and friends had left balloons and gifts and even casseroles to tide them over in the first few days of adjusting to parenthood.

But this was the point in his story where his face dropped. Because in the weeks after Xavier's birth, he'd watched as Elle had sunk deeper and deeper into a depression she'd never experienced before. She struggled to care for the baby, to nurse him, to bathe him. She'd cry and cry and Justin would try to do what he could to help, but he was away from home working during the day and there wasn't much he could do. The doctor said she had postpartum depression, and that it was normal and would pass. She told Justin she didn't know why she couldn't just be happy. She had everything she'd ever wanted, but nothing about it felt right.

It killed him to leave her each morning, seeing how much she was suffering. But keeping a house this size running isn't cheap and he couldn't afford to take any time off work.

When Xavier was twelve weeks old, Elle also had to return to her job as a nurse.

The thing was, Elle was great at putting on a show. To everyone else, she was a woman who had it all together, but at home, her depression was putting a strain on her and Justin's relationship and they began fighting. Then one morning before he left for work, it all came to a head. Elle picked up and left for her mother's house.

"I must have called her ten times that morning, just trying to get through to her to tell her I was sorry. That I loved her and I didn't want to fight. Eventually she picked up, and I talked her into leaving Xavier with her mom so we could meet for dinner to talk."

Justin's coffee is sitting cold in the cup, his finger now tracing a circle around the rim. "The plan was that she would drive home to pick up some expressed milk she had in the freezer for Xavier and drop it back to her mother before meeting me for dinner. I was working that day, so I drove straight to the restaurant to meet her after I'd finished. And I'm sure you already read about the rest from there onwards."

It's evident from the tortured look in Justin's eyes that this is difficult for him to talk about. But if our relationship has any future, I need to hear this. All of it.

"Why did the police suspect you?" I ask.

Justin raises an eyebrow at this. "Why wouldn't they? I was

her husband. She'd just ran away to her mother's house because we were fighting. It all added up."

I guess that's true. The husband is always the first suspect in cases like this.

"But I knew how upset she was that day. And she'd already shared with me in the weeks leading up to it that she'd considered ending her life. I tried to get her to go to therapy, but she didn't want to. When I heard her car was found by a river, I just knew."

"Did you tell the police all this?" I ask.

"Of course I did. And I was there every day alongside them, searching for her. But everything I said and did only made it look like I was trying to cover for myself. There were a lot of questions raised about why one of her tires was flat, but ultimately that led nowhere." Justin leans back in his chair. "They were thorough with their investigation, but there was no obvious signs of an abduction, no signs of a body, and as much as they tried—there was no evidence to pin it on me."

Except it's clear that in the court of public opinion, the blame has been placed firmly on Justin for Elle's disappearance.

"Why did you choose to have her declared legally dead?" I ask.

"There were a lot of reasons. Emotional. Financial. But ultimately, it came down to Xavier's future. I didn't want him growing up always wondering if his mom would ever show up again." Justin looks uncomfortable. "And like I said, running a house like this isn't easy. I struggled for years on just one income after Elle was gone. I needed her life insurance payout just to keep a roof over Xavier's head. Believe you me, getting the insurance company to pay out was damn near impossible. But we won in the end."

I can see how that must have looked in a small town like this. But I can also see that Justin was only doing what he needed to do for his son's future. And my guess is that if it weren't for how special this house is to him, he'd have long since moved away from the judging eyes of Lonerock.

"Is that her?" I point to a photo on the wall.

A woman of about thirty, with flowing blonde hair and gleaming white teeth smiles out from the frame while holding an infant to her shoulder.

Justin nods. "She looked happy, right?"

He's right, at first glance. But I've become wary recently of the smiles captured in fleeting moments on film. And similar to the girls in the photos I found, Elle's smile has a darkness behind it. When I look closer, there are dark circles under her eyes, and rather than a loving hold on her young baby, she seems uncomfortable in that way people tend to look when they hold someone else's baby for the first time.

But a nagging question clenches my gut as I look at Elle's face. How could a beautiful woman like that, who seemed to have everything most others could only ever dream of having—the loving husband, the healthy baby, the huge house, and a stable career on top of it all—have ended up so desperately unhappy that she pulled over on the side of the road, walked to the river below and took her own life without so much as leaving a note?

32

—————

MORY

I'm officially seventeen! Today is my birthday, and also the day Hutch and I go on our first date.

I want to say that seventeen feels different in some way to sixteen, but the only difference I can see so far is that I woke up with a giant pimple on my cheek that wasn't there yesterday. But I'm not going to let that get me down because today marks one year until I'm officially an adult. I have no idea what exactly my plans are for adulthood, but I do know they will not involve living in Lonerock.

And yes, I know the love of my life lives here, but even *he* hates this town. Sometimes I fantasize about us running away together and getting our own place so we can spend every hour of the day with each other.

But while we're still in the soul-sucking pit that is Lonerock, that's not going to happen. Especially while I'm still only seventeen.

I already hated this town enough but since Mrs. Fisher next door was killed, I can't even relax. I lie in bed at night and wonder who that woman pissed off so much they wanted to kill her. And the thought of her body lying there for two weeks, right next to our house while we walked around thinking everything was totally normal really freaks me out. The mailman's son goes to my school and he's been telling everyone that her body was so badly decayed when his dad found her that there were maggots crawling on her. He'd suspected she'd been strangled because he saw marks around her neck.

It turns out he was right and apparently the cops have now launched a murder investigation. They've been to every house in the neighborhood asking people if they saw anything suspicious. As far as I know, they haven't got any leads yet.

Of course, everyone suspects my mom's boyfriend. But my mom is totally sure it wasn't him, and I'm pretty sure she's right. I mean, he could have easily done it. He's definitely strong enough to have strangled Bernice to death. She looked kind of skinny and frail and I'm pretty sure even Cameron would have been able to overpower her. But still, I don't think it was Justin.

I think my mom took Bernice's death hard though, not only because people are pointing the finger at Justin, but also because she'd been arguing with her ever since we got here and she regrets the mean things she'd said about her.

But I don't really understand why everyone is suddenly pretending to feel so sorry for the woman now that she's dead, when they all hated her right up until then. My mom dragged us along to the funeral because she was worried nobody would turn up, but there were a couple of dozen people there, mostly neighbors, because I think all her family are already dead. And the people who stood up to talk seemed as though they had to stretch their minds to come up with anything at all positive to say. They all said things like 'Bernice always watched over her community' and 'she took a passionate interest in the lives of others.'

Kind of like a bunch of gazelles at a lion's funeral saying 'he was a die-hard athlete' or 'he pursued his passion with an unstoppable hunger.' It's all just so phony.

And although she would never say it out loud, I think Mom is secretly happy that Bernice is gone, because now she doesn't have to worry about her complaining over every little thing she does. At the very least, the murder has given everyone in Lonerock something to talk about other than another store in town closing down or the weather.

"You look amazing!" My mom's eyes go wide as I walk into the kitchen.

I've put in effort for my date tonight, straightening my hair and picking out a dress, but I'm never really happy with what I see in the mirror.

"Meh," I reply. "I'm no model, that's for sure."

"I've told you before, Mory, don't ever compare yourself to pictures you see in adverts and online. It's all airbrushed, filtered and fake."

I put my hand to my cheek. "Hold on, are you trying to tell me that television and media portray images that aren't exactly real? You're willing to go on record with that?"

She rolls her eyes. "Well, I think you look great, anyway."

"Wish I could say the same, Mom." I grimace.

She's wearing a decades old Rolling Stones T-shirt, her hair has fallen half out of the lopsided bun on her head and she's on her hands and knees scrubbing the floor.

"Well, you try looking like a beauty queen while cleaning the house."

"No thanks." I sidestep her and check my phone as it chimes with a message.

Happy Birthday. Can't stop thinking about you.

I smile and send back a kissy face.

"I'll take it by the grin on your face that's Hutch," Mom teases. "What time is he picking you up?"

"Five."

"And what time is he dropping you home?"

"Dunno," I say. "And I'm not a child anymore, Mom. I have my own house key, and you don't have to wait up for me."

She frowns. "I know that, Mory. And I'm not babying you. I think Hutch is a responsible young man and I trust him to keep you safe."

"Good." I cross my arms.

"And..." She just can't seem to help herself. "Another form of safety you might be thinking about is—"

"Mom, it's just dinner," I interrupt her. "Maybe a movie. That's it. I appreciate the thought, but I really don't need the *talk*."

"Okay, okay." Mom holds up her pink-gloved hands in defeat. "Just trying to do my job."

I'm sure she thinks I'm just attempting to avoid an awkward conversation, but she really doesn't need to worry. Hutch and I aren't like that with each other, even if my promiscuous mother and father were at our age. A small amount of bile suddenly rises up my throat. Ugh. What a disgusting thought.

Hutch arrives at two minutes to five and my mom waves us off, but not before insisting on getting a picture of us together.

Hutch looks about as adorable as they come in a smart shirt tucked into his jeans. He even opens the passenger door for me to get in. When we pull up outside Caruso's Trattoria, he walks me inside and pulls the chair out for me and treats me like a queen. It's all so romantic and gentlemanly, I'm almost wondering if his mother gave him step-by-step instructions on how to treat a girl, because all the other guys I know his age would count fast food at the mall as a fairly solid first date.

I order the risotto and Hutch gets the chicken parmesan. Conversation flows easily between us throughout our meal and I can see some older couples at nearby tables looking at us, starry-eyed, as though they're seeing themselves young again.

"Here." Hutch reaches into his pocket just as I finish my dessert.

I pull up a napkin and wipe away any remaining traces of the chocolate gelato I just devoured, before taking the small black box from him. "What is it?"

"It's for your birthday, open it up."

I pull the top off and underneath I find a small silver 'M' on a delicate chain. I take the necklace out and admire it. "Hutch, this is beautiful."

"That's why it'll look so great on *you*."

He pushes back his blond hair then reaches over the table and clasps the necklace around my neck, before he sits back to look at me and grins. I smile and force down the tears that try to spring into my eyes.

Hours later, as I lay in bed and picture that grin on his face, I get a strange sensation in my chest. A heaviness that sits on me, uncomfortable, almost smothering.

Hutch is one of the best people I've ever met. He's not only kind and sweet and gorgeous, but he also has a puppy dog innocence about him. And it weighs on my heart like an anvil that I will be the one to shatter that innocence to pieces.

33

RUBY

The house is quiet. Too quiet. It's the second day of March, Mory and Cameron are at school and I'm avoiding the sound of my own footsteps echoing inside the empty house by putting my focus into the backyard.

A few short weeks ago, I was hesitant to so much as mow the lawn in fear of Bernice running out to tell me it was too loud, or that she could smell the grass clippings, or that I was *breathing* too heavily. But today I can work undisturbed on my own property and the task at hand is to finally tackle the flower beds that run along the back fence.

I soak in the warmth of the sunshine on my face as I pull on some gardening gloves and start tugging out the weeds that have taken over. The earthy smell of the soil reminds me of digging up worms as a kid, and I smile to myself as I push my hands into the dirt.

Despite the distraction, my thoughts keep getting pulled back to Bernice. Seeing her casket was a jarring experience. In one way, it made me feel sad for her—that her life was cut short in such a violent way. But the darker part of my mind says this is the most peaceful that woman has ever been and, as horrible as it sounds, I have to wonder if she was done a favor by being killed. Her life seemed to revolve around her own outrage at everyone and everything, always looking for someone to blame for her own misery. What kind of a life is that?

I shake my head, trying to clear all thoughts of Bernice Fisher from my mind. She's gone now, and there's nothing I can do about it, so I may as well move on with my life.

And while that might be easy enough for me, it's a little more complicated for Justin, since he's found himself firmly at the center of yet another police investigation. It's no surprise that they've questioned him about the murder. After all, they had about a hundred witnesses telling them she'd given him motive that night at the meeting. And they already think he had something to do with his wife's disappearance.

But after sitting down with him at his (monstrously large) house and hearing the story in his own words, I feel confident that he didn't kill his wife. And as much as he had cause to want her to shut up, he didn't kill Bernice, either. That investigation is now in the police's hands, and time will only tell where that leads them.

But since the police were here asking questions anyway, I took my chance and tried to garner their interest in the photos of the girls when they came to my door. As I'd anticipated, the officers couldn't have been less interested in some old photos I found around the house. But I know in my heart there's something more there. Something happened to those girls. And I just wish that somebody—anybody—would take it seriously.

Justin, my neighbors, Benton, and now even the cops have all shrugged it off as being nothing. They can't seem to see past the wide smiles and seemingly relaxed poses in those photos to what lies underneath. But I can see it. I can see the fear lurking below the surface.

I yank at the weeds that have knotted their way through the flower beds, having long since strangled the life from the flowers that were once here, much like the life was strangled out of Bernice. Why can I not shake that woman from my mind?

The one good thing going on right now—if I ignore the creepy photos, the murdered neighbor and the fact that everyone in town thinks my boyfriend is a killer—is that Mory finally seems to be more settled here. I have no doubt that the moment she hits eighteen she'll be out of Lonerock like a rocket (likely to live with her father, Caitlyn, and the new baby) but she seems to have fewer bad things to say about this town since she and Hutch have moved up the friendship ladder to dating status. The weird thing is, I don't think she's even lying to me about their PG-rated relationship. Don't get me wrong, it makes me very happy to see a couple their age taking things slowly and getting to know each other well before taking any big steps—but I also remember being their ages. It would have taken a bulldozer to get in the way of Aaron and I getting physical back then.

"Ruby! Hi," comes a man's voice from behind me.

I turn to see Quinten Parker at my side gate.

"Hi, Quinten." I laugh. "Funny, I was just thinking about your son."

He raises an eyebrow and I realize that sounded bad. "I mean, how nice it is to see his and Mory's relationship blossoming."

Quinten nods. "She's all Hutch talks about."

I pull off my gardening gloves and walk over to the gate. "I'll have to send you and Felicity the pictures I took of them before their date for Mory's birthday last week. They make such a sweet couple."

It hits me now that I'm not sure why Quinten is standing at my back gate. "Is there anything I can help you with?"

Quinten grins. "Yes, actually. Speaking of birthdays, Felicity's fortieth is next week and I'm organizing a surprise party for her. I didn't have your number, so I thought I'd come over and invite you in person."

"A surprise party? How are you going to pull that off?" I ask.

Quinten holds a sneaky finger up in the air. "Well, she thinks I'm leaving on the Saturday for a conference in Bayfield. But really, I don't leave until Sunday. So, Hutch and Leo are going to take her out for a birthday dinner Saturday evening, giving me just enough time to use my ninja skills to sneak back into the house to get the party ready."

"She'll be very surprised, I'm sure," I say. "It's really sweet that you're doing all that for her."

Quinten's face clouds over earnestly. "Well, she deserves it. I'm away for work so much of the time, and she runs the whole show. I really wanted this milestone birthday to be special for her."

Lucky Felicity. She's got great kids, a great house, and a hunky husband who cares enough to show her how much she's appreciated. I'm only a little bit jealous. Okay, make that insanely jealous. But I can't hold it against her that her life is all sunshine and roses. Plus, a party is probably exactly what I could do with to unwind. My life these past few weeks has been a whirlwind of anxiety and frustration mixed with endless house renovations.

"So can I count on you to be there Saturday, seven o'clock?" Quinten asks.

"That sounds great, is there anything I can do to help?"

"That's okay, I've got it all under control. Just bring yourself and those two great kids of yours." He winks.

I notice he doesn't mention Justin, whose presence would likely put everyone on edge given the neighborhood have already decided he's Bernice's killer.

"We'll be there," I confirm.

"Great!" He smiles, then taps the side of his nose. "Now don't let the secret out."

"Is that a new dress?" Mory points to the mid-length floral number that cinches right at my waist and flares out around my knees as we make the walk to the Parkers' house.

It's been a week since Quinten dropped by and despite telling myself that I wouldn't make a big effort for this party, I ended up buying a whole new outfit for the night, including heels and earrings. "Yeah, I picked it up at the thrift store the other day."

Does Anthropologie count as a thrift store?

"You look nice." She smiles.

I try not to fall down to the pavement in shock. Mory doesn't throw compliments about recklessly, so either she's buttering me up for something or the effort I put in tonight must have really paid off. I do feel pretty good about myself, though. It took me roughly forty minutes, but my hair is now perfectly styled into the 'effortless bun' from the tutorial I followed online, and I only had to wipe off and redo my smoky eyes twice before I eventually got it right.

Not bitterly, I notice my daughter doesn't need to put in half as much effort in order to look ten times better than I do. At her age, she can run a brush through her hair, throw on any old combination from her wardrobe and come out looking as fresh as a daisy. We were all young once. She's just having her turn now.

"Is Justin coming?" Cameron asks as he teeters along the edge of the curb, balancing like a tightrope walker.

"Not tonight," I say.

"Is that 'cause they think he killed the old lady?" he says, unfiltered.

"Pretty much."

"Did he?"

"No," I say firmly. "And don't listen to anyone who says otherwise."

"Okay." Cameron nods, taking my word as gospel.

This is a trait which seems to end around age ten, so I'm just going to appreciate it for now.

We arrive at the Parkers' and Quinten answers the door with a smile. "Come on in, everyone is hiding out in the kitchen."

He leads us through the immaculate house to the kitchen, where we join a large crowd of other guests. An impressive number, really, since there are no additional cars parked outside. Even Quinten has left his car elsewhere in order to not arouse suspicion from Felicity.

"Okay, people!" Quinten claps his hands to get everyone's attention. "I just got a text from Hutch, they're about to leave the restaurant now. We have about twenty minutes."

There's a cheer of excitement before everyone goes back to mingling amongst themselves. Cameron spots a table of various chips and dips and goes running.

"Ladies, you look absolutely beautiful." Quinten turns to me and Mory. "Thank you so much for coming."

"We wouldn't miss it for the world," I say. "You and Felicity have been so great, having the kids over all the time, doing activities with them, feeding them."

"We love having them here, you raised some great kids, Ruby." Quinten turns to a blushing Mory. "Speaking of activities, Mory, you should see the robotics kit me and Hutch just ordered online."

While Quinten pulls his phone out to show Mory something I'm sure would mean absolutely nothing to me, I excuse myself and head for the bar that's set up on the marble island. Scanning the bottles lined up on top, I spot the bourbon. I grab the bottle and pour a generous amount into a glass, before adding sweet vermouth and a little bitter.

"A Manhattan?" comes a smooth voice.

I turn to see Benton Shepherd standing beside me, glass of white wine in his hand.

"Yeah," I confirm. "Good eye."

"I wasn't always a realtor." He leans closer. "I worked the bar at a hotel to make ends meet during my time studying."

I nod, politely. If I were being honest, I'd say I was more surprised about the fact he's here right now than about him knowing a reasonably common cocktail. I didn't even know he was friends with the Parkers, but apparently they know him well enough for Quinten to invite him here for his wife's birthday party.

I'm still a little wary of this man. He's good-looking, smooth-talking, drives a flashy car and was the only person to have access to my home in the years before I moved in. I have a very hard time believing he isn't responsible for the photos I found.

I can just imagine him being the type of guy that draws young women in with his gleaming smile and flirtatious manner, then... I don't know, forces them to let him take their photos? Kills them? I haven't quite figured out that part yet, but what I do know is that this guy gives me the creeps in a major way.

"So how are the renovations coming along?" Benton's eyes avoid mine as he begins pouring himself another glass of wine. "You know, I've always really liked that house. It just has a charm about it."

I'm not sure what the opposite of charm is exactly, but whatever it is would be a better description of my home. "It's going... slowly."

Benton glances my way. "Oh?"

"I'm doing it mostly by myself," I explain. "So, it'll probably be next year by the time I'm done."

Benton leans on the counter and lowers his voice. "Any word on what happened with Bernice Fisher?"

I drain my drink a little faster than I'd intended to and start making another, wanting to take the edge off the anxiety Benton evokes in me. "I haven't heard anything, no."

Benton shakes his head, solemnly. "It's just so crazy, you know? The last time we all saw her, she was swearing blind that Justin Thomas was the devil incarnate, and then she suddenly shows up dead."

I slam the bottle of vermouth down a little too hard, and liquid jumps out, landing on the shoulder of my dress. Benton grabs a napkin and begins patting the area for me, but I snatch it from him and do it myself.

I've heard the murmurs, the whispers, and I've read the vibe around town, but Benton has basically just come right out and accused Justin of killing Bernice straight to my face. I don't know how Justin manages to keep his composure through all this bull crap but even with only one strong drink in me, my barrier is already down. I throw the napkin to the counter and cross my arms.

"How dare you imply that Justin had something to do with Bernice's death." My voice comes out low between my teeth. "Justin is a—"

I'm interrupted by Quinten's loud clapping again. "Everyone! We have about a minute left until Felicity gets here. Time to quiet down. And phones on silent, please."

I turn back to Benton, whose eyes are still fixed on me. He looks like he wants to say something, but whatever it is, I don't want to hear it. I turn on my heel and walk over to where Mory stands with Cameron.

Quinten switches off the lights and we're plunged into darkness. With nobody able to see me, I take two huge glugs of my drink, draining my glass again. I'm not usually much of a drinker, but I need something to calm me down right now. I shouldn't have exploded at Benton like that, but he really hit a nerve. Thankfully, I don't think anybody else noticed.

We all wait quietly until we hear a car pull up outside the house and doors slam. There are some muffled giggles beside me and people shushing as we all stand motionless in the dark. The door that leads to the foyer is closed and from behind it we all hear the front door opening and then closing.

There must be at least thirty people inside this room, yet not a peep of noise is being made. But I can feel the anticipation of the whole room rising, and along with it, the temperature. I'm pretty sure someone is breathing on my neck. It's way too clammy in here.

There's a noise in the hall outside. Voices. Felicity and Hutch talking. It seems to go on forever. Shouldn't Hutch be encouraging her to open the kitchen door? Imagine if she were to decide to go straight to bed—how long would we all stay standing here until somebody had to go break it to her that there's a party waiting?

Finally, after what feels like an eternity in the blazing inferno that is the Parkers' kitchen, the door slowly opens and a hand reaches for the switch.

In the following moments, three things happen: the crowd collectively inhales, a roar of "SURPRISE!" rings out around the room, and the lights come on, bringing into focus a frazzled looking Felicity, who stands there stunned, with red-rimmed eyes and mascara stains running down both cheeks.

35

RUBY

It's alarming how fast Felicity can go from looking distraught to picture-perfect.

In less than five seconds after the light comes on, she's wiped her cheeks, scooped back her hair and flipped her frown around into a bright smile.

"Oh my God!" she gasps, laughing. "What on earth?"

Quinten grabs her shoulders and pulls her in for a hug. "Happy birthday, darling!"

Everyone joins in wishing her a happy birthday, and as her eyes travel over the room, Felicity looks genuinely shocked to see so many people standing in her kitchen.

"Thank you all so much, this is just... wow." She laughs again. "I had no idea!"

Quinten begins guiding her through the room, stopping to say hello to people as she goes. I spot Hutch standing at the doorway his mother just walked through, a concerned look shadowing his face. Whatever was going on when they arrived home just now is obviously still playing on his mind. I imagine his conscience was torn when he allowed his mother to walk through that door in tears, without warning her of the awaiting crowd. I wonder what upset her? Maybe the fact that she's turning forty? I suppose it *is* quite a big deal. Approaching middle age, your children getting older, deep lines showing up on your face and the realization that you're at roughly the halfway point in life. I'm starting to perspire a little just thinking about it myself. My own fortieth is only two years away.

"Are you okay? You look as though you've seen a ghost." A voice floats into my ear.

I look up from my daze as a drink is placed in my hand.

"A Manhattan," Benton says.

Not this guy again. If this is his way of apologizing for earlier, then it's not nearly good enough. But I *could* do with another drink about now.

"Thanks." I accept it and immediately inhale a sizable gulp. Annoyingly, it's better than the ones I made myself.

"Ruby, I'm sorry if I offended you earlier. I wasn't suggesting Justin killed Bernice, if that's what you thought."

"It sure sounded like that." I take another sip of my drink. "And don't try to tell me you don't think he did it. Everyone here does."

My veins feel like they're buzzing from the alcohol in my system, and I can tell I'm a little drunk because Benton's flashy white smile that usually has me internally rolling my eyes now has me drawn to his words.

"I very much believe that a man is innocent until proven guilty," Benton says. "And as far as I'm aware, they've found nothing linking him to either Bernice's death or his wife's disappearance years ago."

I smile gratefully at this. Finally, I've found somebody in this town who isn't ready to send Justin straight to the gallows.

I look around the party as I sip my drink and see Felicity is now talking animatedly and laughing with a group of her friends, as though she didn't just show up fifteen minutes ago in tears. Mory and Hutch, the magnets they are, have found each other and are chatting away in the corner. Cameron and Leo are over at the snack table, giggling as they mix together a cocktail of fruit juice, crushed potato chips and various other things they've found. I don't really know anyone else here, so I guess I'm stuck talking with Benton.

I drain my glass. "That was *good*. Show me how you did it."

His eyes sparkle and he leads me over to the drinks bar and begins to mix another.

"So, any news on those photos?" he asks.

"What?" My mind goes blank and I blink at Benton in confusion.

"The photos you showed at the meeting. The ones you found at your house?" he clarifies. "You seemed pretty riled up about them."

I maneuver myself onto one of the awkwardly high stools at the island. "Oh. Yeah. The photos."

I watch Benton focus as he works the bottles expertly. He looks as though he might start doing cocktail tricks.

I try to catch his eye. "Do you know who those girls are?"

He passes me the finished drink and leans against cold marble, close to me. "You already asked me that before."

"I know. But I'm asking you again." I take a sip of my fresh drink and enjoy the burn as it runs through my chest. I'm starting to feel a little wild. Maybe I should switch to water. But Benton makes a damn good Manhattan and I can't let the rest of this go to waste.

"Like I told you before, I don't know those girls. But I do think it's weird, those photos all being hidden around your house."

"To say the leasht." I accidentally add an 'h' to the last word. "And it's also kind of weird that you were the only one with a key all those years..."

"You think I left them there?" He raises an eyebrow.

"Yesh." I add another involuntary 'h.'

"Well, I didn't," he says, emphatically. "And what exactly is it you think happened to those girls?"

"I think they're dead." I shock myself, having never voiced this thought out loud. "I think whoever took the photos murdered those girls, and these are his trophies."

"Did you tell the cops that?" Benton asks.

"Pretty much. They aren't interested. Said they're just old photos. All houses have them."

"But you think otherwise," Benton muses. "Why is that?"

"Well for one, they're just weird." I start counting on my fingers. "The old-style dresses, the same grins, the same poses, the same place? And then there's the whole thing of where I found them."

When I've lost count of how many fingers I'm supposed to be holding up I grab my glass again only to see that I've already emptied it.

"And what's with the texts?" I carry on, powerless to control myself. "You texted allll the other people in the neighborhood about that meeting, except me. You didn't want me there!"

Benton is no longer smiling. He's frowning and looks concerned. "What are you talking about? I sent it out to everyone."

"Not me!" I point to my chest.

Maybe I should have that drink of water. My voice is coming out louder than I'm meaning it to.

"No." He shakes his head. "That can't be right."

I grab my phone and pull up the neighborhood text thread, then scroll up, holding it his way. "See?"

He puts a finger to my screen and moves it downwards. After a moment he finds what he's looking for. "There it is."

I look closer and see his finger on a text that sits between two messages I remember ignoring from somebody on the street advertising her daughter's dog walking services. Dammit. He did text me the invite.

"Oh yeah," I say, suddenly feeling stupid. "Sorry."

"That's okay," he says. "It was an honest mistake."

Quinten comes up behind Benton and slaps a hand on his shoulder, before insisting he come talk to his friend, Barry, who is apparently thinking of selling his house.

Alone now, it occurs to me that I've spent the evening so far speaking only with Benton. I should probably start trying to mingle. The problem is, when I try to slide off the stool I've been sitting on, my heel catches on the bottom of it, and I come tumbling to the floor.

A few people turn to stare and Felicity rushes over from where she's been putting out more snacks to help me up. "Ruby! Are you okay?"

I brush my dress down as I stand, laughing to hide my embarrassment. "I'm fine, really. I'm just naturally clumsy."

The look on Felicity's face says she doesn't believe that for a second. She knows I'm skunk as a drunk.

"Happy birthday, by the way." I change the subject. "Forty! Wow."

Felicity smiles politely. "Thanks. I can't believe Quinten managed to pull this party off without me finding out about it."

"You're so lucky to have him," I begin to babble. "That man loves you. And your boys, too. They're good boys. And cute! They look just like their dad! And this house? You've got everything anyone could ever want."

Her brow furrows. She looks like she's about to say something but for some reason my mouth will not shut up. "But you were crying when you arrived! Why were you crying?"

Felicity smiles. "Oh, you know how emotional birthdays can be."

"That's what I thought." I nod, knowingly. "I thought, I'll bet she's just freaked out about getting old. Not that you're old. I don't mean that."

"That's okay." Felicity laughs. "I know what you meant."

Good. So long as someone does. Because at this point, I don't even know what words are going to leave my mouth before they make their exit.

"And really, my life is far from perfect," she says.

I immediately reject this, sweeping my arm around the room. "No way. Look at all of this!"

Nobody has ever thrown me a surprise party, and if they did, there definitely wouldn't be as many people there as there are here.

"My life is a struggle, just like everyone else's," she insists. "My big house comes with big bills, we're still paying off debt from the huge renovation we did on this place years ago, we both had to trade in our nice cars for older models, every bit of money we earn goes into the kids' school fees, my husband is rarely even home and when he is, we're fighting. I'll never live up to the kind of woman his mother was, and since she died, nothing has been the same. When we had Leo eight years ago, I thought things would get better but, no. Turns out another baby can't fix it all!"

I stand with my mouth half open, shocked by Felicity's outburst.

She seems a little shocked, too. "I'm sorry. I don't know why I said all that."

For the first time tonight, I've got nothing to say. I almost want to thank her. She seems a whole lot more human now, and a lot less *Stepford Wives*. I say nothing. Instead, I pull her against me and hug her tightly.

36

———

MORY

My mom is drunk. I've been watching her drink cocktail after cocktail, and she's been getting increasingly louder and more obnoxious with each one.

At first, she was talking to that cute realtor, Benton, and I was pretty sure they were arguing. Then the next time I saw them it looked like they were getting along. At one point, I even saw her on the floor. Mrs. Parker was helping pick her up. I don't know what happened exactly but everyone was staring and now I'm completely mortified.

All the other adults here are drinking too, but nobody else is making an ass out of themselves like my mom is. Although Hutch said his dad doesn't drink, and he's planning on following in his footsteps. Which I think is really cool.

I've been staring at him all night. He looks so good. His blond hair keeps falling over his eyes and I just want to swipe it away for him. Twice tonight, he's pulled me aside where nobody could see us and kissed me passionately before we returned to the crowd and joined back in with the party, like nothing had happened.

Truthfully, I was a little worried about Hutch when he first

188

got here because his mom was visibly upset when she opened the door, and when I went to go talk to him, he seemed distracted. But he's okay now and as we sit together on the back patio, I'm a little surprised when he slides his hand into mine underneath the table. His hand is warm and comforting and I keep hold of it to show him I care.

"You think I should tell her we need to go home now?" I ask him.

"Your mom? I don't know. I think it's kind of funny." He laughs.

I nudge his arm with my elbow. "You wouldn't think it was so funny if it was *your* mom going around drunk, embarrassing you!"

"Actually, I think that would be hilarious. I've only ever seen her drunk once before, at my aunt's wedding, and all she did was giggle the whole night."

We both laugh.

I watch as Mom walks outside, this time with a bottle of beer in her hand. She spots me and Hutch and beelines straight for us.

"*The lovebirds!*" she sings.

Oh God.

"You two are officially the world's cutest couple!" she coos, turning to Hutch. "Did you know that Mory's father and I were also high school sweethearts?"

Hutch doesn't get a chance to answer.

"We were just like you two. Young and in love, thinking the world spun only for us." She's laughing now. "Hopefully you two don't end up like we did!"

"Mom, I think we should be leaving." I start to get up.

"No!" She pushes my shoulders back down gently. "No. No. No. You sit here with your handsome beau. I won't keep embarrassing you, I swear!"

She whispers the last part loudly behind her hand before getting up and wobbling over to a blonde woman who I know to be one of Felicity's friends.

"Kendra!" I hear my mother squeal, before the woman seems to correct her.

My mom snorts loudly. "Well, Harriet, maybe one of you should get a nose ring or something, so people can finally tell you apart!"

I turn and bury my face into Hutch's shoulder. "Kill me. Just kill me now, please."

Hutch is convulsing with laugher and I'm pretty sure my face is beet red. I've never seen my mom have more than one drink before and she must have had ten by now. I take my face from Hutch's shoulder and try to ignore the train wreck happening nearby.

"So, what upset your mom earlier?" I ask.

A crease forms between his brows. "I don't know. She seemed weird when we got to the restaurant and then when we were on the way home, she just burst into tears. I asked her what was wrong, but she wouldn't tell me. Then when we got inside, she wanted to go straight upstairs to bed, but I knew I had to get her into the kitchen."

"What did you do?"

"I didn't know what to do! I knew she wouldn't want to enter her own party in tears, but I didn't have a choice, I knew everyone was waiting. So, I told her I heard a noise in there, and she opened up the door."

I look over to where Felicity is standing with some friends. "She seems fine now."

"Yeah. I guess." Hutch doesn't seem so convinced.

We sit and talk for some time before I spot my mom turning the volume up on a speaker playing music nearby and begin to dance, her beer bottle held high in the air.

"Okay. I'm done." I get up and look around for Cameron. I need to get my mom back home before she ends up doing the can-can on top of a table.

I rush over to her and grab her arm. "Mom, let's go."

"Mory! Dance with me!" Her hips are swaying to a completely different beat than the music and nobody else seems interested in joining her.

"No, Mom, it's late. We need to get Cameron home."

I look around, but I can't see my brother. He's probably inside playing with Leo.

I leave my mom shaking it enthusiastically to 'Crazy in Love' by Beyoncé, and go inside. The first person I see is Benton, by the snack table. "Hey, have you seen my brother?"

"Not any time recently," he says. "But I saw him earlier, running around with Felicity's son."

"Great." I sigh. "That little brat could be anywhere by now."

I'm about to keep searching when Benton puts a hand on my arm. "Hey, is your mom okay?"

I look out the window to see she's stopped dancing and is now leaning back against a wall, looking unstable on her feet.

"No," I reply. "She's completely wasted. I need to find my brother and get them both back home."

This is stupid. I'm seventeen now. Isn't it supposed to be *me* who gets dragged home, misbehaving? Why am I the adult here?

Benton puts down the food he's holding and wipes his hands on a napkin. "Listen, you go find your brother, and I'll walk your mom home."

I narrow my eyes. "Uh... I'm not sure that's—"

"It's fine, really. I don't mind," he insists, smiling. "I'll get her home safely."

Something in the back of my mind is telling me not to let the attractive, smooth-talking man take my blind-drunk mother home, but it's getting late and I really need to find Cameron.

"Um, okay. Thank you."

"No problem." He gives me a wink before heading outside.

I watch him through the window as he walks over to my mom and they talk for a moment before she nods her head affirmatively and he begins to walk her inside.

"You'll bring Cam home?" my mom drawls on the way past.

I promise her I will and watch as she leaves, Benton guiding her gently by the arm.

I ask around some more, but nobody seems to have seen Cameron or Leo. I check the living room, the bedrooms upstairs, the craft room, but I can't find them anywhere. Finally, when I go out to the front of the house I spot them down the street a little, kicking a ball around in the dark. I shout at Cameron to stay where he is while I go back inside to say goodbye.

"You found him?" Hutch asks when I arrive back.

"Yeah. I've got to get him home now. Can you tell your mom and dad that I said thank you for having us and that I'm sorry about my mom?"

Hutch laughs and hugs me goodbye. "Sure."

I walk back through the house, praying Cameron hasn't run off again. I'm glad I got to spend some time talking with Hutch tonight, but I'll bet his dad regrets ever inviting our family to his wife's party.

I'm just out the front door when he rushes out behind me and closes it shut.

"Mory, wait!" He pulls me over to the shadows of the side of the house, pinning me against the wall with his body. "I meant to say something to you tonight."

He kisses me gently on the lips, and my entire body tingles.

"What?" I wrap my arms around his waist and look up into his eyes.

"I was thinking we could go away for the day tomorrow, somewhere special. Just you and me."

"Tomorrow?" I say, confused.

"Yeah. To my parents' vacation home."

Of course this family have a vacation home. They're loaded.

I suddenly realize what he means by this. So far, the most we've done together is kiss. He's never pressured me into anything more. I mean, just a couple of weeks ago it would have technically been illegal. So it makes sense that he was waiting until I turned seventeen to take it further.

"Just come with me for the afternoon. I can drive us out there," he says.

A whole afternoon in a vacation home together. With a bed. Alone. I don't have to think about it for long.

"I'd love to!"

37

———

RUBY

I open up my eyes a sliver, then wince and shut them again tightly. The light sends a pain through my head that makes my skull feel like it's been split open with an axe.

My lips are dry and my throat is stinging with thirst. I badly need a drink of water.

I'm acutely aware that I'm not in my own bed. Something rough and scratchy is underneath me. A sudden image flashes in my mind that makes my blood run cold. The last thing I remember was leaving Felicity's party with Benton. He had my arm, carrying half my sorry weight, and was telling me to come with him. Where was he taking me?

Oh God. Where the hell am I? Where has Benton taken me?

My heart is pounding as I force my eyes open and blink back against the blinding morning light to see... the familiar shapes of my own living room. I sit myself up on the couch. Somebody has left a blanket over me. And there's a glass of water on the coffee table with a note sitting next to it. I down the water greedily before picking up the note and reading it.

Would have left you some aspirin, but I couldn't find any. Don't forget to hydrate! ~ Benton.

Memories of last night come flooding over me and I groan in shame. What was I thinking, drinking that much? I mean, I wasn't thinking, obviously, but who goes to a party with their two children and gets so blind drunk that they can't even remember arriving back home?

How did my kids get home? *Did* they get home?

Oh God. I'm the worst mother in the world. Just wait until their father hears about this, he'll probably gun for full custody to get them as far away from their irresponsible mother as possible.

I stand up and my stomach lurches, but I ignore it, focused solely on finding my children.

"Mory! Cameron!" I shout, and then squeeze my eyes shut in pain from the sound of my own voice.

"In here!" Mory calls from the kitchen.

I make my way through to find the two of them at the table eating cereal.

"Oh, thank God." I walk over and kiss them both on the tops of their heads. "I'm so sorry, guys."

"For what?" Cameron asks, clueless as usual.

"Yeah, Mom. For what?" Mory smirks.

I give my daughter a sour look then begin to rummage around in a drawer until I find a pack of aspirin and wash two down with another full glass of water.

"Why are you still in your dress from last night?" asks Cameron.

"I... um... I just went straight to sleep on the couch when I got home from the party."

He scoops another spoonful of cereal into his mouth. "When is Xavier getting here?"

I stare at my son blankly, not comprehending a word of what he just asked, until I remember Justin and I had arranged to take the two boys to the zoo today. But that was before I went to my neighbor's surprise birthday party and drank myself into a coma.

I look at the clock above the sink at the exact same moment as there's a knock at the door. *Now*, I guess would be the answer to Cameron's last question.

Before I can stop him, he rushes off to answer the door and I have about five seconds to pull my hair down from its lopsided bun and wipe the dried mascara from underneath my eyes.

Mory begins to quietly laugh at me.

"What's so funny?" I narrow my eyes at her.

"This," she says, gesturing to me as a whole. "Just... all of it."

I roll my eyes. "Oh, yeah. Laugh it up."

I brush my dress down with my hands and can only hope I don't look nearly as awful as I feel as I see Justin approaching from the hall. Mory slinks out of the room, leaving us alone.

Justin walks over and looks me up and down. There's no hiding the amusement on his face.

"Good morning." He kisses me.

"Morning," I croak.

"I'm going to take a wild stab in the dark and guess that you may have overindulged a little at the party last night."

"What? Why do you say that?" I stand a little taller, trying to conjure up some dignity.

"Don't you remember calling me at two in the morning?"

What?

"No... I didn't. Did I?" I cross my arms.

"Oh, you betcha." He nods. "I was asleep, so you only got my voicemail. But apparently you think I'm a really great guy. And anyone who thinks differently is a... well, I won't say it out loud, but you used some very colorful language to describe those who think any less of me."

I groan and slump down onto a chair.

"Oh yeah, I've also got a *smokin'* bod," he adds, his lips curling into a crooked smile.

"I didn't say that." I lower my head to hide my radioactive cheeks.

"Baby, I saved that message so fast I nearly tripped over myself doing it. You're welcome to listen to it any time."

I groan louder this time. "I'm sorry."

"Don't be. You didn't say anything that isn't a hundred percent true." He grins.

Cameron and Xavier come running in, shouting in unison. "Can we go now?"

Their voices drive through my brain like a stake and I grab my pounding head.

"Just a minute, boys, I'll be right out. You two go wait in the car." Justin shoos them out with his hands.

I open my mouth to protest, since I'm not nearly ready to go yet, but he holds up a finger to quiet me. "You stay here. Have a shower, get some rest, drink some coffee. I'll take the boys out and I'll drop Cameron home later on today."

"Oh, no, Justin. You don't need to do that. I really just need to change my clothes quickly and I'll—"

"Ruby, you're in no shape for a day at the zoo. We'll be fine by ourselves, I promise. You just enjoy an afternoon to yourself." Justin squeezes my shoulders.

I feel awful about pulling out of our plans today, and I know I should put up more of a fight, but he's right. I need to ride out this hangover at home.

"Okay. I'll stay here," I concede.

"Good." Justin grabs Cameron's full water bottle from the countertop and turns to look at me before he reaches the door.

"What?" I ask.

His face is set in a stony stare. "I just want to be clear. You do understand I'm not kidnapping your son, right?"

I blink back, confused, before I see his mouth twitch upwards and I realize he's mocking me about what happened last Halloween.

"I know, I know," I say, thinking of Mory also laughing at me this morning. "I'm just one big walking joke."

Justin's face softens and he comes to the back of my chair and leans down to kiss my cheek. "No, you're not. You're perfectly imperfect. And to me, that's as perfect as it gets."

38

RUBY

I peel off my dress and try not to retch at the smell of liquor that still clings like a haunting perfume to the creased fabric. The acrid stench of dried-on whiskey immediately summons up visions of last night. Did I really attempt to start a conga line at one point?

Lord, what must the neighbors think of me? For all they know, getting completely hammered beyond all control like that is a common occurrence for Ruby Blake. In truth, I haven't drunk that much in well over a decade. Since before Cameron was even born.

Poor Mory must have been mortified, having her mother show her up like that in front of Hutch. Luckily, he doesn't seem to be holding it against her, since she left to go meet up with him not long after Justin took the boys.

I throw the tainted dress to the floor and when I step into the shower, every water drop that hits my skin feels like needles on a bruise. I tolerate the aggravating sensation for as long as I can, but rather than feeling like a woman refreshed as I step out, I feel more like a drowned rat. Bloodshot, red-rimmed eyes stare back at me as I brush my teeth in front of the small mirror above the sink. In an echo that rebounds all the way back from my college days, I vow to never drink that much again. Some people can handle their liquor. Me, not so much.

I need to do better. I'm a suburban mother of two now. I should really try acting more like Felicity and her cronies. Maybe I should bleach my hair blonde, start going for morning walks in yoga clothes, and take pictures of myself holding a coffee-to-go cup.

Downstairs, I forego eating any breakfast out of concern it could end up making an encore, and as I clear away the kids' cereal bowls from the table, I decide that rather than letting this hangover get the better of me, I'm going to fight back and use this time to clean up the pigsty that is our house.

Twenty minutes later, more flashbacks of Felicity's party are slowly coming to me. The lights flicking on to a rapturous cheer aimed at a woman who was, without a doubt, caught completely off guard. Felicity had been crying. I remember quietly asking her in my inebriated state what the matter was, and her confessing to me that her life isn't exactly as peachy as it always seems. She let her guard down with me, and I saw a vulnerability that I think I really needed to see. We never know what's going on in others' lives and it's easy to forget that everyone is fighting their own silent battles, no matter how perfect it all looks from the outside. But I remember the smile fixed on Felicity's face the rest of the evening. That smile never quite made it to her eyes.

And Benton. Oh God. I don't know if I'll ever be able to look him in the eye again. He'd sat there patiently all night as I'd downed half a dozen Manhattans in front of him while shooting a bunch of accusations his way. Then he'd dragged my sorry behind back home and probably had to make sure I was lying on my side so I wouldn't choke on my own vomit in my near-comatose state.

I guess he's a pretty decent guy after all. Even if he is a little shady as a realtor.

I'm just glad Justin wasn't there to see me like that. But I still can't help but cringe internally when I think about the voicemail I apparently left him. I *still* don't remember that.

I pick up clothes and toys from the floor and dust off surfaces with a cloth. How do other people keep their houses so tidy? I can do all this now, but once the kids get home it'll just go back to the way it was in a matter of minutes. It's a never-ending battle.

I keep finding my thoughts worming back to Felicity. I need to apologize to her. I'll bet she wishes Quinten never invited me to her party. And since Quinten left this morning on a work trip and Hutch is out with Mory, she's been left alone to clean up the mess from last night. That's not right.

What I should be doing is cleaning her house instead of my own. Yes. That's the right thing to do. And a good way to apologize for last night. I put down the armful of shoes I've been collecting from the floor and make my way to my bedroom to grab a sweater, nearly tripping on a row of Hot Wheels cars on the stairs as I go.

In my bedroom I rifle through my closet wondering which color sweater best says, 'I'm sorry I nearly ruined your fortieth birthday party' and after much deliberation end up settling on light blue. Blue has a great calming effect on people, right? I think I heard that somewhere.

Who am I kidding. Felicity probably won't allow me back into her house, even if I promise to clean it top to bottom. And I really wouldn't blame her, either.

I pull the sweater on and walk back out to the hallway, pulling the bedroom door closed behind me. I'm just about to start down the stairs when I feel it. My consciousness on a lag, now summoning me. Something inside my bedroom was wrong.

There was something inside there that was out of place. But what?

I turn back to the closed bedroom door and stare at the chipped white paint for several seconds. It couldn't be. No. I must be wrong about what I saw. A hallucination from the leftover alcohol in my bloodstream. But I'm suddenly feeling more sober than ever. And I'm pretty sure I know exactly what I just saw inside that room.

I reach my arm out slowly and place my hand on the cold brass of the doorknob. It takes me two steady breaths, in and out, before I build up the courage to twist it. The metal creaks in my hand as I push the door open and step inside my bedroom, my heart pounding.

My eyes move straight to the neatly made bed, which I put fresh linen on yesterday morning but never ended up sleeping on. The ruffled dusty-rose pink pillows are right where I left them, the brushed-cotton throw at the foot of the bed still untouched. But there's something laying on the bed that I know I didn't leave there. Something that my tired eyes must have barely skimmed over when I first came in here, but now sticks out like a rattlesnake in a picnic basket.

I walk slowly towards my bed and look down at the photo. A photo I've never seen before. A photo from an instant camera.

Eyes stare up at me from my sheets. But these aren't the eyes of Jessie or Sandra or Erica. These eyes belong to someone else. And somebody has left this photo on my bed for me to find.

I spin around to face the empty room but, of course, there's nobody there.

Did someone put this here when I was out at the party last night? Did they break into our home? Who would do that?

I look down at the photo again and a creeping dread washes over me as I look into the eyes of this woman—fearful eyes, entirely at odds with the smile residing below them—and realize with a stab in my gut that unlike the other three photos I've found, I already know these eyes. I've seen them before, staring out at me from news articles. I've seen them glimmering from a photo hanging proudly on Justin's kitchen wall.

And when I finally manage to rip my gaze from hers and look down to the white strip at the bottom of the photo, the bold letters in black ink send an icy drip down my spine. Four letters that change everything.

Elle.

Elle wipes the tears from her cheeks as the rain pounds on the windshield in front of her, thankful that Xavier isn't in the back seat to hear her cry again.

He may only be a couple of months old, but every time he sees her upset—and that's a lot nowadays—he begins to cry, too. He wails uncontrollably while she tries to soothe him by forcing herself to smile brightly. *See, Mommy's happy! It's okay! Don't cry, sweetie. It's okay!*

But he knows. Somehow, he just knows. And if Mommy isn't happy, then neither is he. Which means he's never happy when he's with her.

But, of course, he's always happy for Justin. Daddy is relaxed. Daddy is fun and his smiles are real. That's because Daddy isn't home all day. Daddy isn't wearing clothes with two-day old milk stains because he hasn't had a second to himself to shower and change because he's always holding a wailing baby who hates to nap.

Elle loves Xavier. She does. She loves him so much that it feels as though her heart is in a vice, about to burst every time she wakes up and sees that sweet little face of his. He is everything she ever wanted. This *life* is everything she ever wanted. The house, the husband, the baby. Everyone is jealous. They coo at little Xavier, they say he's the most beautiful baby they've ever seen. When people come over, they gasp at the size of Elle and Justin's extravagant home. They wink at her and tell her she's lucky to have found a man who is both hot *and* handy around the house.

Elle is the luckiest woman alive.

So why does she feel so empty and hopeless inside?

The doctor said it's postpartum depression. It's totally normal. It's to be expected with all the hormonal changes in her body from pregnancy and breastfeeding. But it doesn't *feel* normal. It feels like there is a bottomless black pit where her hopes and dreams and aspirations used to be.

Two weeks ago, she considered ending it all. She thought that everyone would be better off without her. How could she be a good wife to Justin or a loving mother to Xavier when she couldn't even face getting out of bed in the morning?

When she broke down and shared these thoughts with Justin, he urged her to see a therapist, but she refused. She can't really say why, but the thought of trying to explain the unexplainable sounded worse than just dealing quietly with it herself.

The rain is so thick now that she can barely see two feet in front of the car as the windscreen wipers work overtime to clear the wet glass. Trees whip by, casting ominous shadows on the road ahead.

Xavier is with Elle's mother at her house this evening. And as much as it's nice to be baby-free even for a short time, Elle is really not looking forward to meeting Justin for dinner. But she knows that unless they try to talk it out, their marriage won't last another week. She's pretty sure that Justin asked to meet up at a restaurant so she wouldn't end up shouting at him through tears again. So she would have to control herself in front of others.

The tears have stopped flowing now, likely run dry, but her breath hitches in her chest as she recalls the scene from this morning. The raised voices. The words that neither of them can take back. Elle slamming the door behind her as she stalked off to strap a screaming Xavier into his car seat, headed for her mother's house, Justin begging her not to go. She's not proud of how she acted. And she knows she is just as much to blame as Justin. That's why she agreed to meet him for dinner this evening. To try to fix things and work together. For their marriage. For Xavier.

Over the sound of the pounding raindrops, she hears a loud thud from somewhere and the steering wheel begins to judder in her hand.

"What the..." she mutters as she slows down and uses the indicator—for who's benefit, she doesn't know, since there's nobody else around—before pulling over to the side of the road.

She turns off the engine and opens the door. Water immediately pummels at her face as she steps out to check the source of the problem. She pulls the hood of her jacket up around her face and clutches it tightly as she makes her way slowly around the car until she soon spots the cause of the problem. One of the front tires has blown. Damn.

Elle is no damsel in distress—she does technically know how to replace the wheel of her car—but she doesn't have much practice and to top that off, it's pouring down with rain.

She quickly decides the best thing to do is call Justin and have him come out to help, since he could have it done about ten times quicker than she could. That way they should still have time to make their dinner reservation.

Elle reaches into her bag on the passenger seat and pulls out her phone, but with rain-soaked hands it slips from her grasp and falls down between the seats. She slips her hand down between the crack and wriggles her fingers around trying to locate it, but she can't reach down far enough. Unlike her husband's huge truck with a damn chasm between the seats, her small car has only a hair's width to retrieve lost items. Her phone has now entered the black hole, nestled amongst the likes of granola bar wrappers, loose change and about a half dozen or so pacifiers that have fallen down there previously.

She repositions herself to try to get a glimpse between the seats, but with the storm clouds hanging low in the sky outside it's beginning to get dark and even after switching on the overhead light, she still can't see anything in the space.

A shadow casts over her in the dim light and her whole body freezes as a loud knocking fills the small confines of her car. She whips her head around and sees a man looming outside the window, shadows hiding his face.

Elle is suddenly hyper-aware of the fact she's a relatively small woman alone in her car on a dark, quiet road. Currently without the use of her phone.

He knocks again, this time harder.

Despite her instincts screaming at her to lock the car doors and ignore this man, her manners get the better of her and she rolls down the window and finds herself blinking up into a familiar face.

"Oh, thank God, it's you!" Elle's shoulders sag in relief. "I was worried some psycho murderer was knocking at my window."

He laughs. "Got a flat, huh?"

"Yeah, I was about to call Justin to come out and help, but I've lost my phone to the void." She shoots a thumb towards the gap.

"I wouldn't bother anyway." He shields his face against the pelting drops with the sleeve of his jacket. "Rain's coming down too heavy. I just heard on the radio there's a storm moving in. You'd best leave it until it dies down."

The good news just keeps on coming. Elle sighs and throws her head back against the headrest, at a loss what to do.

He rests his arms on the edge of the car window and leans in closer, his face illuminated by the light inside. "Where are you going? I can give you a lift."

40

MORY

When I left the house this morning, I told Mom that Hutch and I were meeting up in town to get frozen yogurt. A nice innocent date.

There was no way I was going to tell her the truth, because if she found out I was in a car headed for a romantic daybreak at a vacation home right now she would probably lose her mind and lock me up in a tower, never to be seen again. Okay, she's not *that* bad, but I know for sure that she wouldn't approve of this little getaway. I look over at his blond hair rustling in the breeze from the open window—golden curls fluttering around his neck. He has one hand on the wheel and is holding my hand with the other.

"When will we get there?" I ask.

We've been driving for thirty minutes and I just want to get to his parents' vacation home already so we can have as much of the afternoon together there as possible before I have to get back home. When he collected me from our meeting spot by the waterfall he'd gotten out of the car and walked around to open the passenger side door for me. He's always like that. A perfect gentleman.

"Not long now." He shoots a smile my way and my heart does a little flip.

I'd be lying if I said I wasn't nervous. This is going to be a huge jump forward in our relationship and also for me personally. I don't think I'm being too presumptuous that he asked to bring me out to his family's vacation home so we could have a private and comfortable place to make love for the first time. I mean, he's not said it explicitly, but what guy wouldn't want to do it after months of only holding hands and kissing. I know *I'm* ready, so it would be kind of weird if he wasn't.

I'm probably way overthinking this. I've just got to relax and go with the flow. Whatever happens today, it will just be nice to spend some time together, away from everyone else.

We drive by an abandoned old farmhouse, a tangle of weeds growing up its broken walls as though claiming it as their own. Soon the road narrows and trees close over us, a tunnel of green either side. I'm glad to be leaving the small town of Lonerock behind, even if only for the day. There's been a lot of weird stuff going on there recently that's making me feel uneasy. With Bernice Fisher being killed and my mom acting so strangely these past few weeks, obsessing over those photos of complete strangers and then getting so drunk last night that she could barely stand up, I just want a break from the stress of it all.

And while 'frozen yogurt' with Hutch really would have been a nice break too, I can't think of anything better than where I'm headed right now. I'll bet this vacation house is pretty impressive. If their own house is anything to go by, the Parker family must be loaded. They also drive relatively new cars, nothing like Mom's beat-up old car, which has so many dings that it looks like a golf ball. Hutch has told me before that his dad works really hard to maintain their lifestyle.

"Are you okay?"

All my thoughts disappear with a puff of smoke and I look over into his concerned eyes.

"Uh-huh." I nod. "I'm just really excited to get there and see the place."

"Me too." He gives my hand a little squeeze with his before returning it to the steering wheel.

It may be kind of a cliché and I might be building it up to a much bigger deal than it really is, but I just have this feeling that today is going to end up being one of those defining moments in my life. A day I'll never forget.

41

RUBY

Justin stares at the photo in his hands, an unreadable look on his face.

A screech of joy blasts from the backyard where Cameron and Xavier are climbing the tree, a sound starkly at odds with the unbearable weight of tension inside my kitchen as I search Justin's expression.

"It's her, isn't it?" I ask quietly.

Justin's thumb moves with a heartbreaking tenderness over the face in the photo and I see his jaw clench. He doesn't reply. He doesn't need to. Elle's name is right there, written clearly in black ink.

"Where did you find this?" Justin asks, not looking up.

"On my bed." My stomach drops, recalling it.

At this, Justin's eyes flicker in disbelief to mine. "Your bed? What are you talking about?"

"I... I don't know how it got there," I start, feeling the intensity of his eyes boring into mine. "I went up to the room to get a sweater and it was just there. Lying face up on my bed."

Gone are my plans to go help Felicity clean up, she'll have to face the aftermath of her party alone. I need to be here for

Justin right now, because nobody else will be. Everyone already thinks that he killed his wife all those years ago, and once word gets around about what I just found, it's only going to add fuel to the flames. I may be the only person in this town who can see Justin for who he really is. And today, he is just a single father who has clung to the belief for the last eight years that the mother of his son had ended her life on her own terms. A belief now shattered, after seeing this photo.

I don't need to see it again. The image is already pressed so firmly into my memory that if I blink, I still see it. Elle is wearing a green dress that swamps her small frame. Her blonde hair hangs around her face like strings, wet clumps sticking to her cheeks as she bares her teeth in a grin. But there's no happiness there, only fear. Just like the others. And I know now without any doubt that those girls—like Elle—are no longer alive. And I think that whoever left this photo on my bed this morning was the one who killed them.

"It's just like the others. Same camera, same place, same pose," I say softly. "And someone left it there for me to find. I… I think it might be some kind of a warning."

Justin looks a little unsteady on his feet before he pulls out one of the chairs by the table and slumps down onto it. Pain is etched on every part of his face, but somehow he maintains his composure.

I stare out the window at the boys for some time. They're chasing a remote-control monster truck around the backyard. Xavier is laughing the carefree laugh of a boy untroubled. How long before that innocence is ripped from him? I can only hope he never sets eyes on this photo of his mother. I don't think the image would ever leave him.

"Who had access to your house last night?" Justin's low voice cuts through my thoughts.

"Nobody. I mean, I locked the doors before we left for

Felicity's party and there's no sign of a break-in, I already checked. I hadn't even stepped foot inside my bedroom until this morning, because I slept on the couch last night."

Justin narrows his eyes at me in confusion.

"I was... a little drunk when I got home. I actually don't even remember getting home," I admit, my cheeks flushing. "I don't think I would have even made it back if it weren't for Bent—" I stop.

"Benton? Benton Shepherd?" Justin stands up slowly, still holding the photo of Elle. "He came to the house?"

"Well, yes. I mean, he walked me home. He was only being friendly. He didn't stick around or anything. At least... I don't think he did." I suddenly feel queasy again, looking at Justin's face.

I can see the same thoughts are passing through his mind as mine. Benton was here at the house last night while I was passed out on the couch. He even left me a note telling me he'd looked around the place for aspirin. He could have left that photo in my bedroom. It all makes sense. Other than the owners, Benton was the only person who had a key to this house before I bought it. He must have been the one who left the photos hidden around my home. And now he's left this one of Elle to intimidate me. A warning to stop sniffing around. I start to feel dizzy, thinking of what this all means. If there had been any doubt in my mind that the young women in the photographs were being held against their will, seeing this one of Elle has confirmed it. And with Elle having been missing for eight years now—so long that she's been declared legally dead—it's also clear she never escaped. Neither did those other girls.

Benton must have been hiding these photos—these trophies of his—in this house to keep them safe. Did he really expect that they wouldn't be found?

I remember hassling him about the pictures at the party, and not for the first time, either. I phoned him about them, I brought them to his office, I even waved them around at the community meeting.

I'd thought he brought me home last night out of a sense of neighborly duty, a good deed. But now I see he came here to leave me a warning to stop digging. A lump catches in my throat and I swallow it down.

I bought my house from a serial killer.

42

RUBY

I flip on the light switch as I walk into the kitchen and the room floods with a yellow hue. In the glass of the oven door I see my own tired, sallow face reflected back at me as I turn the dial.

Justin is settling Cam and Xavier with a movie while I make a start on dinner. Well, that's if frozen pizza counts as a dinner. I doubt either Justin or I will eat a bite, given the afternoon we've had. But there are still two growing boys to think of who need some kind of sustenance (or what little of which can be derived from pizza).

The cops have come and gone, taking the photos with them and informing me their investigation will likely involve a search of the property, given this is where the photos were hidden. I didn't hold back during their questioning on sharing my suspicions about Benton Shepherd. Although from the looks they gave me, I could tell they were doubtful. He's got this whole town wrapped around his little finger. They think he's the perfect gentleman. The perfect neighbor.

Isn't that what everyone says about serial killers? Or maybe those are just the ones we hear about.

But it doesn't matter how charming or kind or smooth-talking Benton is, the fear in Elle's eyes in that photo was unmistakable. It's clear that even if he used his charm to lure her in—by the time that photo was taken, it had well and truly worn off.

I shudder as I think of the danger I put my kids in, letting Benton into our home last night. He could have done anything while I was passed out on the couch. He could have kidnapped Mory and I would have slept right through it. Thankfully it seems all he did was enter my bedroom and leave a photo for me to find. Benton Shepherd is a twisted man and I don't think I'll sleep a wink again until I know he's locked up.

When the cops left, I told Justin he should go home and get some rest and that Xavier could stay here for the night, but he refused. It's hard to tell how he's taking all this. He's not the kind of guy to wear his emotions on his sleeve. But given that he's spent the past eight years living under the assumption that his wife left this world voluntarily, it must be a major blow to learn that her life didn't end on her own terms at all. She never abandoned him or Xavier. And if she hadn't been killed, maybe she and Justin could have resolved their issues. Maybe she could have gotten the help she needed to get better and enjoy the incredible life that lay ahead of her.

I can't put myself in Justin's position, I have no idea what he must be going through right now. All I know is that I'm going to be here for him and Xavier every step of the way, because the road is only going to get rougher. Until enough proof comes to light that Benton is behind Elle and all those other girls' disappearances, Justin will be the number one suspect around town. Not that he wasn't already.

I'm just glad we managed to keep the boys from finding out why the police were here. They spent the whole afternoon playing in the sandpit outside with a tub of toy animals they picked up at the zoo this morning. And when they asked about the police car, we told them they were just here about Bernice again.

I open up the freezer and debate how many pizzas I should put on. Mory hasn't come home from her fro-yo date with Hutch yet but I suspect she'll be hungry when she does.

I tried calling her after the police left but it just rang out and I've only been getting through to her voicemail since then. Either her battery ran out or she's purposefully ignoring my call, neither would surprise me. I can't call Hutch because I don't have his number. But it's getting close to seven hours since Mory left for their date and I'm finding it hard to imagine they could still be hanging around town, even if they ended up catching a movie or going to the arcade. They've most likely gone back to his house to work on one of their robotics projects.

I pull up Felicity's number in my contacts, then hold the phone between my shoulder and ear as I take the pizzas out of their packages.

"Hello?" A distracted voice answers on the third ring.

"Hey, Felicity," I chime, remembering immediately that I still owe her a huge apology. "I just wanted to call and let you know that I'm really sorry about last night. My behavior."

"Your behavior?" she asks.

I'm suddenly thrown into doubt. Was it not as bad as I remember? Maybe I'm remembering my drunken shenanigans wrong. Maybe nobody noticed I was wasted after all.

"Uh, yeah. I mean, I had a little too much to drink and I was worried that I might have…" I trail off.

"Ruined the party?" Felicity finishes for me. "No. No. You didn't ruin it."

I'm not convinced. There's a faraway tone to her voice that has me concerned.

"Well, anyway. I planned to come over this morning and

help you clean up, but the day kind of got away from me." To say the least.

"Don't worry about it, Ruby. Quinten stayed up last night to get the place cleaned up before he left for Bayfield this morning."

"That was good of him. The party was great by the way. It was so nice of Quinten to surprise you like that. You're a lucky woman."

"Yeah," Felicity says quietly.

"Oh," I say, remembering why I called. "Could you tell Mory that I've got dinner on? I'd tell her myself, but I can't get through to her phone."

"I would," Felicity replies. "But she's not here, sorry."

This surprises me a little. "Oh, I kind of figured she and Hutch would have gotten back from their date by now. It's been hours."

"Date? What date?"

"They met for fro-yo in town this afternoon," I explain. "But that was ages ago, and I think Mory's phone ran out of battery. Maybe you could try calling Hutch to see where they are?"

There's silence for a moment before Felicity's voice comes back over the line, quieter now. "I don't need to phone Hutch, he's right here in the next room. He hasn't left the house all day."

43

────────

MORY

When Quinten said vacation house, I guess I'd been imagining huge glass windows overlooking a pool shimmering in the sunlight.

Well, that's definitely not what this is. Actually, I don't think it could be further from it. Although I think I might see a lake through the trees down the dirt road that leads from where we're parked, but it's hard to tell. Everything here is overgrown.

"That took a lot longer than you said it would," I say, stepping out of the car and evaluating the wooden structure in front of me.

I wouldn't mind, but I know Mom will be expecting me home at any point now. She already tried calling me a little while ago but I let it ring out. Then I turned my phone off and shoved it in the glove compartment for good measure. I figure I'll just tell her my battery ran out and that I ended up meeting a friend in town and went back to her house. I'm seventeen. She doesn't need to worry about me staying out all day.

Quinten stretches out his legs and pushes back his dark blond hair. A single strand falls down before I move it back for him. He smiles and takes my hand in his.

"You ready?" he says, leading me to a wooden door that's so overgrown with ivy it's hard to imagine it'll open.

"Your family actually vacation here?" I ask, trying to keep the judgment hidden from my voice.

"Not anymore," he says quietly. "I mean, my parents used to bring me here as a kid. But since my mother passed away and left it to me, it's not in much shape for a vacation."

You could say that again. This place looks more like a storage shack than a vacation home. But as long as it's clean and dry inside, I'm sure we can still make the most of our time here together.

He unlocks the door and when we step inside the air smells dusty and stale. It's too dark to make anything out, so I stay at the door side until he flips on a switch. One single overhead bulb comes on with a low buzzing noise accompanying an even lower glow from the bulb.

"That probably needs fixing, it's kind of old."

I'm too busy looking around me to reply to this. The fact is, *everything* here looks old. And dirty, too.

"Are you okay?" he asks. "You look disappointed."

I want to say 'duh,' but I don't want to sound like a typical teenager.

"Um... I guess it's just not really what I'd imagined. Is there a bedroom?"

"Yeah." He looks uninterested. "Over there."

He points out a door to the left and then makes his way over to the kitchen area. There's a refrigerator that hums and rattles as he pulls it open and takes out a bottle of cola. I move to the bedroom door and push it open, the rough splinters of the wood pressing into my fingers. The moment the door swings open, the stench of decaying wood and mold descend over me and I put my sleeve to my nose to block the smell. Sure enough, it's a bedroom, but this is not a place anyone could actually sleep in, let alone use for any kind of romantic endeavors. There's dampness in the air and an underlying smell I can't place. And the one bare mattress has a weird-looking stain on it. There's no nice way to put it; the room is disgusting.

I close the door again. There's no way I'm going back in there. This whole shack is old and damp and it's making my skin crawl. I'm completely re-thinking the idea of coming out here. I don't even know why he brought me. I would have been happier meeting up at the falls, like we usually do.

"Here you go." Quinten hands me a glass and I take it from him.

He holds his own out and I reach mine up to clink his, the dark bubbles inside rushing up to the surface, crackling and raining gently down onto my hand.

"To us," he says, and takes a glug.

I smile, relaxing a little, and follow suit. Clearly this isn't brand-name cola because the taste is a little off, but I chug it down before placing the glass on the countertop. He takes my hand and kisses it gently, staring deeply into my eyes.

I can't help it. I melt inside. Suddenly, it doesn't matter where we are or what that weird smell lingering in the background is, because all that's important is that we're together. I can see he feels the same way I do. There's an intensity in his eyes I've never seen before. And that's when he says it. The three words that send fireworks through my veins and make tears spring to my eyes. The words that I've wanted to hear and repeat since the first day I saw him. On every night that we secretly met by the waterfall. On every stolen moment during our robotics builds when Hutch and Mrs. Parker weren't looking.

"I love you, Mory."

I throw my arms around his neck and whisper softly in his ear. "I love you too, Quinten."

44

———

RUBY

"Hutch is on his way over now," I tell Justin as I watch him pull on his coat, getting ready to go search for Mory. "He's not seen or heard from Mory all day either, and wants to help track her down."

Justin straightens the collar of his jacket then puts his hands on my shoulders. "I know you and he are probably jumping to the worst conclusions, but she's likely just out with friends. Do you have any of their numbers?"

"No, I don't," I say, ashamed.

I don't even know any of her friends' names. These are basic things that I should know about my daughter, but she doesn't talk about her friends to me. She only talks about Hutch. Does she even have any friends at school? She says she does, but I've seen no actual proof. She doesn't invite anyone around and I've never heard her talking with anybody but Hutch on the phone. She lied to me about where she was going today—is there somebody she's meeting that she doesn't want me to know about?

"Do you think I should call the cops? I mean, she's been gone for hours now."

Justin rubs at the stubble on his chin. "Ruby, did your mom call the cops every time you lied about where you were going as a teenager?"

He has a point. Once, when I was sixteen years old, I told my parents that I was having a sleepover at Ashley Jenkin's house and even had her call my mom, pretending to be her own mother, to confirm this. My mom bought it hook, line and sinker and Ashley and I spent the whole night at Gordy Abrahams' party, getting drunk on his dad's vodka and making out with boys.

Up until now I've been thanking my lucky stars that Mory is more sensible than I was as a teenager, but the past couple of hours really have me wondering.

Justin kisses me on the forehead and pats his pocket. "I've got my phone, call me if she shows up. I'll start driving around, see if I can spot her."

He gives one last glance at the two boys, who are now taking it in turns to throw popcorn into each other's mouths as a movie blares in the background, then closes the door behind him as he leaves.

I listen to the sound of his engine start up and then grow quieter as he pulls away into the low evening light, and I give silent thanks that I have someone in my life who is looking out for my little family. I don't know what I would do without Justin, he's been the glue that's held everything together over the past few weeks. And he's right, it's too early to be thinking of calling the cops yet. Mory is seventeen and it's been seven hours since she left the house. Soon she'll be an adult, and I may go days without knowing where she is or who she's with. The thought of that makes something jagged stab at my heart.

But the thing that nags at the back of my mind is that I know Mory is a smart girl. If this was just another Ashley Jenkins situation, wouldn't she have come up with a better lie than going out for fro-yo with Hutch and then just choosing not to return home or even text me with a new excuse as to why she's not back yet?

It doesn't make sense.

But if parents started calling the cops every time their teen was a couple of hours late back home, it would be a waste of time and resources. They've already been out here once today about the photos and they'll likely be back tomorrow to continue their search. If Bernice was still with us, she'd have a field day with all this drama.

I wonder now if the cops have visited Benton to question him yet. I made it clear to them that he was the only person who could have left the photos here. I always got the feeling Benton Shepherd was a sleazeball, but now I know he was likely responsible for whatever happened to Elle and those other girls, it chills me to my core that I ever let him into my home. I was so out of it when he dropped me off last night, he could have done anyth— My train of thought is intercepted by a sudden idea that didn't even occur to me until now.

I remember the way Mory was drooling over Benton the day we moved in. She's always had a tendency to gravitate towards older men. That's why I was so happy to see her seemingly pivot and go after Hutch, who at eighteen is an appropriate age for her. But now I'm wondering if Benton managed to sprinkle his charm on my daughter, after all. If he's sick enough to kidnap and torture the women in those photos, he's probably not above going for a girl as young as Mory.

I don't waste any time, pulling my phone out of my pocket and finding his number.

He answers on the third ring. "Benton Shepherd."

"Benton, it's Ruby. Are you with Mory?" I demand.

"What are you talking about? Why would I be with Mory?"

I grit my teeth. "Benton, I swear to God if you are with my daughter I'm going to rip your—"

"Whoa, whoa, whoa!" He cuts me off sternly. "I'm not with your daughter, Ruby. I have no idea what you're talking about."

"I'm supposed to believe that? After you left that photo of Elle on my bed last night?"

I hear a deep sigh on the other end of the line. "Yeah. The police told me about that. I was really sorry to hear about it, that must be rough for Justin. But like I told the police earlier, I had nothing to do with it."

"You were the only other person who was in my house. You brought me home last night, and after you dumped me on the couch, you left that photo on my bed for me to find." I realize my voice is so loud now that the boys can probably hear me in the next room, but I'm furious at this man. And I don't understand why the police just let him go after questioning him. Why didn't they arrest him right then and there?

"Listen, Ruby." Benton's voice is still as smooth as ever, but he's lowered his tone. "I've been as patient as I can be with you. I did you a favor last night by dropping you home. You were completely wasted, and I did nothing wrong. I gave you a blanket and water. I did not go in your bedroom. I have no idea what you're talking about. And I'm sorry if you're having issues at home, but right now, I'm trying to have a nice meal with my girlfriend, and your daughter is definitely not here with us."

I go to open my mouth in retort when I hear it. The background noise. I hadn't noticed before because I was so busy seething, but now that I'm listening, I can hear the familiar sounds of a restaurant in the background behind his voice.

"I..." I don't know what to say next.

Am I wrong? Does Benton really have nothing to do with this?

"Mom?" Cameron appears by my side.

I hold my finger up for him to wait, and he nods when he sees the phone in my hand.

"I have to go," I say, and hang up on Benton before he can say anything else.

I have no idea what to think right now, and I really wish Mory would just walk through the door and put my mind at ease. I put my phone back inside my pocket, then run my hands down my face and groan before I remember Cameron is waiting silently beside me.

"What is it, honey?" I ask.

He has one eyebrow raised. "Um, were you talking about that photo on the bed?"

Crap. I knew I should have kept my voice down. But... I didn't tell Cameron about the photo of Elle. Justin and I made sure the boys were distracted so that Xavier didn't catch word of it. The poor boy has been through enough without seeing a photo like that of his mother.

"Cam, how do you know about the photo?" I ask.

"I found it this morning under the loose tile on the bathroom floor." He shrugs. "I knew you were collecting them so I went to your bedroom to give it to you, but you weren't there, so I left it on your bed."

A groan escapes my chest before I can stop it. I'm an idiot.

"What?" Cameron asks, confused. "Did I do something wrong?"

"No, kid." I sigh. "You didn't do anything wrong. I did."

I think I've lost count of how many things I've accused Benton Shepherd of now. It's seeming less and less likely that he's got anything to do with either the photos left in this house or my daughter running off unannounced.

And Hutch, who I'd assumed she'd spent the day with, hasn't even seen her today.

So, where the hell is Mory?

45

———

MORY

I've always felt a little bad when I'm around Hutch. It's not like I don't enjoy his company, because I do. He has truly become my best friend since we moved to Lonerock. But in the beginning, the main reason I made friends with him was because I knew it was the only way to spend more time with Quinten.

I know it's wrong to have led Hutch on like I have: spending so much time together, letting him take me on a date, holding his hand on occasion. And I'm going to have to think of a way to let him down gently when he eventually makes a real move on me. I don't want to hurt him. But I guess there's no avoiding that, since I'm in love with his father.

One day not so long from now—when Quinten has left Felicity and I'm eighteen and nobody can stop me—he and I will be free to share our love when and where we please.

He's the one. I've always heard people say that, and I guess I didn't know what they meant exactly, but now I get it. From the very first day I walked past Quinten on my way home from school—when he looked back at me, and I looked back at him and our eyes met—I knew there was something between us. An

228

electricity. A meaning. There's just something about him that captured my whole heart and hasn't let me go.

And as cute as Hutch is, he's only eighteen. I know, I know, I'm only seventeen. But girls mature so much faster than guys, and I've always felt like older guys are so much more in control of themselves. More mature. More refined.

Quinten is the definition of all these things. He commands the attention of every room he steps into. Not just because he's ridiculously gorgeous but because he has this air about him, this authority, that makes it difficult not to gravitate towards him. At least that's how I feel about him. Obviously Felicity must have been crazy about him too at one point, to have married him. But from everything that Quinten has told me, that's not how it is anymore. He says it's become stale. That they've only stayed together for the kids, and he's become lonely in their marriage. How sad is that? He's a guy who has everything going for him, he's gorgeous and smart and funny, but he doesn't feel appreciated or loved anymore.

And I know I should probably feel bad about stealing Felicity's husband from her, but will she even care? Like he said, their marriage is dead. Doesn't Quinten deserve to be happy?

I feel his hand on my knee and I scoot myself closer to him on the couch. There's a weird taste in my mouth after the cola; I hope I don't have bad breath when we kiss.

"Is this the necklace Hutch gave you?" Quinten asks, scooping back my hair.

His touch sends tingles all the way down to my toes. I wish he'd just grab me and carry me to the bedroom right now. Okay, maybe not the bedroom, because it smelled like something had died in there. I guess I might end up losing my virginity on this threadbare, scratchy couch. Not exactly how I envisioned it happening, but it's more about *who* it's with and not where it is that makes it special, right?

Although, if Quinten is planning on putting the moves on me, he's going about it slowly. My phone is still turned off in his car, and there doesn't seem to be a clock in here, but based on the fading light outside it's got to be at least dinner time. My mom is probably complaining to Cameron right now about me never answering my phone.

"Yeah, it is." My fingers move to the necklace automatically. "I... I feel kind of bad about Hutch. I don't know if he'll ever forgive me when he finds out about us."

Quinten's eyes narrow just a little. "You don't need to worry about that right now."

I nod, knowing he's right. This moment is about us. Me and Quinten. I want to forget about everything and everyone else in my life. I move forward, bringing my lips towards his. But just before I reach them, he puts a finger to my mouth and I stop.

"Ah, ah, ah," he teases. "Not yet."

I suppress a groan. Why is he putting this off?

I wait for him to elaborate, but instead he gets up from the couch and scurries off towards the bedroom. I make a move to get up but he wiggles a finger and 'ah, ah, ahs' me again, so I sit back down. It's probably for the best, too, because I feel a little lightheaded from standing up too fast. Probably low blood sugar. I get that sometimes, if I skip a meal. Usually, I'd be eating dinner around this time of the evening, and I'm starting to get hungry. Hopefully Mom will leave me some leftovers for when I get home. She'll probably just figure I'm having dinner at Hutch's house tonight. I should probably get my phone from Quinten's car and text her to tell her I'll be home late, otherwise she'll start worrying I've been kidnapped or something.

I can't wait until I'm eighteen and I can live my life without having to report back to her every five minutes. She goes on about the good old days, when kids were so wild that they had to put announcements on the TV at night to ask parents if they knew where their children were—but she's a bucket of contradictions because she literally wants to know what I'm doing at every moment of the day. You can't have it both ways, Mom.

The problem is, it's already getting late and it'd take us over two hours just to get back to Lonerock from here, even if we left now. Quinten better hurry up. What is he doing in that bedroom, anyway?

"Quinten?" I call out. Whoa, my voice sounds weird.

There's no reply.

That's it, I'm going to get my phone. I've got to text my mom before she ends up calling Felicity to see if I'm there and finds out I lied to her about going out with Hutch today. My legs are wobbly as I get up, and I have to use the arm of the couch to steady myself for a second before I move towards the door. Why do I feel so weird?

My fingers have just gripped the cold metal of the door handle when I hear a noise from behind me.

"Where are you going?" Quinten stands by the bedroom door, holding something I can't quite see in his hands.

"I have to get my phone from the car, I've got to text my mom and make up an excuse for why I'll be home late," I say, my voice sounding funny to my ears.

"You don't need to do that," he says. "She won't care."

I laugh, but it comes out a little strangled. "You obviously don't know my mom."

Quinten ignores this and waves me over to him. "Come here."

I obey and walk to him, seeing now that the thing he's holding is fabric. He grabs my waist and kisses me softly on the neck. My legs nearly gave way. I've heard of going weak at the knees but this guy literally makes my limbs collapse.

"You know I love you, Mory," he murmurs in my ear.

"I know." I smile.

He slips the shoulder of my top down and kisses the skin beneath. "Will you do something for me?"

Finally, he wants to take this further. I thought it would never happen.

"Anything," I reply, attempting a sexy voice.

He pulls back a little and passes me the bundle of fabric he's holding. "Great. Put this on for me."

I look down and expect to see some kind of lacy lingerie or a little silk slip, but when I unfurl the green bundle, it unfolds into a long-sleeved dress. It's got brown and yellow flowers printed all over it and looks secondhand.

"What?" I ask. "What is this?"

"It's a dress." He laughs, as though I'm stupid.

I can see that, obviously. I can also see that it's hideous. There's no way I'm putting it on, I don't even know why he'd want me to.

"You're joking, right?" I say.

Quinten looks hurt. "You don't like it?"

Of course I don't like it. It looks more like a pair of ugly curtains than a dress, but I don't want to hurt Quinten's feelings.

"I just thought maybe we could... you know." I place the dress over the end of the couch and try to guide Quinten to come sit back down, but he's not budging.

"I want you to wear the dress, Mory." His eyes are steely and focused on mine.

"Well, I don't want to," I say, crossing my arms defiantly.

His expression stays the same and he remains unmoving. Something about him has changed, he's not acting like he usually does. This is getting annoying. I wanted to come here today so we could be alone together, make love and enjoy one afternoon where we don't have to hide from everyone around us. But instead, he's taken me to a run-down old building that stinks, and he wants me to wear some disgusting old dress that looks as bad as the ones in the photos my mom found of those girls.

My stomach turns. This is all wrong. I look around at the wood-paneled walls.

No. I shake my head to clear away the terrifying thoughts that are now streaming into my mind.

Quinten picks the dress back up and holds it out to me. "Put it on."

"I... I need to get my phone from the car." I back away, my legs barely holding me up. "I really have to call my mom."

Why is my body doing this? Why does my mouth feel sticky every time I talk?

Quinten catches my arm as I stumble, but his grip remains firm once I'm steady. His eyes flash with an intensity I've never seen before. "You're not going anywhere, Mory."

46

RUBY

I open the door to see Hutch looking agitated and Felicity with a soothing hand on his shoulder as they stand in the darkness of my doorstep.

"Has Mory come home yet?" Hutch asks, his voice breaking with concern.

"No, she hasn't."

I usher them both inside, seeing that young Leo is trailing behind them. Cameron wastes no time grabbing him by the arm and dragging him off to play in the living room with him and Xavier.

"Sorry." Felicity grimaces. "I didn't want to intrude on you like this, but with Quinten away on work I couldn't leave Leo alone at home, and I wanted to see if I could be of any help here."

"It's no problem," I say loud enough for her to hear over the three boys' shrieks of joy. "Thanks for coming over."

We move through to the relative quiet of the kitchen and Felicity reaches out and rubs my arm reassuringly. "I'm sure she's fine, Ruby. We all made our parents worry like this as teens at some point."

Hutch's face is twisted in confusion. "She told me she was going to be too busy to meet up today. She said you guys were doing family stuff."

"So, she lied to you, too," I say. "That's not like Mory at all. I mean, she worships the ground you walk on."

"Could've fooled me," Hutch mumbles.

Both mine and Felicity's heads turn at this.

"What do you mean?" Felicity asks her son.

Hutch shifts his weight uncomfortably to the other foot. "I don't know. I mean, we spend a lot of time together, but she always seems distracted. I took her on that one date on her birthday, and I thought that was going to be the start of a real relationship, but... I guess she's not that interested in me."

I glance at Felicity, who looks about as confused as I do.

"You two were holding hands at the party, I remember you sitting together most of the night," Felicity points out.

Hutch laughs gently, but there's no smile on his face. "Yeah. We'll talk for hours on end, she'll hold my hand... but every time I think things are going well, she'll pull away. You guys all keep calling us *lovebirds*." His fingers air quote. "But we've never even kissed."

I can see from the look on Felicity's face that she's as surprised by this as I am. For months, Mory has practically been living over at the Parkers' house and has never corrected me when I've referred to Hutch as her boyfriend. But by the sounds of it, I've gotten it all wrong.

"I guess I just got the wrong impression," I say. "What with how much time you two spend together, doing robotics builds. Not to mention all the nights she sneaks out of the house to meet you."

Hutch cocks his head to the side. "At night? What do you mean?"

I smile. "Don't worry, I've known for a while about your

little night-time rendezvous. She said you guys like to hang out by the falls together."

Hutch shakes his head. "I don't know what you're talking about. I've never met up with Mory at night."

My heart drops and silence washes over the three of us, broken only by the sounds of the kitchen clock ticking its way slowly towards 9pm. It's becoming increasingly clear that I don't actually know my daughter as well as I thought I did. What exactly has she been hiding from me? And from Hutch, for that matter? If her night-time trips aren't to go meet Hutch, then who? My heart begins to race and I feel a little dizzy.

"Ruby, maybe you should sit down," Felicity suggests, pulling out a chair and guiding me into a sitting position.

She gets a glass from the cupboard and pours some water before passing it to me.

I take a sip with trembling hands. "I just wish she'd come home. I want to talk to her. Ask her why she's been lying to me. But what can I even do about it? Ground her? How do I enforce consequences at her age?"

"One step at a time, Ruby. Let's just focus on tracking her down first, before you begin to overreact."

"You think I'm overreacting?" I let out a demented laugh. "You should see how her father will react if he finds out I let her go missing. He'll try to get full custody of both the kids. I'm sure of it."

"Oh, stop it." Felicity shoos off the idea with her hands. "He wouldn't have any grounds to do that."

"How about me being dragged home drunk from your party last night—not even knowing where my kids were?" Tears spring to my eyes. "And now this! Mory up and leaving, and I don't even know any of her friends' names or phone numbers to check if she's with them."

I suddenly feel like the worst mother in the world. Maybe Mory and Cameron *would* be better off living with their father.

Felicity sinks down into a crouch in front of me. "Ruby, look at me."

I sniff and swipe at my wet eyes, lifting my gaze to her determined stare.

"You are doing the very best you can by those kids. It's okay if you make a few mistakes here and there. Lord knows, all of us mothers do."

"She's got that right," Hutch chimes in.

Felicity shoots him an annoyed look before turning back to me. "You're the best mom those kids could ever ask for. Don't you ever think otherwise."

Ugh. Why is this woman so great? It's annoying.

"Thanks, Felicity," I say, feeling a little better. "I just know that if Mory were with her dad, this would never happen. He doesn't even let her fly home from Arizona without—" I stop.

"What?" Felicity asks. "What is it?"

But I don't answer. Instead, I grab my phone and dial Aaron's number.

47

MORY

The rough material of the dress itches at my arms and the collar digs into my neck. I want to rip it off. I want to run out of this old cabin and flag someone down for help, but I can't even get up. I barely have the strength to move. My eyes are trying to close but I won't let them. I refuse to lose what little power I still have left.

"You have such beautiful hair. You know that?" Quinten stands behind the couch, pulling a comb through my hair. "I don't usually have time to do the hair."

I'm not listening. I'm trying to think of a way out of here. But even if I could get to the door, I couldn't run. He put something in my soda earlier, I think. And even if I could run, there's nothing around for miles. We didn't pass any houses for a long time before we arrived.

"You left those photos at my mom's house," I say quietly. "You brought those girls here."

Quinten stops brushing my hair and lowers his head right next to mine above my shoulder. I close my eyes.

"You like my pretty pictures?" he says softly, his breath hot, making the hairs on my neck bristle. "Those are my special girls."

There's something about how he says this that sends a shiver through my core.

"Don't worry," he says, soothingly. "You're special, too."

This does not make me feel any better. I don't know how this is the same man I've come to know. The man who would kiss me the moment Hutch left the room. The man who waited for me by the waterfall all those nights and gave me his jacket to wear when it got cold. The man who wrapped his arms around me in a secret embrace when the lights were out and everyone waited in the darkness ready to surprise his wife last night.

This man looks the same. He has the same floppy blond hair that falls into his eyes as he moves. He has the same clothes, the same face. But the man inside seems to be gone now. I don't know who I'm talking to anymore.

My eyes droop, but I force them back open and when the room comes into focus, I finally see it. I was so caught up in being alone with him here that I didn't notice how familiar those wood-paneled walls looked. They are in the background of each of the pictures Mom found.

"Where are those girls? What did you do to them?" I ask, terrified of what the answer might be.

Quinten resumes brushing my hair. He's silent for a long time, and I can hear my heart beating faster with every second as I wait for him to reply.

"We used to come here every summer. Me. My mother, Beth. My father, Charlie," he says. "I didn't have any brothers or sisters, and there were no neighbors for miles, so I'd make my own fun."

The flickering light from the dim bulb casts his shadow out in front of me as he speaks. I suddenly feel like a child as I look at that shadow. There's a monster behind me and I want more than anything for my mom to come and take it away. But she has no idea I'm here. She has no idea who I'm with.

"I had my own ways of keeping myself entertained. Sometimes, I'd take a stick and carve shapes into the mud. Other times, I'd catch frogs and pin them to tree trunks with my knife. Boyhood exploration. I wanted to see how long they would wriggle around, trying to escape, before they'd stop moving. Gauge their tolerance. Like my father would do to my mother."

I have an eight-year-old brother, I know what kind of games boys play and it's never *that*.

"My memories are wrapped up in these woods. By that lake." He stops brushing my hair and puts down the comb before moving to the window, as though lost in his past.

"Please... just let me go." My whining plea is pitiful even to my own ears, but Quinten pays it no attention.

"You know, when I'd tell my mother about my adventures in the woods, she'd listen so carefully, as if I were narrating the greatest story ever told. She always knew how to see the beauty in the darkness."

Quinten's gaze snaps back to me. His eyes are dark and intense, they bore into mine, almost searching for a reaction.

"You know, my father would punish me for my little experiments, but my mother..." he pauses. "She was the closest thing this world will ever see to an angel. She always wore a smile. It didn't matter what my father did. He'd choke her, kick her, spit in her face, but she'd never let me see her pain. He would roar and rage, throw her around, and I would cry. But she never once let me see her shed a tear. She'd wait until his back was turned and you know what she'd do to let me know she was okay?"

I say nothing but I watch as his dark eyes now begin to

glisten in the low light. I see something in his hands as he spins it absentmindedly. It's an old-style instant camera.

"She'd give me a smile." His voice wavers for just a moment. "A big, beautiful smile. Wide and open. A special, secret smile. A smile just for me."

48

RUBY

"What do you mean you can't find her, what's happening?" Aaron's voice rises.

I hear a worried Caitlyn in the background asking what's going on.

"I'm sure it's nothing." My confident tone belies my fear. "She's probably just with a friend."

"Well did you try calling around? Have any of her friends seen her today?"

I try to bypass this, not knowing how to break the news to my ex-husband that I know exactly zero of our daughter's friends. Well, that's not entirely true, I guess, since Hutch revealed that Mory has kept him strictly in the friend zone.

"She's a sensible girl, Aaron. She's not a small child anymore, she's seventeen. We aren't always going to know where she is." I pause for a moment before continuing. "But even so, can you give me her location from your tracker?"

There's a sigh on the other end of the line. "Yeah. Yeah. I'll check the app now and text you the location. But, Ruby, if I haven't heard back from you in the next hour that she's home safe and well, I'm calling the cops."

"That's fair," I say before we hang up.

It's well after dark now and the boisterous noises from upstairs seem to have quieted down. Maybe the three boys have fallen asleep.

Felicity brings me a cup of herbal tea, which I take gratefully. The warm liquid soothes my chest as it goes down, somewhat calming my nerves.

"Any word from Justin?" Hutch asks. He looks tired, dark bags beginning to form under his eyes.

"Nothing yet. But if he does spot her around town, I know he'll call me straight away," I assure him.

A warm feeling of gratitude washes over me. At least Mory has one friend who is looking out for her. It seems so strange, though, for her to have shied away from taking their relationship further. I know how much she cares for him. A memory suddenly hits me; that phone call we had over the summer, while she was staying in Arizona with her father. I remember she was so torn up, crying—sobbing big, choked tears—and telling me she missed him so much and that she loved him. But... if she wasn't talking about Hutch, then who *was* she talking about?

My phone dings with a message and I open it to see that Aaron has sent me a screen shot of the tracking app.

> This is the last place her phone was located
> before it turned off. Familiar at all?

I stare at the image. There is a red pin stuck in a map, green terrain surrounding it for what looks like miles. Above the pin reads 'White Crane Road'.

"What the hell?" I murmur.

"What?" Felicity is suddenly behind me, looking over my shoulder.

"This is where her phone was last tracked to. Nearly two hundred miles north of here," I say, incredulously. "What on earth is she doing out there in the middle of nowhere?"

Hutch jumps up and joins his mother, looking down at the screen in my hands.

"White Crane Road," he reads. "That... that kind of sounds familiar."

I whip my head around. "Do you know anybody who lives out that way? Someone from school?"

Hutch shakes his head. "No. I mean, I don't think so. But I... I don't know. It just rings a bell is all."

I try not to get frustrated with Hutch, but he's giving me enough to think there might be a good reason for Mory to be out there, miles from home, but not enough to actually help me.

My phone pings again. Aaron.

Ruby, this is all wrong. I'm calling the cops.

Two minutes ago, I might have protested out of fear we were overreacting. But now that I've seen the image from the tracking app, I know he's right. I type back:

Okay. I'm going to drive out to that location now.

I quickly pull up the map on my phone, which determines the pinpointed area is nearly a three-hour drive from here. I'm not waiting around for the cops. I need to find Mory and see for myself that she's okay.

I call Justin and give him the update. He says he'll come back now to stay with the boys while I make the drive.

"Felicity, do you think you could stay here and look after the boys until Justin gets back?" I ask. "He won't be long, and I need to leave right now."

There's no response from Felicity who is staring at the window, into the darkness outside.

"Felicity?" I say again.

She looks back at me, apparently only just hearing me now. She opens her mouth to say something and then stops. "Sorry, what?" she finally mutters.

"I said could you stay here with the boys? I'm going to drive out to White Crane Road. Hopefully Mory isn't far from where her phone was last tracked."

Felicity looks dazed. I'm not sure what's wrong with her. It's not like it's *her* daughter who's missing, but she looks as white as a ghost.

"Um... yes. Of course. I'll stay here with the boys." There's a strange warble to her voice, but I don't have time to worry about what's going on with her right now.

"Thanks." I grab my keys from my purse and start for the door. "If Cameron asks, just tell him I'll be back in a while."

I wait for a response from Felicity, but she's gone back to staring out the window.

Inside my car I prop my phone up inside the holder on the dash, punch in the location and listen as the robotic female voice starts giving me orders. I pull on my seat belt and start the engine up, but before I can put my foot on the gas, the passenger side door suddenly opens and a figure jumps in beside me.

"Hutch, what are you doing?" I ask.

He pulls on his seat belt.

"Something's wrong. And there's no way I'm sitting around doing nothing while Mory is still missing," he says resolutely. "I'm coming with you."

49

MORY

"Felicity begged me to sell this place. She only ever came here once." Quinten runs his hand gently up the wooden wall. "But she didn't like it. Said it was too far gone. That we could use the money from the sale to help do up our house."

I blink slowly, trying to push through the haze that clings to my mind. It's like a thick, suffocating blanket that I can't push off myself. I'm not interested in anything Quinten has to say. He's certifiably insane. I know that now. But I nod along as I try to focus hard on staying awake because if I fall asleep, I don't know if I'll ever wake up again. I don't want to die. If I can just stay awake and make him think I'm on his side, play along, maybe he won't kill me like he did those other girls.

"So, I told her that I sold it. I took out a huge loan, we did up the house, and she was none the wiser. She got what she wanted and I get my little slice of happiness here to visit whenever I like. With whoever I like."

Did the other girls jump in his car and travel out here to the middle of nowhere as willingly as I did? I feel so stupid. I should never have fallen for Quinten's charm. I should have just been a normal teenager and fallen in love with his cute son. Had a normal relationship that I didn't have to hide and wouldn't end up getting me killed.

My stomach turns at the thought of Hutch. He's been the best friend I could have asked for, and he's made it glaringly clear that he's fallen for me. But I just strung him along while seeing his father behind his back. What is wrong with me?

"Felicity never liked my mother's dresses." He looks me up and down. "But you like them. All my girls do."

He's wrong. I hate this dress. And I think all those girls did, too, judging from the looks in their eyes in those photos. But I don't tell him that. I just remain motionless, slumped on the couch.

I don't want to hear any more about his dead mother. It's creeping me out. He dressed all those girls up in her dresses and now me, as though this will bring her back or something. I don't know much about psychology, but I'm pretty sure all of this stems from his screwed-up childhood here at the cabin. I mean, if it was so bad, why is he trying to relive it?

His mouth is still moving but it all sounds fuzzy to me. I think he's saying something about his camera, I can't tell. I'm so tired. I just want to go to sleep.

Maybe he'll just keep talking while I sleep. Maybe it will be okay.

The dim light overhead makes the shadows on the walls dance and move about almost cheerily. For some reason I find this soothing and I feel a warmth come over me. Maybe everything is going to be okay.

I look at Quinten. This is the man that I have loved for so long, shouldn't I trust him?

My head feels blurry, like it's filled with cotton candy, and every time I try to focus the fog only deepens. I watch Quinten's lips make shapes as he talks, and I remember the first time we kissed. He was so gentle, so careful to check I was okay with it.

Of course I was. I love him. Or... do I? Isn't there a reason I'm supposed to not like him now? Did something happen? I'm having a hard time remembering. I'm just so tired. I can't think clearly. My thoughts begin slipping, like grains of sand through my fingers. My eyelids begin to fall and it feels so good to just let go and embrace the darkness that lives behind them.

But my peace is short-lived because suddenly I'm being picked up and when my eyes open again, I'm in the bedroom sitting on the floor. Quinten places my back against a cold wooden wall and adjusts me when I begin to slump to the side.

"Not yet, sweetheart, we need to get a picture first. Wake up."

Oh. Yeah. I remember him mentioning that before. Why does he want to take a picture? I just want to sleep. Can't this wait?

My eyes close again, but this time I'm instantly snapped back to consciousness by a hot stinging sensation on my cheek and I see Quinten's hand pulling away.

"I said wake up!" he yells.

I grab my cheek. He hit me. Why would Quinten hit me? Then it floods back to me. The girls, the pictures, the dress I'm wearing.

I feel the rough wooden paneling, the splinters biting into the skin of my back, but I'm too numb to care. I brace myself against the floor to keep from flopping sideways again as I watch him kneel down in front of me, the camera covering his face.

"Okay, honey, give me a smile." His voice is suddenly sickly-sweet again.

I'm not going to give him what he wants. That's what the other girls did, and where did that get them? "No. Why should I? You're just going to kill me anyway."

The room goes quiet. The only sound I can hear is the leaves outside rustling against the windows. Every breath I take feels like a struggle. The air is thick and stale. It smells faintly of mold and something much worse. I try to shift, to find a more comfortable position, but my limbs feel so heavy.

His eyes glint now with a twisted kind of pleasure. "Mory, Mory, Mory. I didn't think you'd be the one to give me trouble. You're usually such a good girl."

He gently strokes my chin before gripping it harder, digging his fingers into my skin. I squeeze my eyes shut, trying to make myself smaller, wishing I could disappear into the wall behind me. I wish I'd never met this man. I wish I'd never started seeing him behind everyone's back. I wish we'd never moved to Lonerock. I wish I could be back in Arizona with Dad and Caitlyn, playing games and jumping into the pool.

Quinten lets go of my chin and I gasp in pain, clutching my face.

He raises the camera again as he kneels there, a dull silhouette, his features softened by shadows. All remnants of hope feel like they squeeze from my chest as a sense of utter defeat washes over me. There's nothing I can do. I'm going to die tonight. And nobody even knows where I am or who I'm with. I'm not the first, and I won't be the last girl Quinten brings back here to dress up as his mother and smile up to the camera, playing out this sick memory of his.

He leans down, his face coming into focus, his eyes wide and expectant. "Now, Mory. Give me a big smile."

50

RUBY

The tires bounce along the road and I find myself gripping the steering wheel so hard my knuckles turn white as I navigate the unfamiliar roads far from Lonerock.

The trees that surround us sway gently, their leaves rustling in the darkness. I glance at the clock on the dashboard for the hundredth time, and the minutes seem to stretch on. Time is slipping away, just like Mory.

Seventeen years. How is it possible that so much time has passed in what feels like the blink of an eye? In my mind I can still see her as a toddler, her laughter ringing through our home. I swear it's the sweetest sound that's ever reached my ears. She would bounce on her tiptoes, her curly hair flopping over her eyes as she squeezed her stuffed bunny, Boppy, to her chest. I remember when I couldn't leave the room for a second without her searching for me. She'd call for me with that sweet high-pitched voice the second I was out of sight. But now that little girl feels like a ghost, a fleeting memory that lives on only in my mind. Mory's life has taken her down a path she has made sure I can't follow. I knew the innocence that I so adored wouldn't last forever. I knew she would change and grow and become her own person, exactly who she was supposed to be. But what I didn't expect was that we would one day grow so far apart that I'd find myself driving down back roads desperately searching for her, having no idea where she is or who she's with.

Did she run away? Is she alone? With friends? I wish she'd have just told me where she was going today rather than lie to me about being with Hutch. I shake my head, trying to rid myself of the spiraling thoughts.

Where are you, sweet girl?

I glance at the passenger seat. Hutch hasn't said much since we left and there's a peculiar look on his face as he stares at the road ahead.

"Do you recognize this area?" I ask, knowing it's unlikely given there's practically no houses or landmarks to be seen. Just trees and bushes as far as the eye can see.

"I... I don't know," he mutters.

"Hutch, if you know anything at all, you need to tell me now. Why would Mory's phone say she was all the way out here?"

"I don't know!" he shouts before slamming his head back against the headrest and lowering his voice. "I don't know. I thought I knew Mory. I thought she told me everything. But now I have no idea what to think."

We drive in silence for a few minutes before Hutch speaks again. "I'm starting to think she's been seeing another guy."

"Yeah," I agree. "I think so, too."

Now the question I'm asking myself is why she was keeping it a secret. And if she was really meeting up with this secret guy today then why is her phone now off, and why did she never make it home?

We drive on in silence until my phone abruptly informs us that we've arrived at White Crane Road, which looks exactly like all the other nondescript roads we've just driven down.

There are no houses, no farms, no nothing. There's no party, no friend's house, no place for a quiet rendezvous with a secret boyfriend. There is literally zero good reason for Mory to have come all the way out here. This is all wrong. And from the look on Hutch's face, I can see he knows it too.

I check my phone and see Justin has just sent me a message saying there's still no sign of Mory at home. There's nothing left to do but call Aaron.

He answers on the second ring. "Did you find her?"

"No. There's nothing out here. Did you call the cops?"

"Yeah, there's a patrol car already on its way out there."

"Well I'm already here, and I'm not sure what good that's going to do because there's nothing but an empty road. Aaron, I'm scared."

Aaron sounds about as terrified as I am, but tries to calm my nerves, telling me we're going to find her soon and not to panic. I know it must be killing him to be so far away, unable to help search for her.

I hang up and keep driving slowly enough that I can look in every direction as I go. I try to tell myself that Mory is okay and this is all just a big misunderstanding, but in my mind all I can think of are the pictures of those girls. Of Elle. My stomach knots with the knowledge that whoever took those photos was in our neighborhood—in our home—and now my daughter is missing.

It's not until a few minutes later that I think I see something amongst the trees ahead. A building, maybe. I can't make out what it is, but when I look over at Hutch I can tell he's seen it too as I watch him tense up.

He's not said a word since I got off the phone with Aaron, but now his voice comes out in a choke. "I think I was wrong. I... I think I know where we are."

51

———

MORY

The flash blinds me momentarily, before Quinten lowers the camera and pulls the film out, shaking it lightly in his hand. He grins. "That wasn't so hard, was it?"

The wooden floor is cold beneath me. I blink slowly, trying to shake the yellow rectangles from my vision. The remnants of whatever he drugged me with are still clinging to my senses, and the edges of the room look as though they blur and bend. I try to focus on Quinten as he moves around the room.

He's staring at the photo as it develops in his hand. "Beautiful. So beautiful. I'll keep it forever."

His energy is visible, he looks like he's preparing for something, but I don't want to imagine what. When he turns my way, I pretend to be weaker than I really am, my body limp, breathing shallow. Inside, I scream and fight against the fog, but I can't let him see.

The stink of mildew stings my sinuses. I think it's coming from the mattress over there. It feels like I'll never get the smell out of my nose, even if by some miracle I escape this place. Which is looking more and more doubtful by the second.

I try to focus on the sound of his footsteps, the creaking of the floorboards. Hours have passed since we first got here and I know my mom will have figured out I'm missing by now, but since I stupidly covered my tracks when I came to meet Quinten today there's no hope of anyone finding me here now. And even if they do, I'll probably be dead by then.

No, I can't think like that. The only way out of this is to fight, and for that I can't afford to lose my grip and give up. I just need to clear my head and wait for the right moment.

"I'm going to miss our little midnight meet ups at the falls," Quinten muses. "I really have grown fond of you."

Emotion catches in my throat as I think about the nights we spent huddled together under the stars, listening to the water flowing. I really believed we had a future together. That he and Felicity would separate and we'd leave town together, able to share our love freely. No more hiding from everyone or sneaking around. But every feeling that I had for him has now gone. Disintegrated. I can't believe I ever fell for this sick bastard. Everything he told me was a lie. He probably convinced all of the girls he brought out here that he'd fallen for them, that he was taking them to his vacation house. I wonder how he killed them? What's in store for me now that he's gotten his precious photo of me to add to his collection?

"Why did you leave them there?" I ask quietly. "The photos at my mom's house."

He sits down on the edge of the bed and looks at me for a long time before speaking. "Elle was my first. Eight years ago."

Elle? That wasn't one of the names on the photos my mom showed me. But it soon hits me right in the chest: Elle Thomas, Xavier's mom.

"You killed Justin's wife," I mutter in disbelief.

Quinten ignores this. "She was a beautiful woman. I always thought so. Of course, my wife was friends with her, so we knew each other a little. Enough for her to trust me when I offered her a lift that night."

Poor Elle, Xavier would have only been a baby back then. Justin lost his wife and their son lost the chance to ever know his mother, all because of Quinten.

"My mother had just died, and the cabin was now mine. Maybe Felicity hated this place but I still loved it. I kept coming here, even after I told her I'd sold it."

It doesn't surprise me Felicity wanted this place gone from their lives. It's the stuff nightmares are made of.

"Elle, though. Seeing Elle in the cabin was like being brought back to my childhood. My mother's clothes were still here and I couldn't resist. When she put on that dress, she looked just like my mother had. Nobody has a smile quite like my mother did, but Elle's was so beautiful I had to get a photo to remember it by."

A shiver runs through me as I look down at the dress I'm wearing. His dead mother's dress. Gross. And I know he did this to at least three more girls, I've seen the photos. This is so twisted, I don't want to hear any more. I squeeze my eyes shut but he won't stop talking, confiding in me what he couldn't with anyone else.

"When we started renovations on our house, we needed to move some stuff out of the way for the work to be done. And since we'd been friends with the Desmonds—the couple who used to own your mother's house—they agreed to let us store some of our furniture there while our renovations were being done. I also needed somewhere to keep my photos where Felicity wouldn't find them, so I hid them around that house. It had been empty for so long, I guess I thought nobody would ever buy it. I went back to see my girls often, but I had to be careful with Bernice Fisher living next door, that woman never missed a thing. Then last year, I had been away for a week on business and when I got home Felicity told me in passing that the Desmonds' house had been sold. By that time, it was too late to go back and retrieve my photos because your family had already moved in."

As he talks, I work on flexing my fingers and toes, building my strength.

"So, I could no longer come back and see my girls. I missed them very much. Of course, it didn't take your mother long to find them. Luckily, when she showed them around, Felicity didn't seem to notice the walls of the cabin or think for a moment that I had anything to do with it. But it didn't take long for old Bernice Fisher to put two and two together, that it had been me who left them there. When she went berserk and pointed me out at the town meeting as being the one who had been coming and going from the house over the years, it was sheer luck that Justin Thomas was sitting right next to me, and since she'd already been ranting about him killing his wife, everyone assumed she was still talking about him."

I don't even ask the question that comes into my mind, because I already know the answer. Quinten killed Bernice that night to keep her quiet, to keep his secret safe, and the blame still pointed firmly at Justin. And it worked. Everyone thinks Justin killed Bernice, and they probably always will.

Quinten will kill me too, then go home to Felicity and his two sons who still worship his every move. I bet he and Felicity don't even have any relationship problems, and he was just lying about that to lead me on.

There's a quiet hum in my head now, low and rumbling.

"I won't lie," Quinten continues. "Seeing those photos again at the meeting was one of the biggest thrills of my life. My beautiful girls there for all to see. I only wished I could tell everyone that they were mine. That their smiles were just for me."

Through the haze of my mind, I hear it louder now. A distant rumble that continues to grow. My heart races. Is that a car?

Quinten must hear it too because his body tenses and he jumps up to move toward the door. Before I can second guess myself, I seize my chance. With every ounce of strength I can muster I spring upwards, launching myself toward him. My mind has switched off, it's all instinct and adrenaline. I swing the door backwards with all my might, the wood meeting his face with a loud thud. He screams in agony and stumbles back, stunned. I dart past him, my bare feet slapping against the filthy floor as I use every bit of my concentration to keep moving my body forward. The front door is just a few steps away, I can make it, I know I can!

I can hear the car getting closer and if I can just get outside and flag it down, I'll be saved. I just need to move faster.

I can hear Quinten behind me, screaming at me as he advances. My fingers just reach the cold metal of the door handle before my hair is yanked back, his fingers tangled inside it, my head snapping backwards as my feet leave the ground and I fall to the floor, hard.

Quinten jumps on top of me, holding me down as I struggle and kick against him.

"You're not going anywhere!" The words are laced with a sick sense of ownership that makes my skin crawl.

I kick and thrash, but he's stronger and his grip is like iron. I can feel the heat radiating off him, a repulsive blend of sweat and anger.

"Let me go!" I scream, desperation clawing at my throat.

My heart is hammering against my ribcage as he pushes my arms down, pinning them against the floor. I try to pull them free but it's no use, I don't have the strength. All I can do is scream and scream in the hope that whoever is in the car can hear me. But Quinten leans down closer, his breath hot against my ear.

"Shut up." His voice is low, almost a growl.

I twist my body, trying to break free, but I'm no match for Quinten's strength as he drags me up off the floor and pulls me back toward the bedroom.

52

MORY

I hit the floor face first. My heart races, drumming against my ribs, sending pain soaring through my core. I whimper as I shuffle myself backwards toward the wall to get away from him.

Quinten's eyes narrow, pinpricks of rage. "Who did you tell you were coming here?"

I swallow hard, tasting blood. "Nobody," I croak, the word barely escaping my throat.

I so badly want to believe that someone has found me, that maybe this is my chance. But how could they know? I didn't tell a soul we were coming here. Nobody has any reason to believe me and Quinten have been seeing each other, and from what he told me, nobody even knows he still owns the cabin.

"You better be telling the truth, Mory," he hisses, leaning in close to my face, his breath hot and fetid. "I need you to listen to me. Stay in this room and be quiet. I will gut you like a fish if I hear so much as a cry."

Something about how he says this makes me believe him. Is that how he killed those other girls?

I nod and watch as he stalks toward the door, every step

heavy. The door creaks open, and just like that, he's gone. I'm left alone in the darkness. In silence.

I don't know what to do. If I obey him, he might convince whoever is outside that he's here alone and then kill me when they leave. But if I try to run outside and flag down help, then he'll kill me right then and there.

I need to think, but the air inside this room is thick and suffocating. I squeeze my eyes shut, willing myself to breathe, to think. What do I do? I can't just sit here and wait to die. What if it's my mom out there, coming to look for me? But of course, that's not possible because there's no way she could know that I'm here.

Through the remaining fog filling my head, I suddenly remember: Dad's tracker! Maybe she told him I was missing and he helped her track me down. She could be right outside, ready to save me! The hope in my heart carries the weight of possibilities but my new-found optimism is shattered in a moment when I hear it.

A single gunshot, sharp and jarring, slicing through the night outside. Then another. The sounds echo in my head and freeze my blood. Panic floods over me and I scramble to my feet, my thoughts racing. Did Quinten shoot someone? Did he shoot himself? I'm frozen to the spot, every cell in my body screaming at me to run and hide, but I can't move. Fear keeps me anchored in place. But as though a cloud parts in my mind, there's suddenly no question about what to do. I need to run, or I am going to die. I make a dash for the window, ready to face whatever's outside. But before I can get to it, the door opens and Quinten steps back into the room. My stomach drops. Even in the dim light, I can see it. Blood spatters, wet and glistening, cover his hands, his clothes. He's now holding a gun, the metal gleaming in the shadows.

I stop and back up against the wall and cling to it, paralyzed by terror, my body betraying me. He strides toward me, grabbing my arm and yanking me forward.

"We have to get out of here. Now! Move!" His grip tightens as he pulls me toward the door.

I don't dare put up a fight. Not now I've seen the gun. The blood.

I shiver, my body trembling uncontrollably as he drags me outside. The cold night air hits me like a slap in the face and I stumble behind him, my legs unsteady. And then I see it.

A body lies sprawled on the ground, the figure twisted and unnatural in the dark. Blood pools around it, glistening under the moonlight, and a metallic odor bites at my throat. I can't process what I'm seeing; my eyes widen as horror washes over me like a tidal wave.

"No," I whisper, shaking my head in disbelief. "No, no, no..."

Quinten's grip tightens on my arm as he drags me closer to the grisly scene, and I stare in horror, unable to believe this is possible.

"Look! Look at what you made me do!" His voice is frantic, a wild edge creeping in as he tries to catch his breath. "This is your fault!"

I can't breathe. The world tilts on its axis, and I feel like I'm going to be sick. "How could you do this?" I croak, every syllable sticking in my throat like shards of glass.

"Shut up!" he barks, his eyes darting around before they settle on his car. "We need to get out of here before anyone else comes."

He shoves me forward and I stumble, catching my balance just in time to keep from falling. I don't want to follow him; I want to scream, to run, to escape this nightmare. But I have no choice but to do as he says.

He shoves me forward and points at his car. "Get in!"

I take a step toward the car but suddenly stop when I see lights approaching on the road. Quinten sees it too and before I can make another move, he grabs me from behind and raises the gun upwards, pushing the cold metal to my temple just as a car comes to a screeching halt by the cabin.

53

RUBY

Gravel crunches underneath the tires as I pull the car to a stop.

The crumbling wooden building before us is almost swallowed by the blackness, but the headlights illuminate the scene in front of it, depicting something far darker than I could have ever let myself imagine. A police car sits with its door wide open, like a gaping mouth screaming. An officer lies sprawled on the ground, his gun holster empty, a river of blood spreading across the earth beneath him. Because of the shadows, I can't tell if he's young or old but the lifelessness of his face leaves no question about it. He's dead.

"Dad!" Hutch's pained voice yells and it's only then that I see them beside the cabin door.

Quinten and Mory stand in the darkness. His arm is tightly around her, and he's holding a gun to her head. I can barely comprehend what I'm seeing because nothing here makes any sense.

"Mory!" I scream as Hutch and I exit the car simultaneously.

"Mom, help!" Mory cries and I begin to rush forward but stop when Quinten takes a step back, dragging Mory with him.

"Don't come any closer!" Quinten orders, his eyes wild.

He's staring back and forth between me and Hutch and he looks nothing like I've ever seen him before. Felicity's cool, calm husband has been replaced by a madman. What is happening? Why has he brought my daughter here? But it takes only a moment for me to register the dress Mory is wearing and the reality of what this all means to slot together in my mind.

"It... it was you," I mutter.

The girls. The photos. It was Quinten all this time. The whole neighborhood has been rallying against Justin for years, convinced that he murdered his wife, but they've been overlooking the wolf dressed in sheep's clothing amongst them all these years. He fooled Felicity and he fooled his boys. He fooled us all.

"Dad... what... what's happening?" Hutch's voice cracks. "What are you doing?"

"What am I doing?" Quinten shouts. "Well, son, I was spending some quality time with your cute little friend here before you all showed up."

Tears are pouring down Mory's face and it takes everything I have not to rush over and grab her.

"You ever wonder why she just wasn't that into you, Hutch?" Quinten's eyes glimmer with some kind of sick pride. "It's because she was with me. She wanted *me*."

"I don't want anything to do with you, you asshole!" Mory screams and thrashes, but Quinten holds her tighter.

"That's not what you were saying all those nights we met at the falls. All those weekends helping out with robotics, your lips on mine every time Hutch left the room. See, son," he looks Hutch dead in the eyes, "Mory is one of *my* girls."

My stomach turns. This man is sicker than I could have ever imagined. Hutch just stares ahead, seemingly unable to process the fact that his father isn't the man he thought he was.

I take one step forward, my teeth gritted. "Mory isn't yours, Quinten. And neither were those other girls. Let her go!"

He laughs and shakes his head. "That's not going to happen."

My chest fills with rage. This is my daughter—my baby—I can't let anything happen to her.

"No," Quinten says slowly. "Mory will be going to join my other girls."

He looks off into the night for a moment and I shudder to think of where their bodies lie now. One thing is for sure; so long as there's breath still in my lungs, my daughter will not be joining them.

"Dad, why are you doing this?" Hutch cries. "This isn't you!"

"Son, if you had more time in life, you'd realize that people are rarely who you think they are."

There's no question in my mind of what he means by this. He plans to kill Mory and then us. I can't let this happen. There must be more officers on their way. If I can just keep him talking, maybe they'll get here before he can kill us all.

"You don't have to do this. Let Mory and Hutch go, they're just kids!"

"Sorry to disappoint you, Ruby, but your daughter isn't nearly as innocent as you'd like to think." He kisses the side of her head, and I see her flinch. "Mory has spent the best part of a year leading my son on like an idiot. She came here with me behind your back, behind his. Because it's me that she loves."

"No I don't! No I don't!" Mory screams and sends an elbow backwards into Quinten's ribcage so hard the breath gets knocked from his lungs.

Quinten groans in pain and loses his footing, stumbling backwards. The gun goes off above him, sending a shock wave through the still night air. Mory rushes forwards into my arms and I hold her tight, squeezing her head to my chest and breathing in the smell of my beautiful daughter. I've never known a scent so sweet.

With one hand holding the gun and the other grasping his injured side, Quinten tries to recompose himself. He steadies his arm and points the gun in our direction, but it's too late as Hutch runs at him from the side and collides with his father, both of them falling to the ground.

Quinten struggles and pushes at his son but Hutch is a younger and stronger man than his father, and overpowers him easily before grabbing the gun from his hand and slamming it into his head. Quinten is stunned momentarily. Hutch jumps off of him and stands over him with the gun pointed his way.

"Why... why, Dad?" Hutch sobs. "Why did you do this?"

Quinten gets up slowly, his head streaming blood. He backs up against the wall of the cabin. "I wouldn't expect you to understand, Hutch. I... I wouldn't want you to understand."

His tone almost sounds sorrowful, but I don't pity this man one bit.

It doesn't seem Hutch is fooled either, as he holds the gun with both hands shaking violently. "How could you do this to Mom? To Leo? To me?"

I see Hutch's finger tightening on the trigger. "Don't shoot him!" I cry.

Whatever Hutch is going through right now, killing his own father will only make it worse. But Hutch doesn't seem to hear me. He's laser-focused on his father, and the tears of pain in his eyes are heartbreaking to witness.

I squeeze Mory closer to me, shielding her from the scene in front of us.

"He's not going to shoot me," Quinten spits. "Just put the gun down, Hutch."

But Hutch only steadies his shaking hands around the gun.

"No! I'm not going to let you hurt anyone else ever again," he shouts through tears before lowering his voice to a near whisper. "I'm... I'm sorry, Dad."

I squeeze my eyes waiting for the inevitable, but instead of the sound of a gunshot, I hear an engine revving. I open my eyes to see a stunned Hutch lit up by headlights and a car driving straight for the cabin, no signs of slowing down. Hutch watches on, jaw slack as the car hurtles forward, headed straight for Quinten.

Quinten is frozen, a look of terror on his face as he sees the vehicle coming for him. The driver is staring dead ahead at him, their face a picture of determination.

I don't have time to turn away before it happens.

The tires screech, rubber grating against gravel, as the force slams Quinten against the rough wooden wall of the cabin. The sound of the impact reverberates through my chest, hitting my senses like a sledgehammer. Everything stops and for a fleeting moment, time seems to stretch on as the air settles around us. Quinten chokes under the crushing weight of the car that pins him helplessly, squeezing the breath from his lungs. He gasps, a strangled sound bubbling up, as blood drips from his mouth, the life draining from his gaze, before his neck goes limp.

His final view as he stares straight ahead is the intent eyes of his killer, who sits behind the wheel glaring resolutely back.

54

RUBY

Felicity steps slowly from her car, shaken but uninjured. A long time goes by without any of us uttering so much as a word. Mory and I wait inside my car for help to arrive, giving Felicity and Hutch time to process what just happened. Although I doubt they will ever truly process it all.

When the area is taken over by officials and Mory is sitting in the back of an ambulance being seen to by a medic for her injuries, I find a moment with Felicity.

"How did you know?" I ask solemnly.

She lowers her red-rimmed eyes. "I've suspected he was having affairs for years now. But I didn't know about *this* until... well, I guess until you traced Mory's phone to this address. But now. Now I'm wondering if maybe part of me knew since the day you showed us those photographs. I thought I saw a little glint of recognition in Quinten's eyes, but when he said he'd never seen them I quickly put it out of my mind. I didn't recognize the cabin in the photos, but when you said you'd traced Mory's phone to this area... it all clicked."

She explains how Quinten convinced her years ago that he'd sold the cabin his mother had left him when she died and since then, the frequency of his work trips had increased. She tells me of the renovations they did a few years back and how they'd asked the Desmonds to let them store some furniture in their empty house. When Felicity learned about the photos I'd found, she'd convinced herself that it couldn't have anything to do with Quinten. She suspected he was cheating, but she'd figured it was with someone from work. Then on the morning of her surprise birthday party—when Quinten was getting ready to leave town on a 'work trip'—she'd done something she'd never done before. She'd waited until he was in the shower and gone behind his back to check his phone, something he would never have allowed her to do. How Felicity never saw this fact alone as a blinding red flag, I don't know. But I guess she'd just been so intent on keeping up appearances that she knew to keep those stray threads firmly in place, so as not to unravel their whole lives.

"There were messages on there from a contact called *M* that confirmed what I'd suspected. Quinten was seeing someone else. But I didn't consider for a second that it could be your daughter."

A heavy silence falls between us. We've both been under the illusion for a long time that Mory had fallen for Hutch. The revelation that she'd actually been seeing Quinten all this time is one that neither one of us wants to accept. I can see the pain in Felicity's eyes, just as I'd seen on the night of her surprise party. She'd been crying when she arrived, which at the time I'd thought was just normal emotions about getting older, but now I know it was because she'd just confirmed that her husband was having an affair.

Felicity takes a deep breath. "I think Bernice tried to tell us the photos were Quinten's at the meeting," she explains. "Everyone thought she was talking about Justin, but I saw her pointing dead on at my husband. When I found out she was killed, I didn't consider for a second that it could have been Quinten who strangled her, so I latched on to the idea that it was Justin, like everyone else did. But now I know. Quinten killed Bernice to keep her quiet."

I say nothing, but the cogs in my mind are beginning to turn. What Felicity just said makes complete sense and something inside me relaxes, knowing that Justin won't get the blame for Bernice's death.

But my heart still breaks for Felicity. For Hutch.

Felicity glances at the officers behind us and lowers her voice. "You won't... you won't tell them, will you?"

I know exactly what she's asking. "Quinten had a gun. He was going to kill us all. You did what you had to do."

Nobody ever has to know that Hutch was the one pointing the gun at Quinten when Felicity arrived.

Who knows? If I were in her shoes, I might have done the exact same thing. All I know for sure is that the world is now a better place without Quinten Parker in it.

Felicity returns to Hutch, whose eyes stare blankly ahead. I can't imagine what's going through his mind right now. Yesterday he had a stable family, a loving relationship with his father, and what he'd hoped was a budding relationship with Mory. But all of that was shattered to pieces tonight. He's been betrayed by a life that once seemed to be firmly on his side.

Then there's Mory. I don't know how we're going to navigate the coming days, after everything she's gone through. It's going to be difficult, but she's here and she's alive and that's all that matters.

When the medic steps away, I wrap my arms around her and she clings on to me like she did as a small girl.

"I'm so sorry, Mom," she sobs. "I'm so sorry for lying to you. This is all my fault!"

Her words send a searing streak of fire through my chest.

"Don't you ever say that, Mory!" I grab her shoulders. "None of this was your fault. I don't know what Quinten did to make you trust him, but everything he told you was a lie. Everything that happened tonight is because of him, not you."

What I don't say is that I'm still stung by the lies she told everyone. But ultimately, I know that's not what led us here. Quinten is. And thankfully, he's out of her life forever now. Though I doubt that she and Hutch will ever be able to resurrect their friendship again after what's happened.

The gruesome scene has been cordoned off and is now shielded by white tents, but behind them I know there lies the body of a man who has destroyed many lives. And I came frighteningly close to losing my daughter at his hands tonight.

I kiss Mory's head and hold her tighter as heaving sobs shake her body. "It's okay, baby. It's all over now."

EPILOGUE
MORY

ONE YEAR LATER

I lean on the wooden railing of our newly-built deck and let the sunshine warm my face.

Justin has been calling it 'Mory's Deck' since I pitched in and helped him build it, but really, he did most of the work. Like ninety percent of it. But it was kind of a fun experience, and I think it made Mom happy that I got to know him a bit better during the process. Justin and Xavier spend a lot of time here now, and we even go to their house sometimes. It's huge, like a cattle ranch but with no cows. Justin says he's going to build a climbing wall out there this summer for the three boys, who are literally inseparable. Cameron, Xavier and Leo. We call them The Three Amigos.

I take off my cardigan and the warmth instantly hits my shoulders. The sun sits in a cloudless sky, glowing brightly over our backyard as bursts of laughter and the smell of grilled burgers drift about the air.

I watch Mom move from guest to guest, looking surprisingly

comfortable in her unfamiliar role as hostess. She's worked so hard on this house. On making it a home. It felt like it would never happen, but the renovations are finally complete and the inside space cleaned up pretty great. We no longer live amongst the chaos of mess and power tools. I used to dread people coming over, I'd cringe even at the thought of anyone seeing the inside of our house and I resented Mom for moving us here. But today, with the sun shining and the yard alive with neighbors and friends, I actually feel kind of proud of her. She worked really hard for this. She deserves to enjoy it.

Felicity Parker is here with Leo. Hutch didn't come, of course. He doesn't really talk to me anymore. I think he's said hi to me twice in total since that night at the cabin—once when he came to our house to bring Leo home and once when I went over to his house to collect Cameron. I don't blame him for not wanting to talk to me.

I've had a lot of time to think about what happened with Quinten and even if he hadn't been a psycho murderer, I still made a huge mistake ever starting a relationship with him behind our families' backs. I thought him being interested in me meant I was mature, a woman. But that's not why he was seeing me. I don't even know if he was ever really into me that way, or if it was all just a ruse to get me to his cabin to kill me like he did all those other girls. The police suspect he hid the photos in various locations around the house while it was abandoned for all those years, before my mom bought it, so as not to arouse suspicion if they were all found together one day. They're probably right, one lone photo wouldn't have anyone thinking much of it. Mom didn't sense anything unusual about it until she found enough of them to start seeing a pattern.

They found six bodies in total, buried deep in the woodland behind his cabin. Who knows? There could still be ones they missed. It's not exactly easy to tell what killed a person whose body is that badly decomposed, but they said there's enough evidence to suggest they were all strangled to death. Not a day goes by that I don't think about how that could have been me, too, if Mom and Hutch and then Felicity hadn't shown up when they did.

A shiver runs through my body now, making me shake a little despite the blazing heat.

They've identified all of the bodies they found, including Elle, who Justin held a funeral for at the start of this year. It was heartbreaking, but he told us it was healing for him, since he'd never gotten closure when he'd first had her declared legally dead.

It's strange to think how much has changed in the past year. Just a month ago, I turned eighteen. An adult. I keep having to remind myself of that, but the word still feels weird in my head. Especially since I just became a big sister again recently. Dad and Caitlyn welcomed little Mildred Rose a few months back, and even though I think that's clearly an old lady's name, I do think she's pretty cute. Cam and I have flown to Arizona a couple of times since she was born and I have to admit, when I first met her I started bawling like a baby. Her toes... they're just so tiny. I never thought I'd feel this way about getting a baby sister, but I can't deny there's something super special about her. Cameron is totally in love with his little sister too, of course.

"Hi," comes a voice from behind me and I startle at the sound.

I turn around to see Hutch standing there, his blond hair glistening in the sunlight. "Hi," I say quietly. "I didn't think you'd come today."

Hutch scratches his shoulder, awkwardly. "Well, I'm here."

We're both quiet for too long, and I don't know what to say. I start to sweat under the heat before the silence becomes too much and the words I've wanted to say for so long burst from my mouth without me meaning them to. "Hutch, I'm so sorry for everything. I should never have done what I did. I never wanted you to get hurt and I'll never forgive myself for it. I was just completely deluded, and I can't believe I jeopardized our friendship like that when you mean so much to me and I—"

"Mory, slow down!" Hutch looks amused as he grabs my shoulders.

My heart is drumming a hundred beats per second in my chest, and I'm nearly shaking as I slowly close my mouth, embarrassed. "I'm... I'm sorry, is what I'm trying to say."

"It's okay." A smile pulls at the side of his mouth. "Well, it's not okay, it was actually super messed up. But it's... the whole thing is complicated, and I don't want to spend my whole life angry. I'm trying to move past everything that happened, for my mom and for Leo."

"I'm so sorry, Hutch," I repeat.

"You said that already." He laughs.

"I know." I sigh. "But I just wish I could take it all away and go back to how we were before. You were my best friend. My only friend. I miss seeing you," I admit.

Although I've settled into Lonerock and there are a few people I hang out with around the place now, I've never felt more comfortable than when I was with Hutch. And despite what happened with Quinten, I've always thought Hutch was super cute. I'd even go as far as to say *hot*, now.

"I've missed you, too." Hutch leans his arms on the wooden railing beside me and looks into my eyes. "You know, I could actually do with your help with something."

I raise my eyebrows but try not to sound too excited. "Sure. What is it?"

He smiles. "Well, I've got this project I'm working on. It's like a small autonomous robot that can navigate through a maze, but I'm still trying to figure out how to make it so the ultrasonic sensors can detect obstacles without interference. I could really do with some help... What do you think?"

I think I didn't really understand anything he just said but he could ask me if I wanted to go pick up litter from the sidewalks and I would jump at the chance to do it beside him.

"Sure." I smile. "It's a date."

———

RUBY

I feel arms wrap around me from behind and I jump before Justin laughs and kisses my neck.

"You can't sneak up on a girl like that," I complain, putting down the tongs and leaving the burgers to sizzle.

I turn around and melt into Justin's arms. "Pretty good party, right?"

"It's amazing, I'm so proud of you, Ruby. For everything." He presses his forehead against mine.

"I couldn't have done all this without you. And thank you for keeping everyone entertained while I cook, I saw you out there schmoozing," I say. "You and Harriet looked like you had a lot to talk about."

Justin pulls back sharply and stares at me, horrified.

"What? What's wrong?" I ask.

"That was Harriet?" His face is twisted in dismay. "I thought it was Kendra. I was *calling* her Kendra! Oh my God."

I nearly double over laughing, watching his cheeks turn a deep shade of red. I quickly change the subject, hoping to ease his embarrassment.

"Hey, are you seeing this?" I nod to where Mory stands with Hutch.

They keep moving closer to each other as they talk, and it

warms my heart to see them together again. I know how much she's missed him this past year, she still talks about him all the time but she's been resolute in giving him time and space to heal with his family.

"Wow. There's hope for those two after all. Love always wins." Justin squeezes me once more before heading back into the crowd to entertain the guests.

I plate up some burgers for my hungry neighbors and when it's Benton Shepherd's turn I stop and pull him aside. "Benton, I want to thank you again, for what you did. Especially after all the horrible things I accused you of. It really means a lot to us."

It turns out that Benton Shepherd is actually a pretty decent guy. After the cops concluded that Quinten had killed Elle, Benton had taken it upon himself to use the next community meeting to clear Justin's name publicly. It also turns out that there was nothing nefarious about the delay in selling our house. He was never stringing the Desmonds along, in fact, he was jumping through hoops for years with the city planners to get this house cleared for sale. I still feel awful for all the things I said to Benton, and what I accused him of.

"Water under the bridge!" He waves away my concerns with a hand before aiming his gleaming smile my way. "And I must say, Ruby, you've done amazing things with this place. It really looks great."

When Benton disappears into the crowd, I take some time to absorb the compliments I've been getting on my finished home and garden. I'm so proud of this place. When we first arrived here, it was old and outdated and the sheer amount of work it needed was so overwhelming that I doubted my sanity more than a few times for having taken on such a huge project. But I poured my heart and soul into this place and the work really shows. I do have to give a lot of credit to Justin, though.

He stepped in and took on the task of helping to fix up this house without me ever having to ask.

"Look at that." Felicity appears at my side, nodding over at Justin. "Last year, not one person in this town would so much as speak a word to him. Now he's the life of the party. He's a good man. I just wish it hadn't taken so long for our community to realize it."

"I'm a lucky woman." I laugh.

"He's a lucky man, Ruby," Felicity says, meaningfully.

Felicity's and my friendship has grown strong since that night a year ago. With the trauma that bonds us, as well as both of our boys being a part of The Three Amigos, we've spent a lot of time helping each other heal and been a shoulder for each other's frustration and tears.

"It's so good to see those two talking again," Felicity says of Mory and Hutch. "He still holds a candle for her."

"You never know, we could end up becoming mothers-in-law one day." We both cackle like witches at this.

"I'd better go wrangle the boys." Felicity sighs. "They've been running around with toy swords all afternoon. They must be getting hungry by now."

I wave her off and watch as she attempts to herd the three wild children from their game to the food table, which is overflowing with salads, breads, and desserts that this amazing community has shown up at my door with. The boys dig in like they've been starved for months.

The Three Amigos: Cameron, Xavier and Leo. Watching their boisterous, innocent play always evokes a bittersweet feeling for me. All three boys are so innocent. So clueless to the pain and suffering that has enveloped the rest of their families.

Cameron still doesn't know that his sister was kidnapped and nearly killed.

Xavier already knows that his mom, Elle, has been dead since he was a baby but how can Justin explain to him that it turns out she was abducted and murdered by his own friend's father.

And Leo. God. My heart breaks for the boy who thought the sun rose and set for his father. He knows his dad passed away that night, but one day he will inevitably learn of the sick, vile things his father did before he died.

There will come a day that all three friends will have to count on each other for support when they find out the truth about their pasts. But for now, I truly believe in the saying, let them be kids. The rest will come when it comes.

I look around at my friends, my community, my family and I feel a sense of pride in having made a home here in Lonerock. We got off to a shaky start, but I truly believe that we belong here now.

The only question left in my mind is whether I regret killing Bernice Fisher.

Of course, I didn't *plan* to kill the old bag that night, after the meeting. I only went to her house because I was upset with her for accusing Justin of killing his wife in front of the whole town. I was going to try to settle the air between us and explain why she was wrong about him. But she wouldn't listen. She spat her angry words at me and told me I didn't belong here. That she wouldn't rest until Justin was thrown in jail for what he did to Elle. Her bony finger was in my face and I only meant to push her away from me, but that woman was about as light as a bag of feathers. Her tiny frame betrayed the weight of all the hatred sunken into her brittle bones. Her head hit the marble countertop, and blood began to stain her hair.

"You... you tried to kill me!" she'd wheezed, clutching her head.

"What? No I didn't! I just pushed you lightly," I protested.

"No, you just tried to kill me! You want me dead. You're no better than *him*. You and Justin belong together, you're both sick in the head. I'm calling the police!"

She began to get up, holding tight to the countertop, crawling along as she reached for the phone on the wall. I don't know what happened then. It's as though something primal came over me, an urge to protect my family. To protect Justin.

Bernice Fisher made my life a living hell from the moment I moved into this house, and she wasn't going to stop until she drove me away for good. If she'd called the cops, who would believe it was an accident that I pushed her that hard, especially after she'd just been cursing me out at the meeting?

No. I couldn't let her do it. I couldn't let her continue to harass me, to accuse me of doing things I hadn't done.

It felt as though I was outside of my own body, looking down at myself as I took off my scarf and wrapped it around that nasty old woman's neck. She shook and fought, but it took almost no effort to hold that scarf tight until her body went limp and her eyes glazed over. I strangled her. I strangled her just like Quinten strangled all those girls. And because of that eerie similarity, nobody will ever suspect that it was me who killed her.

Quinten is gone now, and as far as anyone else knows, he took Bernice Fisher down with him.

I watch as my guests laugh and mingle, enjoying the harmony of a warm day and good company, safe in the knowledge that the murderer who once lived among them is now dead and in the ground. And as much as I have struggled to come to terms with what I did, I know that this beautiful scene in my backyard today would never have happened if Bernice were still alive and living next door.

So, do I regret what I did? No. I don't think I do.

I just want to enjoy this beautiful day with my new-found friends. My community. They never need to know that a killer still lives among them.

ALSO BY NANCY SAVAGE

The Couple in Cabin 14

The Motel

AUTHOR'S NOTE

Thank you so much for picking up this book and joining Ruby in her journey, I hope you enjoyed reading it a fraction of how much I enjoyed writing it.

If you liked *Pretty Pictures,* please consider taking a moment and leaving a review for it on Amazon or Goodreads, as this will help new readers discover my books.

If you would be interested in being a part of my advanced reader team in the future, or just want to drop me a message, you can contact me via the form my website: nancysavagebooks.com.

ACKNOWLEDGMENTS

A huge thank you to the incredible team at Bloodhound Books! Betsy Reavley, Fred Freeman, Tara Lyons, Hannah Deuce, Lexi Curtis, and everyone else who played a part in bringing this book to life. A big thanks also to the folks at Dreamscape Media.

A very special thank you to my wonderful editor, Abbie Rutherford. Not only do you work magic, but you always seem to know exactly what to say to lift my spirits!

To Jared, thank you for spending the last twenty-two years supporting me at every turn. Without your belief in me, I would not be writing.

To my mother, Kerri—thank you for dropping everything (even your beautiful garden!) to comb through my pages with your careful eye. Your support is everything to me.

Thank you to my wonderful children! You inspire me every single day.

And finally, thank you, dear reader, for picking up this book and spending time with a story that means so much to me. I'm so grateful you're here.

A NOTE FROM THE PUBLISHER

Thank you for reading this book. If you enjoyed it please do consider leaving a review on Amazon to help others find it too.

We hate typos. All of our books have been rigorously edited and proofread, but sometimes mistakes do slip through. If you have spotted a typo, please do let us know and we can get it amended within hours.

info@bloodhoundbooks.com